Deborah Forster grew  rked as a staff and freelan vas a 'This Life' columnist

Deborah is marrie three children. *The Book of E*

G000146734

...grew up in Footscray, Melbourne. She work...
...freelance journalist for many years and was...
...on *The Age* and *The Sunday Age*.
...married to Alan Kohler and they have t...
... is her first novel.

THE BOOK OF
EMMETT

DEBORAH FORSTER

VINTAGE BOOKS
AUSTRALIA

A Vintage book
Published by Random House Australia Pty Ltd
Level 3, 100 Pacific Highway, North Sydney NSW 2060
www.randomhouse.com.au

First published by Vintage in 2009

Copyright © Deborah Forster 2009

The moral right of the author has been asserted.

All rights reserved. No part of this book may be reproduced or transmitted by
any person or entity, including internet search engines or retailers, in any form
or by any means, electronic or mechanical, including photocopying (except
under the statutory exceptions provisions of the Australian *Copyright Act
1968*), recording, scanning or by any information storage and retrieval system
without the prior written permission of Random House Australia.

Addresses for companies within the Random House Group can be found at
www.randomhouse.com.au/offices.

National Library of Australia
Cataloguing-in-Publication Entry

Forster, Deborah.
The book of Emmett.

ISBN 978 1 74166 786 8 (pbk).

A823.4

Cover design by Natalie Winter
Text design by Midland Typesetters
Typeset by Midland Typesetters, Australia
Printed and bound by Griffin Press, South Australia

Random House Australia uses papers that are natural, renewable and recyclable
products and made from wood grown in sustainable forests. The logging
and manufacturing processes are expected to conform to the environmental
regulations of the country of origin.

10 9 8 7 6 5 4 3 2

For my mother

1

On the day of Emmett Brown's funeral, Tuesday the tenth of January, the temperature is 40.4 degrees in the quivering shade. Out the front of Gilberts Funeral Parlour in Footscray, someone suggests that there's no need for a crematorium to dispose of Emmett, just leave him hanging around in this heat and he will surely self-combust. Smiles, sly with memory, surface like fish rising up in wide rivers. People fan the slow, thick air around their hot faces with funeral programs, and by degrees the smiles fade.

Gilberts lost most of its land when the snaking concrete overpass the locals call Mount Mistake went up and now the front yard is an odd shape because it's truncated and almost tucked underneath the thing. The funeral parlour is a creaking old Edwardian joint full of corners and bow windows and little fireplaces lined with cracked tiles.

It's right across from the Western Oval, a patchy green heart glowing in the dull streets where both Brown boys played footy as kids. Rob remembers it best. He'd been a middling footballer, one who liked being in the team more than he liked winning, who loved the thought of footy more than the game.

He remembers walking past Gilberts and those mornings, full of the loose strands of the day, still stand out sharply because they were rich with anticipation. He still believes hope is the best part of everything.

And even now if he closes his eyes he can see himself and his mates, small shapes against the pale winter skies threading through long treeless streets where the houses are low and hunched, backs always to the weather, bouncing the footy and talking fast.

After a frost there might be puddles sealed with panes of glassy ice that Rob and his mates would break with their heels so as not to wet their feet and all the while the boys yapped on constantly, boasting about how much beer they'd be able to drink when they were grown, about how much their fathers drank and about whose father was the biggest pisspot. (Rob won hands down.)

Sometimes the talk was more mundane, about where to get wheels for billycarts or who really was the best footballer even though this always boiled down to Ted Whitten.

They dragged everything into the conversation but no matter where they were in the river of talk, they always hurried past Gilberts because it gave them the creeps. One of them would start running and soon enough, another would break into a sprint and then they'd shoot past the place, hearts banging around in the caves of their skinny chests, and they'd show up at footy puffing and blowing.

Now Rob is forty-five-years-old, standing under the eaves of Gilberts being watched by the sole terracotta dragon still hanging onto the roof, and his past is washing by him like sticks set down on a river. Yeah, he remembers those footy days, but mostly he remembers his father, Emmett. Every bloody inch of him.

He looks up at the dragon and into the oven of the sky and he steadies himself for the task of burying the old bastard. About time it all ended he thinks. Something has made him recall George Harrison's 'All Things Must Pass'. He secretly likes the song but doesn't mind stirring his sister Louisa for declaring George her favourite Beatle. How could anyone go past Lennon? For a smart girl she's still pretty damn wet. Yet, he concedes, today George you got it spot on. I am ready to enjoy the passing of all things.

*

After Emmett died his wife, Anne, was determined that there be a quick funeral. No mucking around, she said, and this despite the fact that Louisa, the eldest Brown, was in Italy. No, the thing would proceed. Funerals aren't a big deal, they are just something to be done with. What's the point of waiting, she wanted to know, especially in summer.

No one seriously argued with her, though Rob did mention that it was possible to put bodies in fridges these days, they made them big enough. But without Louisa there to laugh, the crack fell flat and was ignored. Anne was never one for jokes and in better times was stumped that anyone would want such a troubling thing as a sense of humour.

So plans were made. Louisa would hurry home with some urgency and three quotes for the disposal of the earthly remains of Emmett Brown would be sought. The three quotes were for form's sake because Gilberts was the only place really considered. In Anne's opinion, only locals could really be trusted at such a time.

*

Outside the funeral home while they wait for the others to arrive, the Browns keep to the narrow cut of shade cast by the overpass wall. They edge back as the sun erases the shadow and from above they look like a string of beads.

3

They're waiting for Peter, the second youngest Brown, to arrive but it could be a long wait because Peter's idea of time has always been elastic. Still, there'll be no funeral without him, so the wait goes on.

Though it isn't a big turnout, maybe thirty or so, some people drift towards the Browns in dribs and drabs and hands are shaken and cheeks are kissed and remarks about the baking weather are made. Then the hot, heavy arms of the day take them.

Standing by the radiating concrete wall, Anne's hot but she's not letting on. She's never been much bothered by heat. People make far too much of such things, she thinks. Heat is heat and the best thing to do about such extreme displays is to pay them no attention. This makes things more bearable. So she doesn't fan herself with the funeral program she's already collected, she simply takes her mind off the heat by reflecting on the miracle of her children.

In that trench of shade, dressed in her reliable fawn pants-suit and her new tan sandals with soles like tyre treads, she marvels that these people are actually hers. They've grown up so well, all things considered. And so tall, given that she just scrapes in at a bit over five feet. For the children she silently thanks Emmett. Without him they would not be who they are.

In the sky, the glare dulls as if someone has turned it down and twigs carried so far by the wind are tossed at their feet like offerings. Against it, some people clutch hats to their heads and women hold their summer dresses down as the gust swells skirts like sails. Some raise their voices over the bullying wind, remarking about the strength of it. The Browns seem outside of such things, they just watch and wait for Peter.

*

Rob Brown grew later than most of the others but now he reaches nearly six feet. His shoulders are broad and because of his outdoor work he's fit and strong and lean. He keeps his hair longish (can't be bothered with hairdressers) and it suits his broad face. He shaves when he remembers.

His dark eyebrows are wing-shaped and it's acknowledged that Rob has the best eyes of all of the Browns, they're lighter than both Emmett's and Anne's and though there seems something Nordic in them, the aquamarine colour is a gift from his English grandfather, George Alfred Griffin, the kindest man Rob ever knew.

Rob is an arborist. Today he reckons the best perk of any outdoor job is that you need decent sunglasses which give you a place to hide. And even though his hands are hard from years of handling trees, today, standing there in his suit, face shaved, dark hair slicked back, the sunnies make him look sophisticated. He wouldn't mind keeping them on all day.

He stands beside his sisters Louisa, forty-six, and Jessie, thirty-two, both of them handsome dark-haired women who seem to be clinically observing the arrival of Peter as his car rattles and lurches into the yard. Even though she appears to be concentrating, it's possible that Louisa is not because today she is porous and possibly the only active thing about her is the sweat slipping from her temples. But then the burring sound of Peter's old car awakens her.

'For God's sake,' Rob says at the farting of the van's engine as it cools, 'that old kombi can't possibly hold out much longer and anyway, the bloody thing handles like a dog on lino.'

Out of old habit, Jessie snaps, 'We're not *all* as materialistic as you are Robert,' as they examine the faded orange pop-top kombi with Anne's floral curtains, noting a rainbow sticker, another one reading 'I ♥ Footscray' and a surfboard leaning on the back window. Tyres are a bit down too.

Rob, a tad wounded by Jessie's go at him, grumbles, 'Come off it Jess, even you drive something built in the last ten years.'

Jessie pulls her handbag in close over her shoulder. 'At least it's not a fuel-guzzling V8,' she sniffs, and considers that she might be allergic to something around here.

'And neither is mine,' he replies indignantly, lifting his hair with one hand and wiping the sweat from his brow with the back of the other one. He flicks a few drops onto the concrete and watching them disappear he reflects that such arguments are typical of the incendiary one. Always has to have the bloody last word, he complains to himself, and wonders whether all families have flame-throwers, even at funerals. If not, he'd be willing to hire her out.

Louisa pays no attention to their bickering, it's background noise and even kind of comforting in its way. No, she has other concerns. Actually, she thinks she might be hallucinating. When she looks at Peter's car she swears it's changed colour, wasn't it red? And he's been driving the thing forever. Can he really have got it when he was twenty-one? Scrambled eggs, she thinks with a sense of panic, my brains are scrambled eggs.

Anne was the first to declare that Louisa was overtired. As soon as she clapped eyes on her last night, she summed her up with, 'That girl needs a good long sleep.' But considering she'd just stepped off a plane from Italy, Louisa didn't think this particularly insightful. And it had been a long time since she was a girl.

She'd had one day in Venice when the call came through late that first night announcing the end of Emmett, so she'd packed up and headed straight home, and after flying for nearly forty-eight hours she had been bowled over by jetlag.

At Melbourne airport there was the usual jostling of passengers to be the first in to grab bags from the carousel. With a sinking heart Louisa entered into the fray with the men and minutes later, elbows out, she lurched back dragging someone else's bag. Of course. A big bloke helped her set the thing free again, but in the end she was the last person standing at the deserted carousel. It seemed her luggage was lost.

After long laps of circling time, some kind of officer stepped forward wearing a shining badge and a shirt the washed-out buff colour of Australian officialdom. His broad hat was slightly tipped back and a fine film of sweat bubbles glazed his big face.

'Everything all right here Miss? You've been here quite a while,' he said, planting his big feet. And all of a sudden, at that plain voice, Louisa felt she was home. And the lump in her throat was now a boulder.

When it became clear that her bag really *was* lost, for some reason she strangely and unexpectedly let slip to the officer that her father had just died and tears spilled over and she found herself sinking into sentences that wouldn't hold and she stuttered to a halt. It took a serious harnessing of all the shreds of her composure to stop herself from leaning into him and weeping.

'I'm very sorry to hear such sad news Miss,' the officer said and briskly led Louisa from the labyrinth of the sprawling airport. She trailed him like a lost child.

Outside in the bright day, with cars trundling past as though they were on tracks, he found a canary-yellow cab and got her into the back of it, took her name and address and said he'd see to the lost luggage. Then he stood up and like a magician, tapped the top of the cab three times to send it on its way.

From the speeding car, the flatness of the landscape lassoed Louisa's tired heart. This was bleached, practical country. Nothing flashy going on here, just parched land and thirsty air and it hadn't changed much in three days.

A flock of milky cockatoos lifted from a paddock and scattered upwards like seed on the wind. Louisa watched listlessly. The last few days had taken a toll. The skin on her lips was as dry as Cornflakes and her hair badly needed a wash. A solid magenta pimple had emerged near the corner of her mouth and had begun to throb. The volcano is ready to blow, she thought dully.

Louisa felt the reality of life. Father dead and here she was ageing fast, almost visibly, but she spoke sharply to herself about getting a grip. She'd hated her father and now she was getting weepy in front of strangers. Still, she argued, at times the old man could be okay. Sinking into the comfort of memory, she remembered the red children's encyclopaedias he bought for them and how he'd seen something special in the story of the ugly duckling and said sometimes there's a little ugly ducking in each of us. And later there was the time he'd won the double and given her money so she could lay-by the black dress covered with small flowers. The dress she wore when she got married.

The taxi driver, whose name according to a curling card sticking up on the dashboard was Hussein, had noticed her sniffling in the rear-vision mirror and put his foot down as if there were an emergency. Soon enough the paddocks were gone and Melbourne could well have been any of ten Australian cities, anonymous and closed up against the heat.

In Footscray, after Louisa leaned over to pay, the driver said in stumbling English, 'Please Miss, I hope you will be well,' and looked away tactfully. Didn't seem much, but she was felled by him and couldn't speak. Kindness always made her feel guilty; she doubted she deserved it. To explain it she harboured the strange thought that Hussein and the airport official might have been angels.

Still, seeing herself through Hussein's eyes, she realised she must look a sight so she smoothed her clothes, pushed her hair back and got ready for all that was coming. She mumbled thanks and gave him a mighty tip which made her feel exposed as a fool and then watched his cab move into the distance, a small bright piece of disappearing kindness. Then under the verandah next to the overflowing rubbish bin out the front of her mother's shop, she stood like a dolt. She was just getting her bearings.

That Anne still lives in the shop even though it's long been closed is an outward sign of her inner stubbornness. She sold all the stock but the shop itself was harder to shift. The idea of renting it and living upstairs was inconceivable. Anne likes her privacy. So, because she couldn't stand the thought of renting it to strangers, she decided to use the shop as a lounge room; the old display dummies in their skew-whiff wigs stand around in the background looking into the distance like family ghosts, their wrists forever at right angles.

It wasn't too long before the door burst open and Peter was dragging her inside. In the cool dark of the old shop her brothers and sister held out arms as though they were harbours and Louisa sailed right in; even the warmth of their hands on her back was comfort itself. So much had happened so fast.

Sadly though, she didn't wait long enough before she told them about the airport officer and the lost bags. The reticent girl was long gone, these days Louisa was a blurter. 'It was his accent that finished me off. I missed it so much, it was so good to hear one of us again.'

Pete and Jessie nodded; they understood. But Rob narrowed his eyes ever so slightly and said brusquely, 'For God's sake Louisa, you've only been gone a couple of days.' Blabbing about Emmett to strangers in airports was not on. And neither was whingeing.

Louisa read the message from Rob but it was too late, she was fully committed. She ploughed on, 'Well, he reminded

9

me of Dad,' she allowed herself to say and knew this was worse than lame, that she was revealing, even in this sideways fashion, that there might be more than just hate at work here.

The agreement between Rob and Louisa was being stretched but she was too tired to get into it. He'd always forgive her anyway. Always. She rubbed her raw eyes. The lack of sleep made them hot and it seemed all her history was crushed behind them. Time she went to bed.

The funeral was the next day. Rob said he'd drive her home. Gingerly, as though she were fragile cargo, she loaded herself into his ute, her legs moving heavily. Nothing was real and she was absorbing everything. He tried to ruffle her dirty hair but it stayed resolutely flat. They drove in a comfortable kind of silence.

'I'm glad you came back for the big day,' he said as the car slid through the streets. When they stopped, she put her hand on his shoulder, didn't want to let go. Tried a smile. 'See you tomorrow mate,' she said and stepped into the hot air.

From the front porch she watched the ute disappear and then, in slow motion, she let herself into the house, heading to the bedroom thinking, I have been awake for a thousand days. Didn't change, just lay down on the bed and pulled the bedspread up, glad her children were still at their father's.

*

Next morning, she'd driven to Gilberts in a state between sleeping and waking, hot-faced, gripping the steering wheel hard and driving with so much caution that she was beeped twice. But today she didn't even notice the impatient head-shaking of other drivers. The world was surreal this morning, the city tender from the weight of the heat and the sky the colour of roses.

As usual Louisa hadn't really looked in the mirror, just a glance to check that she didn't have toothpaste trailing from her mouth. She wasn't in the mood to be fussing with make-up, it was too damned hot and tears were expected. And anyway, she'd already had one miracle that morning.

Her white linen shirt had been hanging clean and ironed in the wardrobe and finding it had been such an enormous relief that it had felt like a gift. Small things, she muttered to herself as she forced on her good grey trousers and sucked in her stomach hoping the seams would hold. Though it was so damn hot, she'd have to wear the black shoes, she had no sandals apart from thongs. The endless little negotiations with the tyranny of everyday things.

Louisa had spoken to her kids at their father John Keele's house. No, they didn't want to come and though at heart she was disappointed and a sense of loneliness swam up around her, she didn't let it show, she just agreed with the kids that it would be for the best. Louisa never pushed things with them.

There was no suggestion that John would come, even though he had known and even liked Emmett. Ah people, she thought, when you get down to it, who really needs them? And how like mum that sounds, she realised and smiled.

*

So when that morning at Gilberts she looks up to see her former husband, John Keele, for the first time in nearly a year leaning blithely on a car in the blanched sunlight, she feels assaulted by the shock of him. He's wearing a grey jacket and his hair is long and fair and, unfortunately, he looks pretty good. 'Hi,' they say to each other smiling tightly. 'Thought you weren't coming,' she says. He shrugs and looks down Geelong Road, following a swaying semi.

Striding away from him she catches her heel on something and stumbles slightly. Jessie reaches out and grabs her sister to steady her. Louisa gestures towards John, and Jessie nods and says, 'I've already spoken to him, vile toad.' Jessie loved John as a child but when he left Louisa, she hated him. Loyalty is simple for Jess, though this wasn't always so. 'Don't even think about him,' she says fiercely and pats Louisa's shoulder. 'This is about getting rid of Dad, not him. His turn will come. All the bastards will go down in the end.' She smiles, grimly, Louisa thinks. They hold hands briefly. This is not what they usually do.

Louisa finds herself wondering what John's thinking and whether any of his poems have been published. Jessie grabs her arm harder than she means to. 'Louisa, this is not the day for ex-husbands,' she says firmly, looking her right in the eye. 'This is the day for burying fathers. Come on. We're doing it for Mum.'

Soon enough Peter is striding towards them, tall, dark and shining in his ironed white shirt, a shield against the heat. And almost immediately on seeing him, there's a release in Louisa. Here is Daniel's twin and while Danny is lost to them, Peter holds them together. Though they don't talk about it, they all believe he's the best of the family. Lou holds onto him as though he were a tree. 'Shoosh now,' he says, assuming all these tears are about Emmett. 'Shoosh Lou. It was the right time for him to go.' Jessie pats little circles on her back and the wind lifts her hair like a wing.

In the moment of being held by Peter there in the yard at Gilberts, Louisa understands this as the purest relationship she will ever have. Brothers and sisters want nothing from you. They know who you are and they love you anyway. These are the ones who know and in the war against Emmett, they'd been in the trenches with her.

Jessie scans the yard like a sentry. Rob and Anne watch while Peter and Louisa head inside Gilberts, then they follow. Inside, the dull light swallows them and Emmett's coffin dominates the room. Native flowers are splayed across the dark wood. Red waratahs so perfect they might be plastic lay upon gum leaves shaped like long tears. But no shiny metal gleams on Emmett's coffin because while Louisa was flying home it was decided that such folderols would be a waste of money and the one thing the Browns do not waste is money.

The family moves to the front of the big room and relatives and friends and old codgers who wouldn't miss a funeral for quids drift into the seats behind them. Rob walks to the wooden podium and slides a sheet of paper out of his breast pocket, unfolds it and somewhat reluctantly it seems, takes off his sunglasses.

He clears his throat tentatively and then in a calm voice says, 'Thank you for coming here today on this very warm day, it's much appreciated by all of us.' He pauses, smoothes out the folds in his sheet of paper. Clears his throat again and pushes off into the deep.

'In all the world Emmett really only had us four kids and Mum. He had two old uncles who were basically his parents but they died a while ago. He never knew his father and his mother put him into the orphanages when he was young. He did have a half-brother, Jimmy, and a couple of half-sisters, but they were fostered out and there wasn't much contact there.

'Emmett kept diaries on and off for most of his life. A few are still kicking around. I want to read something to you from one of Emmett's diaries, this one from February 25, 1974. Emmett was aged forty-two when he wrote, "When I die, I don't want any mealy-mouthed, psalm-singing hypocrite talking bullshit about me. I just want my mob and I want them to cry for me. Cry for me, but not too much and, please, I ask you all now to forgive me for doing some of the wrong things I did. Remember me and laugh about the funny times. Laugh about me. Laugh at me. Doesn't matter. Remember, I was nothing but a drunken old bum."'

Rob looks up into the little room and sees the small crowd of mostly dark heads looking down.

'We are Emmett's mob and we are here to say goodbye. Emmett was a tough father and we had our problems, to be honest there were many problems. The best I can say is that I remember him clearly. Emmett was a teacher, always a teacher. He taught me how to cut an apple. He taught me how to bowl a cricket ball. He taught me how to make compost and he taught me a lot of things I would rather not have known.'

Rob is gripping the podium and holding on to his place in the flow of his sentences with one hand. He's not sure there's anything more to say. Emmett loved music so each of the kids has chosen a song for him. Sinatra singing 'The Summer Wind' begins and somehow the music brings Emmett to life. Tears start again.

As the music sways through the hot room, Rob walks stiffly from the podium and sits down next to Jessie, bowing his head to listen with the rest of them. Jessie puts a hand on his arm. He's folded his speech and grasps it like he might want to hit someone with it. The music has got to him. He angrily dashes away a tear with the back of his hand.

By the time it's Louisa's turn to speak, she's beetroot-faced and it's becoming clear that she slept on one side all night because that side of her hair still prefers to be up. Louisa is known to be a truly terrible public speaker and the Browns are bracing themselves for her speech. They've seen it all before at weddings and even at small family birthday parties. Things begin almost normally and then with unnerving speed the speech veers off. Stretches of anxious silence arise in the audience, sympathetic murmuring and sometimes even clucks can be heard.

She once explained the terror to Peter. 'When people look at me all at once I feel like I'm disappearing. Like I'm being eaten.' He thought about this and put both hands behind his head. 'Think of the sea Louie, the sea doesn't panic. Sometimes you remind me of the sea.' And Louisa said, 'Yeah, vast and all encompassing,' and laughed dolefully, swiftly dodging the compliment.

In most speeches, after a few words her eyes spring leaks and soon enough she's actually crying, and not even at the sad parts. Today, the people at the funeral duly wonder when the tears will begin.

Louisa has written something and is damned if she isn't going to read the thing. She's the eldest after all, and she feels the magnitude of this. She launches into her speech with an uneven, 'Hello, I am Louisa, eldest of Emmett's children,' then bizarrely qualifies with, 'though Rob is only a year younger, so there's not much in it.'

She takes a deep breath and ominously feels a sob rising like a big bird stretching its wings within her and the words stall. The audience thinks, *and so soon* and sighs a fateful sigh. With effort, she wrestles the sob down and after a pause begins again.

'We spend a lot of time talking about Emmett in the Brown household and much about him will always be inexplicable because he towered over us. He was a giant and giants, you'll agree, are unusual creatures.' She doesn't look up but holds the paper in front of her as if it were a screen between herself and the audience and she reads fast to beat the tears. 'He encouraged my love of words and that's how I ended up in my first career in journalism, so I'll give him that. When Dad was in a good mood he'd wander around, making a cup of tea checking on his "System" stats and sometimes saying "branch" again and again because he loved the bloody sound of it. When I asked him once why he kept saying "branch" he said he "liked the song the word made in the air".

'And he wanted us to love words too. When Rob and I were kids he got us to define words. We tried so hard to get them right.' Here her voice rocks unevenly and tears slip from her eyes. She tries to push them back in but it doesn't work, so she clears her throat, takes a sip of water and ploughs on. 'He taught us to spit properly, none of that dribbling. He said, "If you're going to spit, make it straight and fast." We are all excellent spitters,' she says to an unexpected wave of laughter which she reads through, head down, galloping like a riding school pony in sight of the home gate.

'And he taught the boys to shake hands like men. He said, "Look people straight in the eye and then one shake and release – hand fully into the palm, none of this fingertip bullshit."' Again laughter falls softly about her and startles her, making her look up so she loses her place and for a moment the thudding of her heart is all there is. She finds the place again and races on.

'He told me reading was the best way to understand the world, no bloody doubts about that. He believed writing was the greatest art form. Though he thought dancing was an art too and that Rudolf Nureyev was as great an artist as the footballer Alex Jesaulenko. He loved anything written by Hemingway, Steinbeck, Tolkein, by Henry Lawson, or by his beloved Banjo Paterson, and his favourite music was by Tchaikovsky and Beethoven.

'He was a man who loved to feel things strongly. I want you to hear this simple little song by Cat Stevens because I remember listening to it by the old radiogram in the front room one day when Dad walked in and I thought he'd yell at me and tell me to get out, but he said the music was nice. This is 'The Wind' by Cat Stevens. Also the other choice, the *1812 Overture*, would probably take up a bit too much time.'

When she comes back to the wooden seat, Anne clasps Louisa's hand in her own knotty hands. Louisa knows this is clearly the worst speech she's ever given but by now it doesn't even matter. There is a wrenching going on within her. Some kind of old pain is finding its way out right there in the little chapel at Gilberts and while she's shuddering with grief, she is also honestly beyond caring. That her children won't see it is the only thing that matters.

Beside her Jessie is sobbing steadily, her shoulders rocking. The tissues in her hand are a mesh of snot and tears. She barely raises her head. Peter doesn't want to speak. Says he can't think of anything that hasn't been said. The odd tear slides down his face as he sits with an arm around Jess.

Outside the hot north wind pounds the ragged little funeral parlour and whips under the overpass. The palm tree out the front stoops before the wind and sheds papery fronds that curl on the hot concrete. Eva Cassidy is singing 'Fields of Gold' as Louisa and Rob and Peter and Jessie carry Emmett's coffin down the length of the chapel, and the music gives them strength.

Apparently there are those who believe that women shouldn't carry coffins. Well, thinks Louisa, here they bloody do. She looks across at her sister and is glad at last that there's another woman in the family. They feel each other supporting their father and now that the load is shared, he seems a lighter man.

Turning right with the coffin isn't easy. There's some mild straining and the sweat flows. Outside, the silver hearse shaped like a bullet is ready to take Emmett away. They wait for the back to open and then in a slipping moment the coffin is lowered and swallowed by the wide mouth of the shining vehicle and then the door comes down and Emmett Brown is stowed away forever.

Outside Rob slips his sunglasses back on and waits for Anne to emerge. He studies the sky intensely. Notes that the dust storm is edging closer. A blotchy Louisa reckons the coffin in the hearse seems far too final for something connected to Emmett.

She looks over at her mother and her brothers and Jessie, slim and tawny as a lioness today, and thinks, well, freedom opens many doors and we will be free of him. She walks over to Rob and Peter and puts an arm around each brother. There's a space in them where the tears have been sheltering. Each of them feels exposed, there's been too much crying today and all feel weakened by the display. The worst of it is that they know people believe they've been weeping for their father and that they are simply bereaved by his death.

The truth is something else. Louisa closes her eyes and sees a flash of him in the kitchen, the light streaming in, making them fill his beer glass and God help them if they spilled a drop. Beating them, terrorising them, humiliating or exalting them – and she still doesn't know which was worse.

And the sad irony is that she realised this wasn't love only when she was far too old to have such doubts. She feels a pulse of rage at the pathetic man in the coffin. And then recalls his shaggy grey head, sees him old and stumbling in the hostel before he died, and once again pity for the poor old bastard takes the place of rage.

And she realises how tainted is anything connected with Emmett. Themselves included. With their arms around each other, their heads down, the four of them so different, yet so united by their father. They feel the strength of each other.

They meet eyes and recognise their oldest grief – for a stolen childhood.

Before the hearse moves off, Peter reaches out and puts his hand on the back of the thing. He doesn't want to let him go, wants to keep Emmett with him, and he couldn't explain it even to himself but he understands there will be no slowing this completion. A wash of boiled afternoon sun is sifting through the gauzy dust as the hearse moves off slowly and makes its way towards the crematorium at Altona, further west again. As it climbs Mount Mistake, Peter is the only one of them to be glad that the old man will have one last view of his great, flat, baking city before the darkening sky closes over them, but then Peter has a forgiving nature.

2

Louisa's first memory is of a plate of food lifting through the kitchen then ramming into a wall and sliding down slowly with the suction of a squid. Other times the plate would leap off the wall and smash into a tangle of sharpness and food. Apparently Emmett doesn't like pumpkin. Or bastard chops. Can't you get it through your head that he's sick to fucking death of chops?

'For God's sake!' he roars, 'Can't a man have a decent fucking meal ready for him you pathetic bitch? Is that too much to ask after a hard fucking day at work? You slave your guts out every fucking day and you come home to this putrid slop.' You can see he's briefly pleased with something and if Louisa were older she would reason that it was probably the word 'putrid', an excellent choice if harsh in this context. Still, he wastes no time gloating about good words now because he's in full flight, holding her small mother by the face.

'Is this good? No. What is this? I don't know, I don't . . .' The smacking sounds are loud and hard. Her mother is on her knees. Louisa is nearly two and Rob about one. The screaming that goes with the throwing has been eliminated and the plates slide in a resounding silence. The child has stopped hearing. Her eyes are doing all the work now, pulling in images like a satellite dish. She must stay quiet, stay small and stay near her brother. She must not watch the hurting.

Right from the very beginning she understands that one day Emmett will kill her or one of them or all of them and then it'll be their own fault. The certainty of it edges into her life. He is the paw of the bear on her head, heavy with the promise of its nature.

*

Friday nights are pay nights. Summer is grass green and it's the blue of high skies and it's the honey colour of sun. Days are spent in the envelope of yard in the housing commission place where the sea of grass waves high above their heads because Emmett doesn't like to mow.

Children chasing and squealing and playing Blackfoot, their game of stalking lizards and each other. Playing hard and laughing and chasing each other until all are breathless and sagging like spent sacks onto the grass to laugh and then again to play some more. To make soup with flowers with the sun falling around them like a cloak of light.

There are only two Brown kids and all the other kids are from down the street. They're allowed into the Brown yard but never into the house. Emmett doesn't like other people's brats. They are gathered around the bucket making daisy-weed soup when Emmett appears at the corner coming in from the street with a big box balanced on his shoulder like a greengrocer.

'Come on you mob,' he yells loud and happy tonight. 'Come and see what I got.' He's been to see his old mates at the market. When he was young he lived near there and worked its long aisles sweeping and scrounging. There was no choice, he said, either you gave the family a chop-out or you went back to the orphanage.

Anne makes a space on the table. The screen door swings and the Brown children surge in on the wave of their father and there on the table is the biggest box of fruit they've ever seen. The neighbour kids watch for a while at the wire door but soon they are pulled away like small ghosts.

A bristly pineapple and a watermelon like a striped submarine and grapes as green as eyes and apples and cherries so dark and hard, all spill out of the box. The kids and Anne and even Emmett make earrings out of the cherries and eat some until their teeth turn red. Then Emmett takes out the big knife and swings it down into the watermelon and the slicing, sucking sound as he pulls it out is tidal. He cuts them slices bigger than their faces. They spit shiny black pips into the box and then Emmett is cutting pears and serving thin slices skewered onto the tip of the knife like a priest offering communion.

Rob, his mouth full of cherries, says, 'Dad, you should work at the market and we can always have fruit like this forever, wouldn't that be good?' Emmett pats the boy's head, his hair so short his skull is visible. He smiles, his teeth still dark from the cherries.

3

Emmett explains it to the kids in the square little kitchen. Nan's rose plate is stuck high on the wall, Louisa thinks, like a portal to a better world. 'Words,' her father says, 'are *the* key to life. There is nothin' they can't do.' He glares at Rob, daring him to move. Rob, the boy who has trouble keeping still, looks down and boldly decides to fidget with his fork.

When Emmett moves his searchlight gaze from him, Rob sneaks the fork off the table and under his leg, just to see if he can get away with something, anything. Sometimes Louisa feels winded by the high daring of her little brother. Why would you risk it?

They understand Emmett loves words. Always has. He wanted to be a poet but he has to work for a living supporting these ungrateful brats instead. They all know he's read Jack London's book *The Call of the Wild* so many times that he can practically recite the thing from cover to cover. They don't have a copy of it in the house so they can't read it themselves, but boy do they know the story. Triumph over adversity – all the best stories have it. That, and a hero, you gotta have a hero. Emmett's drummed it all into them.

Emmett doesn't write poems anymore. His words are cast into the amber liquid. These days he reasons he'll just make the kids clever and this will reflect well. So on good days

Emmett the quizmaster tosses questions around and waits for the kids to catch them and open them up as though they were boxes of treasure.

'What is a hedge?' he asks one night after tea when the plates are pushed back and the blue laminex table cleared enough for questions and elbows. This is a night when there will be a bit of entertainment. The question hangs and the silence stretches and eyes dart between the children. Competition is king and which kid is the smartest? Louisa or Rob?

The kids, at six and seven, are astounded and stumped by the word 'hedge'. Nothing grows around the housing commission but weeds.

'That's one for ya,' Emmett laughs and pushes back his hair and when he laughs there's that eyetooth, sharp and yellow.

'Hedge! Come on now! Think about it,' Emmett urges and the word hangs above them solid and impregnable. Louisa thinks it's a word like 'edge' and Emmett says 'maybe' and 'you may well be right my dear'. Rob, still fooling with the fork, will not be outdone by Louisa smarming up to Emmett. That the old man sometimes likes her makes her someone to beat. He hatches an answer. 'A hedge is something green,' he declares and Emmett says that together they are completely one hundred bloody per cent right and he suspends the moment for a long time and spins it out until you can hear time moving away in inches with each tick of the clock.

And then, all theatre, he says that yes it is so, that 'a hedge is indeed a green edge, an edge of green'. The kids are pleased but you wouldn't know it. They're both subdued, Louisa with worry and Rob with sharing victory. She hisses to Rob to put the stupid fork away.

The twins, Peter and Daniel, are in their wicker carrycots on the floor, cooing and batting away time as if it's nothing at all and Louisa wishes she was still a baby, safe from questions.

Rob decides Louisa is acting like Lady Muck, typical pain-in-the-neck-know-all-girl, and she's watching with owl eyes. Patient, waiting, willing Emmett not to change, to let this night finish without incident.

The boy hates her encompassing stare. Sometimes it seems not to be aimed at you, though most often it is. Still, he reckons, she's a worthy rival because she can pursue you without seeming to hunt and she's always alert. Always ready to get you and always wishing for a better Emmett.

In this wish they're united, but Rob doesn't leave it at wishing. He places his own hopes on time. On being a grown-up. Then Emmett will be gone and there will be just him and his mum.

'Watch out Rob,' Lou hisses urgently, spitting on her finger and smearing the red territory of a mozzie bite on her leg, 'and listen. Might be a story coming.'

Louisa understands the way to be. Be silent until he wants to speak to you and then be polite. Your eyes should not be boastful. Hold yourself inside. She doesn't share her under-standing with Rob, there's no way he'd listen anyway, he's too full of himself for listening.

But a peaceful night is not on the agenda. Not long after the triumph of the hedge definition, the fork inevitably stabs Rob in the leg and he leaps away from the table with a revealing scream. A little row of blood beads stands out from his thigh. That's it, game over.

Emmett leans over, his long arm heavy in the yellow kitchen, and swats the boy hard as he passes, so hard that he reels back. Louisa, standing appalled beside the chair, is belted across the face for good measure.

4

The walls of Wolf Street are coated with old smoke from the fire when the couch went up a while ago. Grandpa George thought it was the fireplace and put a match to it. Pretty soon smoke was rolling out from the house and Stan Williams from next door, a big soft pillow of a man, just happened to be getting home late from his Red Cross meeting. He was a volunteer.

When he saw the hot mesh of smoke emerging, he ran round the back and pushed through the door of the smoky house. Choking, he grabbed Louisa, who seemed to always be at her grandparents' house in those days, and pulled her out of bed. He surged down the front with the child in his arms like a hero emerging from the surf.

Outside in the street Nan and Pa sat on kitchen chairs with blankets across their shoulders. The red of the fire truck throbbed through the night and smoke, a slinking animal, just kept slipping through the door.

Because of the fire, Grandpa George went to live at the big mental home in the parched paddocks further west at Sunbury and Nan stayed on at Wolf Street alone. Anne took the kids to Sunbury on Sundays.

To get there they'd walk the long paths through brown paddocks. The paths were shaded from the white hot sun by corrugated iron strips and after many turns they'd find Pa standing alone among many in a vast room, bruised from thumps from other patients.

Though his pants were held up with braces, he'd lost so much weight they sagged like a half-mast flag. His eyes were gaps. Even in photographs it was apparent that he was fading out. When the kids held his hands they could have been holding moths.

He died at Sunbury and Nan forgot about eating and survived on smokes alone. So in 1969, Emmett and Anne and Louisa and Rob and the twins Peter and Daniel moved into Wolf Street, West Footscray. They brought their beds, their noise, their fights and not much else.

*

The Maribyrnong River pushes inland from the ports on the marshy edges of the horse-head-shaped Port Phillip Bay deep into Footscray. If you rise up above, you'll see that the city works on a grid and also, that there are so few trees, it's a blasted landscape.

Regardless of trees, Emmett believes Footscray is a better bet than the housing commission and Wolf Street has the advantage that the War Service loan on Nan's house is cheaper. More money for booze and the ponies.

Although Wolf Street is to the west of the river, on warm evenings when the kids are playing kick-to-kick on the deserted Total service station behind the house, they imagine that in the lull between kicks and in the spaces of silence when cars are not roaring down Williamstown Road, they can just about hear tug boats moving about in some blue distance. It's highly doubtful the Browns can hear any boats. Still, they persist in the illusion. Such fancies make life better. And though they seldom discuss them, they uphold them with each other.

Number fifty-five Wolf Street is one in a row of boxy wooden places that line both sides of the long narrow street. It has four rooms, two on each side divided by a skinny passageway. First is the lounge room where in winter Emmett stokes the fire until the throbbing orange of it forces the kids and their cushions back like retreating seals. Next comes Emmett and Anne's room, then Nan's, and the kids are in the last room. The kitchen runs along the back and is connected to a small bathroom with a sliding door. A lean-to fernery slouches up against the kitchen and the washhouse and toilet hang onto that. There's no electric light and no windows and sitting on the throne in the dunny in the dark, the kids' feet swing high and loose.

A modified Hills hoist dominates the yard. An amateur inventor once lived at fifty-five, a bloke named Herb Hawkins, long since dead. Herb took it into his head to improve upon the clothesline with a hydraulic lift device (a hose) attached to the tap beside the house. The water was meant to push up the clothesline and save all the effort of winding. Possibly it once worked but when the Browns live there it doesn't, and now tilts heavily to one side.

Since the hydraulics packed up (oozing for weeks like a wound) the clothesline offers no lift at all and so remains fixed. Sheets can't go on the low side because they drag in the dirt. Still, the frame of the thing is sturdy enough for kids to swing on and as a wizzy-giver it's unbeatable.

The kids aren't allowed inside much when Emmett's around, so the backyard and the street are theirs. For a little yard, there's a lot going on. In one corner is the big shed which is seldom used by adults anymore since Emmett made beer and most of the bottles exploded.

Now the big shed is calm though slightly creepy and the kids reckon there may be someone buried inside in a shallow grave, just going by the atmosphere. A curtain of spiders' webs hangs over the crooked little window.

The dog who became Frank was hidden in there for six days until his scratching and howling got him discovered and turfed out by Emmett who raged red-faced that he refused to take on any more bloody dogs . . . or kids. 'They shit everywhere and bite people and then a man has to sort the whole bloody mess out. NOT HAVING IT!'

But the dog was never really impressed by Emmett. He just sat there in the shed watching and even seemed bored, as if he'd seen better displays. He propped outside on the concrete and scratched himself lazily. And the kids had seen worse displays about less, so they weren't without hope either.

For two days the dog sat at the front gate of number fifty-five without food. He took a bit of water from the gutter when he could find it but it seemed he had chosen his family and that was it. In the end, coming home from work one day, Emmett saw him there, invited him in for a feed of Rice Bubbles and gave him a name.

'Francis Xavier O'Hooligan,' Emmett declared in the kitchen that night standing beside Frank as the dog enthusiastically knocked back his Rice Bubbles, 'is a Catholic dog.' Pause, while the kids absorbed the detail. 'And as such, will need to be treated with respect and affection. These Micks get touchy if you don't love 'em,' he explained sagely to the kids, drawing on his time in a Catholic orphanage but not saying so. 'They are very fond of a bit of ceremony,' he said. 'Love a bit of a fuss.'

The kids thought their father was off and raving again and they knew that the dog was unlikely to have a religion, but listening was the way of peace, and they were deeply glad to have the sane and wise Frank on board.

*

The little shed was where Pa used to finish off cricket bats, planing them patiently and knocking them in with a wooden mallet. It was even said that some of his bats had been used by test cricketers.

And when he was working, the knocking of wood on wood rang out in hollow circles. Pa once worked at a little bat factory down the road in Seddon. He made a bat for Rob but it got pinched which was said to be Rob's own fault, yet no one suffered more at the loss of the mystical bat than Rob. He yearned for it, dreamed about it. Emmett called the boy pathetic for losing the bat and said he ought to be whipped but right at that moment, he couldn't be bothered. He did say that giving the boy a bat was a waste. 'Never be much of a batsman, would ya anyway? Never be much good at anybloodything.'

Still when the boy made his first century in the schoolyard Emmett was mildly aroused. He was stacking the week's beer supply into the fridge leaving not much space for anything else. Bending over, he was illuminated by the fridge light and for a while it seemed he might even be impressed. But then flipping the lid off the first for the day, he dismissed it as schoolboy cricket and not worth a pinch of shit.

After Pa died each of the kids claimed the little shed at various times – the boys for a fort with sticks poking through the windows like weapons. For a while the war theme was uppermost and they made hand grenades out of tins stuffed with oily rags and chucked them out onto the petrol station where Dimitri, the transcendently dark bloke who ran the servo, kicked them aside or chucked them back. The bombs made a racket on the tin roof and his curses were like nothing they'd ever heard.

In time, another project beckoned, making a machine or a kite or a billycart. Rob was always in charge but Peter and Dan, three years younger, were usually the inspiration. Louisa was neither invited nor interested but when the boys tired of the shed, she inherited it. Tried to make a home of it and put up pictures of flowers laboriously cut from faded magazines and draped scraps of her mother's fabrics at the window.

A moat of concrete surrounds the house and beyond the shed the backyard is a square of dust and weeds dominated by the clothesline skeleton and a skinny apple tree grown from a core Louisa buried in the dust and watered. Sometimes Rob mows the patch of weeds with the rusty hand-mower.

The front of the house faces west and cops the full force of the afternoon sun as it heaves into the lounge room and the front bedroom. On summer afternoons the venom in that sun feels personal, but somehow the narrow sideway stays cool with fishbone ferns and moss unfurling slow and green in shallow furrows along the fence.

Anne tries to soften the old house by putting pale pebbles around the one established plant at Wolf Street, a barbed old mother-in-law's tongue jutting victoriously from the triangle garden bed under the lounge-room window. But unfortunately, the pebbles reflect sunlight upwards into the room like a searchlight and make it hotter. The pointy plant grows bigger and sharper.

Anne lays black plastic under the pebbles to suppress the oxalis and kikuyu but soon, with the pure resolve of freedom fighters, the weeds surge through the plastic and engulf the pebbles until she admits defeat and gardens no more. A hanging basket that once held red petunias still swings with ghostly menace on the verandah now, heavy with dry dirt.

On the house, the paint has been shed down to the naked slug-coloured wood but for the kids even paint has its uses. It's possible in idle moments to conscientiously ease off long shreds of it and then to scrunch them into younger ones' heads so that it looks like they have appalling dandruff with the added bonus that it's very hard to remove.

All the neighbourhood kids agree that the Browns live in the worst house in the street and some even say it's haunted. Johnno Johnson from Louisa's grade rides past regularly on his sister's bike yelling, 'Ghostie . . . Wooooooo Louisa Brown lives in a ghost house.' After the second time he does it Louisa is convinced this can only mean he likes her. Therefore, she reasons, he must be cracked.

Soon after the move to Wolf Street, the Brown kids discover a hedge down the street and they find out what hedges are best for: hiding in. It's a big, shaggy cypress hedge on a corner. The apex is deep and comfortable and in there, in that dry little room, the roots of the hedge push down into the earth, protecting the children like the ankles of giants.

5

Matchbox cars are the most prized toy. The boys covet them, hoard them and steal them from each other. One Saturday morning when Anne is at the shops, a hushed scuffle breaks out over a little red matchbox truck. It's hushed because Emmett is working at his statistics in the front room and the kids are in the passageway in front of their room. Daniel starts wailing because Rob has pinched his favourite matchbox.

'Give it back to me, you know it's mine, you know it's my best one,' the four-year-old cries thinly, loudly, and for far too long. Emmett sends a little warning through the door of his room. 'You are starting to give me THE IRRITS,' he shouts into the pool of temporary silence.

And then Rob comes back to life. 'Nick off,' he jeers softly to Daniel, 'it's mine wormhead and you can go jump.' He holds the red truck up at full stretch in his dirty hand and smirks at his little brother. Peter and Louisa emerge. 'Sshhh,' Louisa whispers and then hisses loudly, 'JUST SHUT UP!' No one listens. Then somehow Daniel's tears get fuller and Peter steps in to help with a brave and bold, 'Give it to him! You rat, you rotten rat!' And all of a sudden Rob loses his temper and hurls the matchbox hard at Peter and it clips the top of his head and cuts him.

The boy puts his hand up and with a throb of panic, feels the slippery stickiness of blood. 'Oh!' he yells and gets ready to yell it again. Instead he begins to cry in earnest and spins around in search of an adult and at that exact moment Emmett bursts out of the bedroom like a big grey hurricane.

There are times when the kids see him as the Tasmanian Devil, the tornado from the cartoons. There are days when he seems to whirl and froth, to have too many arms. Today he stands there considering for a moment and then decides. He swoops down and grabs Rob by the back of his shirt and drags him all the way down the passageway to the bathroom.

The other kids are still knotted together near the bedroom doorway watching their brother being hauled away by their father. They long remember his toes pointing up as he is pulled away. His eyes are locked to Louisa's but they all witness the crying boy who knows what's coming. It's a long way down that passage when you know what's coming.

Emmett throws the boy into the bathroom and takes off his belt and then he belts his son until he's exhausted and the boy is just a sobbing lump on the floor. It takes a long time. Each time the belt lands, they hear it cut into him and then they hear the boy who hates tears, they hear him sob.

They wait outside the sliding bathroom door, a little posse of dread. When Emmett steps out like a man who's done his business, Rob is slumped in a heap against the bath, crying and bleeding. They huddle back against the wall, waiting for the shock to leave and release them. Peter and Daniel believe it's their fault and hold each other, and the grief of causing such a thing weighs heavy.

At the sight of her brother's face, Louisa feels her stomach rise. It's swollen beyond recognition. He's not making a noise and yet tears still flow from his closed eyes. Maybe he's unconscious. Louisa doesn't know. He's been sick on the floor. She picks him up and half carries him to the bedroom. The twins hover like duplicate ghosts.

Rob is shivering and crying and so is she, but she must think, not give in. She runs back to the bathroom and gets a face washer hot under the tap and wrings it out tight. She finds the Dispirin bottle and makes him a half glass full of it and gets him to drink it. Red welts rise up all over him and blood drops steadily from his mouth and nose. Carefully, she touches his cheek with the hot face washer and he closes his eyes. 'Lou,' he murmurs, 'we'll have to kill him. I think we will.'

The twins sit on the other bed close together, still shaking. Louisa climbs onto the bed and holds her brother. 'Don't think about him now,' she says, 'you're alive, just be glad.'

In the back of his throat Rob makes a noise. 'Not glad,' are the words she later understands him to have said.

Then Peter and Daniel come over and weld themselves to the older kids and Louisa sees that Rob is still holding the red matchbox car in his small filthy hand. He must have picked it up before Emmett descended.

*

Rob sees himself as an astronaut stepping onto the biscuity moon. In 1969 this is not an original idea but after the moon landing, even in Australia, such things seem possible.

Louisa tells him he's mental to even think about it, be damn lucky to get a decent job much less one as an astronaut. And while he sees what she is driving at, he won't let her stop his dreams. He nurtures them and collects bits of junk to make air hoses for space suits and hooks them up to the old washing-machine tank in the shed. For a while he even calls it mission control.

He likes to think surrounded by the length of the sky, all that emptiness seems welcoming to him after the crowded little place they live in, and he loves to get up high on the fernery roof. Up there he feels safe.

One side of his room is wallpapered with vintage cars. Anne had thought about doing the whole room but it might have looked too much and besides there was the cost to consider, wallpaper is quite pricey you know. On the other side of the room his younger brother Peter is dreaming of fishing, his favourite thing. Rob doesn't know what he sees in it. Peter sleeps in the bottom bunk under the balding blue candlewick bedspread and Daniel is up top.

Peter whimpers a bit when he sleeps, always has, but tonight, a Tuesday night in July, he's having a good dream of fishing at a beach where it's sunny and still and the fish, beautiful little silver flatties, are lining up to be dragged in. Daniel snores. The ashy moon filters through the gingham curtains.

It's about four am when Emmett appears at Rob's bedside and shakes him awake. 'Get up boy. We're going fishing,' he says low and dark and then stalks out. What? Rob says to himself, wondering if he's really seen his father. He unglues his eyes, sticky from the depth of sleep. He knows not to argue. In the other beds Peter whinnies on, happy enough with the night, and Daniel is silent now.

Blinking and stumbling, Rob gets himself into the glary kitchen in his school pants and green moss-stitch jumper that Nan knitted years ago for Louisa. Emmett is a hulking dark shape sitting at the table fully dressed in his work coat and boots. 'Get your shoes on boy,' he says, and Rob stuffs his feet into his school shoes. He doesn't bother with laces or socks. These are the only shoes he owns and without socks they hold his feet loosely.

When they step outside into the dark mid-winter morning past Frank curled outside the back door, it's so cold the dog doesn't move. He could be made of stone.

The Browns' car is a 1964 EH Holden, white with red bench seats and white piping. It's Emmett's pride and joy and not more than five years old. Sitting out there all night in wintry Wolf Street, it might as well be refrigerated.

With each breath, steam rolls from Rob's mouth onto the windows. Emmett is hurling something into the boot and the boy has no clue what it might be. He slams the boot down and then he's back, a big man heaving himself into the car, making the seat drop with the weight of him and lifting the child up with a puff.

Emmett causes the mist to grow thicker on the windows but the demister is on the blink so he rubs a porthole in the glass in front of him and pushes the car into gear. With a protest and a lurch from the frozen engine that hasn't had long enough to warm, they are away and sliding down the thin street like a barge on a canal.

Rob doesn't know where they're going. He looks at the street lights slipping past and he thinks, this is it. He's going to kill me and dump me. Must be. Well, it makes sense, seeing as how he hates me. I'm a runt.

He sneaks little sideways looks at Emmett sitting hunched in his big blanket of a jacket. Holding the steering wheel lightly and staring into the cautious morning, he thinks Emmett looks like an Indian from a Western.

The father smokes steadily and the haze of it swims around and the orange tip of the cigarette lingers in the corner of the boy's eye. Disapprovingly, the boy thinks that he might cry and this will prove he's a weakling, which he thinks is true but he knows it will be the end of him if he does cry. So he fiercely looks down at his white legs as the light changes outside the car and he studies those legs very carefully.

And the legs in the short pants are thin as stems. Scabs drift across the knees and shins, healing at different rates.

The newest are still raw and tight but others have set as hard as lids. The oldest scabs are at the wafer stage, light and thin and nearly ready to flick. He draws comfort in thinking about picking his scabs, but he doesn't try it in the car. The old man wouldn't like that.

Emmett doesn't speak and that's all the boy hears, and anyway he doesn't know what to say to his father. He's filled with a circle of thoughts and most of them involve dying. At least it's going to be over, he says to himself. He hates me, hates me, I'm too small, I wish I was bigger. He'd like me then, maybe. Nah, I'm just too bad. It's the end now. He's going to get rid of me, maybe then things will get better for the others.

He says such things to himself again and again with the rhythm of the road as it cuts through the milky light of morning. Tears stall on his eyelids and then slip sideways and he wills them not to fall. The boy holds his own hands all the way through the sleeping city just for the warmth they offer.

On that school morning after three hours driving out along the coast, they pull off the bitumen at a bleak and empty beach. The sky is steel grey and the wind has picked up and is whipping the stinging sand in the carpark against them, and the beach has a malignant feel.

Rob stands beside the car door shivering in his short pants and pulling his sleeves over his hands. Emmett steps out of the car and stretches himself lazily as if he were a lion penned up too long. From the boot he gets out a bag of bait and a couple of broken-down rods and turns to the beach.

Like a stray dog, Rob follows his father down the track until the sea is revealed, so much of it spilling over the sand. He sees a lot of sky, maybe too much, and it's all grey this morning. Emmett strides across the pale horizon like a dark god and the boy follows at a distance, trudging through sand, shivering, and thinking about what will happen next. Blood, he reckons, there'll be lots of it.

Then Emmett stops and throws down the gear, snaps the rods together, drags some bait out of a bag and weaves frozen tubes of octopus onto the hook. With a practised arm he begins casting.

Should the boy do what the old man is doing? He doesn't know. He sits at a distance from Emmett and takes in the Southern Ocean through his mirror eyes and decides it looks cold. What lives under there? Sharks. I bet there's an awful lot of sharks he concludes.

After a while, somehow, he begins to feel calmer and time edges in and settles him and he thinks of the kids at school, sees them sitting at their desks and then outside running and playing and kicking the footy. Probably for the first time in his life he wishes he was at school.

He burrows his hands and his feet, even in their shoes, into the cold sand because it's warmer under there than the air. He wishes he'd found a pair of socks before they left.

Emmett fishes for ages, whipping the line through the air again and again and into the sea until the bait is gone and the tide has changed. He catches nothing. Then suddenly he turns and walks back to the car and Rob follows.

On the drive home to Footscray Emmett is silent just as he was all the way there, but it does seem to Rob that going home doesn't take nearly so long and he reckons he probably isn't going to get killed today so he relaxes and breathes, looks at the houses and thinks about what he might have missed at school.

When they pull up in Wolf Street, Rob sees Peter and Louisa and Daniel further down the street playing kick-to-kick, dodging the parked cars with the other kids. They wave to him, Louisa with the ball under her arm. 'C'mon Robbie!

Come and have a kick!' she yells all out of breath. But he isn't in the mood and just shakes his head and follows his father inside.

Once in the house he slips away from Emmett but not before he's told to get him a beer. In his bedroom, the boy crawls under his bed and there among the fluff and old toys he cries silently for so long, his arms wrapped around himself, that in end he is gathered by sleep.

6

If the Browns want a shower they have to tip briquettes, small chunks of brown coal, into the top of the old briquette heater. The big tank stands about six feet tall not far from the back door and when it's going, they place their hands on the skin of it and feel the hot water waiting inside. When there's fire in its belly the kids open the latch at the bottom where the ash pan slides in and out and see a roaring orange place and it seems that things aren't too bad really. But when it's out, coldness seems to spread.

It is Rob's job to fill the hot water tank but everyone knows he's irresponsible, so Louisa is used to humping the hessian bag of briquettes on her back over to the heater, then climbing onto the chair beside it, heaving up the sack and tipping it. Then hearing the long slide as the coal falls.

Rob, never so fussy about showers, watches his sister go through the ritual. He's stumped and peeved. Good, he thinks stewing on it, let her. How can she be bothered anyway? Bloody girls.

But he doesn't say anything. Instead, as he passes on his way towards the back door, he sneers, 'You're such a suck Louisa. In fact, I reckon you're a suck *and* a slut.' He seems pleased with the word. He heard it at school today. He smirks and the smirk says, Top That Miss Louisa Smart-Arse.

She's not even slightly impressed. 'Piss off you little weed,' she yells back louder than she means to, grunting and wondering while she lifts her load what exactly a slut is. The briquettes are so heavy she feels her legs buckle. She's now at the tricky bit, moving the second sack off her back and into the heater and her strength is just about gone.

Rob drops his bag near the step and moves towards her. He places one hand on the chair and gives it a sharp little jolt that wobbles it and she screams, a gratifyingly loud scream. 'Ahhh Rob, you little dickhead, cut it out, just cut it out . . . what's the matter with you?'

By the time she jumps down off the chair, she's covered in briquette dust. She takes off after Rob and corners him by the big shed and smears black all over him. When he spits at her she scoops it off and rubs it hard into his face before she lets him go. 'Good!' he yells, triumphant to have riled her, and sagging against the shed, he adds, 'Ha! Now they'll think I filled the bloody heater.' Louisa shakes her head in disgust and walks away from her filthy little brother, her long dark plait dividing her back. 'Fair dinkum Rob, you can be such an unbelievable shit.'

And then out of nowhere, Emmett's at the back door and Louisa is blabbing, 'Hi Dad,' and when she gauges the mood as fair, she plunges on, asking, 'Dad, what's a slut?' as if it's any other word. Emmett turns to her and, low and dark, says, 'Who called you that?'

'Rob,' she answers without thinking much, because Emmett seems calm enough today and maybe even pleased she's filled the hot water service but no, once again, she's got it all wrong.

Emmett turns and hits Rob across the face hard enough to loosen a couple of his side teeth. He walks inside without looking back at them, saying low, but almost casually, 'Don't you ever call my daughter a slut, boy.' The words fall onto the huddled child. Louisa kneels down beside Rob, tears slicing tracks down their black faces. Their careful eyes lock. 'Sorry,' she says, 'sorry Robbie.'

*

For a twelve-year-old, Rob is pretty small but not outlandishly so anymore. Still, his size seems to be the thing that really bothers his father. His first-born son should by rights reflect well on him and here's this boy, this puny runt of a boy. Honestly, thinks Emmett, it's pathetic. Nothing like a son of mine should be. Nothing at all. Having a boy so small offends his sense of his own manhood which is the most important thing in the world. Without your manhood, what are you?

And fighting and manhood are twins. Emmett often comes home with chunks out of his face and red tears like angry little zips round his mouth. He's been known to lift up his shirt to show the kids evidence of the fights. Swelling bruises bloom like eggplants all over his stomach and even across the lightening scar of a childhood liver operation.

Until he was thirteen or so, Rob always assumed the old man won most of the fights and he even took some comfort from the idea of that. Then, after school one day, he hears something in Johnno Bond's lounge room that changes everything.

Over in Harold Street, Rob hears Johnno's dad, Billy, mention Emmett and his ears prick up — since there's only one Emmett, this must be his. Trouble is, it's not always easy to work out what Billy's on about because his New Zealand accent sits heavily on words.

Billy Bond is a Maori wharfie who looks a bit like Elvis Presley. He encourages this by slicking back a thick wave of his gorgeous hair. Similarity trails off there though because Billy's face is cratered with acne potholes. His nose is as wide as a bath plug, his teeth look like peanuts and his eyes are granite chips. His immense blue arms are teeming with faded tattoos but when he smiles, you fear not.

The door to the pale blue kitchen is ajar and Billy is chatting amiably to his wife, Shirley, a hefty woman in a floral housecoat and thongs, while she gets the tea on. It's coming up to five o'clock on this warm afternoon. This is all strange to the boy, a man talking to his wife and no beer in sight, but Billy's always been a bit on the weird side.

'That Immitt Brown's difinitely got some kynda dith wush,' he declares. A blue mug on the table before him sighs tea fumes and his forearms surround the mug like illustrated hams.

Over at the sink Shirl takes a good quarter-inch off the surface of the carrot she holds in her red-raw hand. 'Is he?' she asks distractedly, keeping her eye on her youngest who's yelling something at her about the dog from outside the kitchen window.

Billy pushes on regardless. 'Well, he takes on enyone who'll kick his head en and et's pathetic. Used to be all right, least he could look after hiself. Don't know what's wrong with him. Bin worse lately no doubt about thet.' He takes a gulp of hot sweet tea and, looking through the window onto next door's sagging grey fence, reflects on life. 'Funny old world eh?'

Shirley couldn't care less about Emmett Brown but over in the lounge room Rob Brown certainly could. Even his favourite show *The Jetsons* can't compete with gossip about the old man. Still, for appearance he waits till the show ends before he unfolds his legs from the floor and bounces up saying, 'See ya', looking Billy square in the eye. Then he burns home with his nugget of news.

The Bond's flywire door is still banging by the time Rob

reaches Wolf Street and bursts down the barrel of the sideway brushing past the ferns and nearly ploughs into Louisa near the clothesline. In the still of the afternoon the girl is bringing in the washing. A great pile of clothes stiff with sun spills out of the basket. He gets close enough for her to see sweat pearling on him.

'Come 'ere,' he spits out breathlessly, bending over with his hands on his knees, panting and sucking air in deep. 'Wanna tell ya something.' She's intrigued but won't show it. Casually she drops the pegs into the peg tin, leaves the clothes under the line and heads for the big shed, absently pulling her dark plait over her shoulder for comfort.

Inside, it's dark except for where the old timbers on the walls are slipping. Slices of sun slash through the wall. Five tea-chests seem to hold up the other wall. The washing-machine tank with hoses sticking out everywhere and *missio* . . . painted on it stands in the front, a relic from Rob's astronaut period. Up one end, an old work bench sinks reluctantly into the dirt. The place smells of dust and mice and time and they sit on the dirt floor in the circle they have drawn to make them safe. They firmly believe in the power of circles.

Still panting slightly, Rob delivers his news solemnly. 'The old man wants to die, Johnno's dad said so, reckons he's got a death wish, that's what it means doesn't it, that you want to die?'

Louisa stares at him through the gloom, by now she should have begun to get tea on, she doesn't have time for this rubbish. 'What? What are you talking about?' she retorts as if he's retarded. Rob stares back, calm and sure. Louisa raises her voice a notch. 'Anyway, Dad doesn't know anyone else, any grown-ups. How does Johnno's dad know him?'

Rob doesn't even have to think about that one, it's just too obvious. 'The pub, course it's the pub,' he says, feeling good and grown-up for a few seconds, but the feeling doesn't last. What does all this really mean?

Louisa and Rob are used to working together on the subject of the old man but neither of them has thought of killing yourself, that people really do such a thing. 'Is he going to get worse?' Louisa asks. 'What's a death wish anyway?'

Rob draws a square in the dirt with a stick. 'I told ya it means he wants to die. Means he's like . . . going to kill himself.' He wonders how he knows this because no one has told him, he just knows it from the way Johnno's dad looked at him before he went home. With some kind of sadness. Something he might one day name as pity.

Louisa's eyes are enormous. She's long thought this day would come but she's not worried about what Emmett will do to himself. 'Is he going to kill us too? You reckon it's going happen?' Rob, with the wisdom of a sage, says, 'Could be. It could be.'

7

Emmett seems to work to a different rhythm from anyone else. There are times when he's at home and times when he's not. When he's at Wolf Street you can't escape. When he's gone, peace settles slowly. You never know when he'll show up because he tells no one what he's doing.

Food is often behind Emmett's rages. He simply demands better. One Saturday around tea-time they are sitting down to fish and chips when the back door is flung open. Perhaps it's their completeness without him that arouses his anger but whatever it is he waits there in the doorway, the eternal outsider. With the light behind the open door outlining him, he examines them like insects. Then he leans over to the table and points. The kids flinch. The fumes of the pub ebb out of him. He takes his time.

'This food is fucking rubbish,' he spits venomously, starting low and getting louder. 'Why don't you give them proper food?' he roars at Anne. Now he's an immense frothing man whose mouth swallows all the air in the small kitchen. Their heads sink above their laps. Nan and Anne are very still.

Then in another moment Anne says quietly, even gently, 'This *is* proper food, Emmett. They are just potato cakes from the local shop, made of spuds and flour. They're nice, have some.' She stands to move a plate towards him. There's a plate of them in the middle of the table and a plate of bread and butter and because it's Saturday there is Fanta for the kids, something a bit special on the weekend.

It's as if she's poured petrol onto a fire and he explodes. 'You want them, you fucking eat them bitch,' he screams and grabbing a potato cake, he smashes it into her face then rubs it in, and says, 'You want this shit, you eat it.'

The tide of dread fills the children's hearts as they watch their father take their mother. It is happening. Terror stills them. And then in the humming of the smallest amount of time the trance moment is over and they leap back from the table as if it's electrified. Now time is faster than they would have believed possible.

Emmett holds their mother by the back of her head and with the other hand he rams the food into her face. He might be smothering her or maybe will cut her throat. Each of them thinks different things.

Louisa thinks he is trying to push it up Anne's nose and that she won't be able to breathe. Rob wants to do something to him, maybe stab him, but he hates himself for not being brave enough. Peter and Daniel hold each other, weeping.

Anne can't breathe and bits are breaking off and going back through her nose into her throat. She can't breathe or speak. Louisa grabs the broom in the corner and wielding it like an axe chops at her father's legs. Rob leaps up onto his back. Peter and Daniel hold onto Nan as though she can save them. Rob tries to gouge his eyes from behind. When Emmett shakes the kids off and turns towards them lying there against the wall, both of them think today is the day they will die.

Emmett still has Anne under his arm and when Louisa swings the broom again, it hits her mother. The girl is stricken but her mother doesn't seem to notice. She seems scarcely alive. Time has slowed or maybe, Louisa thinks, something has slowed him. Still, she knows she must act.

She pulls Rob up from off the floor by the fridge where he's landed and turns and grabs the twins by the hand. They run down the passageway to the front door and flee to the hedge, to the corner hedge down the street. Through their special parting they dive and enter the darkness of the dusty greenness and wait for quiet, hardly believing they can really be safe.

Their breathing comes and goes and they hear the pounding in their ears as if in that quiet space they are under water. Even as he unlaces his fear, Rob is aware of the way their breathing makes them one solid planet. He and Louisa don't look at each other. Their faces remind them too much of what has just happened. Crying isn't an option.

They hide under the hedge within the world of the dry dusty stems, within their sanctuary, for longer than they know. Truth is, Emmett is beyond looking for them once they're across the boundary of the property. He's never going to go tearing up the street, pursuing them. He likes to keep his terrorising private. And besides, once he's finished he'll be pretty well buggered.

Much later in the dark, the children creep back into the quiet house, one of them acting as lookout to see where he is. But he's always gone by the time the kids come back. They put themselves to bed, the older kids helping the younger ones. They're as quiet as they need to be. They have suspended any idea of a normal life. They have survived again and that's enough for one night. In a while, Louisa will go and stand at the bedroom door to watch her mother sleep. Count the breaths.

8

Emmett is a linesman. He works for the Postmaster General as a grade two technician and hankers after the idea of making it to a grade three. Probably won't happen, he concedes.

In the end Emmett accepts that it's his lot at work to fix faults in all weather on all days. Management, with its cushy rewards, will never be for him. Somehow he just doesn't have a way with people.

Much of his work is done outdoors connecting up phone lines to houses and fixing faults way up high. He's an outdoor man and the sun has turned his forearms the colour of oak, but in the secret territory under his shirt, he's as white as scars.

Once he brings home a bird that landed unwisely on a power line junction and got zapped with thousands of volts. It sits on the table, hard and black, a cricket ball with a beak. 'That,' he says wearily, taking off his sweaty smudged hard hat and setting it down next to the bird, 'is what happens if you fuck around with electricity. Get me a beer, Dan.' The kids all long to touch the bird. This will come, but for now the theatre of the moment must unfold. The withholding of information.

But he's not really in the mood today. Peter, huge eyes level with the table edge, stares ardently at the black bird. Emmett rubs his hair roughly and laughs, 'You'll be right mate, just stay away from bloody power lines, that's all I'm saying.' He hands the bird to them by order of age and each child weighs it reverently before passing it on. After they've all held it, the bird goes to a shelf on the olive green dresser with the square biting latches and there it perches, scanning their lives for years.

*

To make up for the disappointments of work, Emmett concentrates on his Famous and Completely Original System. Its mathematical probabilities are multi-purpose and are meant to deliver winning lottery tickets and horses. It's a broad strategy based on records of winnings which he keeps with a kind of religious fervour. Despite there being little evidence of his genius, he's convinced.

Some days, a row of seagulls line up on the picket fence out the front of Wolf Street, idly peering in through the venetians like bored patients in a waiting room. Somehow though, the seagulls can be forgiven because they bring with them the good feeling that the sea knows them, even in Footscray. When one of the kids opens the gate, the birds lift lazily, hover, and then come right on back again.

Day after day, the crooked stripes of light cleave through the wonky blinds and Emmett sits in that irradiated bedroom absorbing his smokes and his beer and sweating out sour alcoholic funk as he slaves away on his probabilities, nutting out all those numbers at the big green desk, firmly believing he's working for his family.

While beer is the only true constant in his life, for a man who doesn't believe in much, God crops up a lot. When things are going well with the stats, he talks to himself. You bloody little bee-uty. God, he says, is in all things! And he smiles and chucks beer down as if he were a man standing on the edge of a cliff tossing everything he owns into the abyss. When his confidence swells his heart is a billowing red balloon rising slowly. He'll show the rotten bastards.

But when the figures don't line up, the tone changes to fury and again he appeals to God. Jesus wept, a man is doing his best here and I just keep coming up against it. Why can't you give a bloke a break? I don't ask for much in this fucking bastard of a world, he snarls to himself and hurls his pencil down, draining the glass and glaring at the poxy little seagulls perving on him out there, thinking, a man oughta grab the bloody shotgun.

Emmett reckons probabilities explain the laws of the universe. '*This* is the big one,' he tells Rob one day at a backyard barbie at Wolf Street when the boy is a bit older. 'This is how you understand every bloody thing there is mate. Everything. This is the rule that applies to all things and let me tell you, nothing, not one paltry thing, is random.'

Rob doesn't say anything because he thinks everything *is* random, especially Emmett. He smiles and just to be polite and keep him in the good zone asks, 'And how does it work Dad?'

Emmett waves his hand airily, and foam from his beer slops on his faded orange Hawaiian shirt, always a summer favourite. 'Bugger,' he says, brushing absently at it. He's drunk a fair whack by now and isn't in the mood for detailed explaining. Besides, his grasp on the concept isn't entirely finalised and he doesn't want to risk making a total arse of himself. 'I'll explain it all to you one day son and that will be my legacy to you. One day, you too will understand the universe.'

Grouse, thinks Rob. This'll make me the only person in the whole world who understands the universe (apart from that well-known genius, Emmett Brown). But he keeps his opinions to himself and slips off to get a sausage from the barbie. He wraps the charred thing in white bread and douses it with tomato sauce and is ready to sink his teeth in when Emmett intervenes with, 'Wouldn't shout in a shark attack would you mate?' and Rob looks at him blankly. 'Dense too,' sighs Emmett. 'Get us one of those will you mate? Plenty of dead horse on it,' and lowers himself into a weather-beaten deckchair propped skittishly near the house.

Rob does so and on handing the snag over manages to spurt sauce all over Emmett's foot which looks disturbingly naked in its thong. But Frank, snoring on the concrete, is up in a flash and obligingly licks up the sauce in under a second so real harm is averted.

Emmett aims a mild swipe at the boy with his other foot. 'Useless fucking idiot child,' he mutters benignly and asks the air conversationally, 'Why would you have them?' And he leans back with snag in one hand and beer glass in the other and he lets the sun warm his face. Probabilities can wait.

Emmett is firmly convinced that one day he'll make it big with these probabilities and it's only a matter of time. It *will* happen. One day he's going to be a rich bastard, he tells himself as the amber fluid flows through his veins like a yellow river, and then he'll be happy. He just knows it.

9

Nan is so small. She seems to be dissolving into the air. Still works hard though she breaks up all her jobs with little rests. Still loves a smoke and keeps her fags in her apron pocket till after she's hung out the washing and then sits on the box in the sun savouring the work that's behind her. Above her the washing flies like empty people.

She makes the beds early and does a bit of washing every day plus any dishes hanging around. When all her work is done, she sits at the table with a cup of tea, her smokes and her pack of cards and plays Patience, her fag burning long in the ashtray beside her. She seldom eats but when she does, she loves bread and jam and choc wedges. Sometimes she's still at cards when the kids get home.

*

In the days of Nan, being the first one home is worth something. At ten Louisa is the same height as her grandmother and, getting home, she slides her bag into the corner and puts her arms around her. Nan smells of ironing and of Lily of the Valley talc. Her softness, her mildness is an antidote to Emmett, and Louisa thinks of her Nan as purely good. When Lou gets home she says, 'Hello little darl, what's cooking today?' and before long she'll be dealing Louisa a hand after she's put the kettle on, saying, 'I saved you a tic-toc, last in the packet, and while Louisa is licking the biscuit, she'll think that if he would only stay away, life could be like this. Could be perfect.

*

Sharon James' old man runs Jim's Butcher Shop on Willy Road, a blue-and-white striped shop with a sawdust floor and more than the occasional low-flying blowfly making passes at the meat. Sharon, who's in Louisa's class at school, has curly blonde hair and plenty of dough because, according to Nan, there's one certainty in life, and this is that publicans and butchers are always rich. Louisa knows Nan says this to soothe her because Louisa wildly envies Sharon's blonde hair and her popularity, even if the girl does look like a pig. Something about the nose. When she mentions the snout to Nan, they laugh with a hilarious shame until Nan says, 'Well, my darlin' girl, we should not be passing remarks, Louie, the poor wee lassie can't help her schnoz,' and they're off again.

Louisa's the only girl not invited to the party at the James's house and though she hates herself for it, she follows the group home instead of taking her usual route through the lanes. At Field Street, Mrs James, a large version of her daughter, nose and all, is ushering the girls into the house and when she sees Louisa straggling behind, she calls, 'Sweetheart, don't dawdle, the others have all gone in,' and gestures towards the front door. 'Hello, Mrs James,' Louisa says glumly, coming to a halt at the picket fence.

At the questioning she replies, 'Um. Well, I wasn't invited to the party.' Though Louisa is transfixed by the possibility of going inside, shame surges through her like a tidal wave. Just as she guessed, the woman takes pity on her and will have none of her leaving. 'But what about the party? We've got lots of lovely

55

food. Oh, how awful you weren't invited, there must have been a mistake. Sharon would never leave one of her little class-mates out. It's Louisa Brown, isn't it, from down in Wolf Street? Would you like to come darling? Of course you would. Just nip home and get your party dress on and we'll be underway.'

And before another second has passed, Louisa is sprint-ing towards home like a runaway racehorse, cutting a swathe through the street. At home, the boys are having a sedate little game of kick-to-kick and the footy bangs against the house, which means Emmett's not home. She's too winded to speak. In the fernery she grabs Nan, gasping, 'Dress. Party. Sharon.' They both know there's no party dress, but Nan makes straight for the ironing pile and soon extracts something Anne made for Louisa years ago. It has lace, which qualifies it. 'I'll run over it with the iron, my darling, and you'll be the most beautiful girl there. And what about we let you wear your hair out for a change?'

Nan unearths a block of chocolate for a present from some-where in her bowerbird room and brushes Louisa's long hair until it reaches a semblance of decency. Of course the summer dress is too small and slight for winter. The lace is torn but the old green jumper covers much. Her grandmother walks halfway to Field Street with Louisa and watches her all the rest of the way down that needle-straight street, worrying whether the chocolate will be enough.

*

Louisa's singing 'Yellow Bird' loud and flat when she hears of the death of her grandmother. She's just home from school, walking down the sideway, past the ferns with their long green fingers when Emmett's voice reaches her before she sees him. 'Stop singing, Louisa,' he commands. As she walks through the door he says, 'It's not a day for singing. Your grandmother has died today.'

Her father is in the kitchen with her mother. They don't spend much time in the same room. It must be true. She looks at her mother leaning against the Kookaburra stove, all cream and green, cream and green and Anne nods and makes it true. Louisa's eyes rest on the small picture of the kookaburra on the stove, covered by a slick of dusty grease, and as she notes this, the crushing weight of the universe settles in forever.

Nan had gone down to the milkbar for a packet of smokes and in the shop she had a heart attack and fell to the crazed red concrete floor and died.

She's now lying on her bed. The stillness of Rose strikes Louisa with the force of a truck but this is the last time Louisa will see her because Anne believes kids should not go to funerals, that they should be shielded from death.

The girl cries for a month. Nothing can stop her. She goes to school and does her school work and cleans and does the potatoes for tea. She walks the lanes to school with Frank leading the way like a pilot but she's in a trance and the tears just keep coming. Whether she's at school or in her room, at the shop or at the table, they seep forth as if there's a spring inside her.

She decides dying is a good option. She can't live without her Nan. Simple really. Why doesn't everyone just leave her alone? Rob and Peter and Daniel manage to keep going though there is a flatness to their eyes. And then, with the suddenness that is pure Emmett, he has seen enough.

It's one Saturday morning when he decides it has to end. 'Louisa,' he roars from the kitchen, 'get out here.' Carefully the girl edges from her grey bedroom like a sea creature stranded in a tidal pool. Her hair is unwashed and her clothes smell of every single day she's worn them. 'Get yourself cleaned up. We are going for a walk.' Louisa is shocked into waking. Into thinking. Emmett has never taken the kids for a walk.

They walk down to the shop where Rose died. It isn't far. Emmett holds Louisa's hand and she barely notices despite not being able to remember it happening before. Rob and Peter and Daniel trail behind like a chorus. 'Now,' he says patiently, 'we are going in here and we are buying the newspaper.'

She steps inside behind him and looks at the red floor and wonders where her Nan's head fell. Which spot was it? They buy the paper and he shoves it under his arm and it flaps as if it were a dying bird.

Outside a tide of cars passes and the sun shines with morning hope. Emmett stands Louisa on the step of the shop and looks her in the eye, a pair of matching indigo eyes, and says, 'This, and you know what I'm talking about, this is going to end now. Finished. Finito. This is it.' He makes a sideways cutting motion with his hands.

'I know you're sad and that is right, she was your grandmother and you loved her and you know Louisa, she loved you too, but she has died and it's time to stop grieving. I'm your father and I'm telling you that now is the time to stop. It can't go on. Your Nan would not want to see you sad. It's all over now Lou.'

Her brothers are cantering around, close enough to hear but far enough to be out of clouting range. They notice Louisa nodding and hiccoughing through streaming tears, but then she always cries when people speak up close to her. Such a sook.

Emmett grabs her hand and he swings it towards home, making an effort towards joy, and now Emmett's palm seems like a bit of wood but it feels like they're leaving her Nan behind and that's got to be some kind of betrayal. And she knows it is. Even so, she feels the burden of her grief leaving her like a boat slipping its moorings.

10

There's something sacred about the races. They are a continuum and their currency is hope. Emmett studies the form all week and by Saturday he's ready. Sussed it right out. Bloody organised.

To the kids, the form guide, that perfectly folded paper, is the divine document and the key to their futures. At Wolf Street it's the Bible.

They're proud that this is the thing Emmett devotes himself to because when he eventually wins, they'll stop being poor. And then things will get better. Their father will be happy, their mother will not have to work so hard and then they'll be allowed to breathe like other kids. Money will make everything better. But despite all the quiet they give him, the wide berth, the tiptoeing and the nervous, watchful looks they shoot him in passing, it hasn't happened yet.

Like horses, the Brown kids notice with their skin; the ripples along a flank that show a fly has landed, the waves beneath flesh. They're as alert as antennas to their father's mood.

'I told ya he wouldn't win anything today. He didn't have enough time on the probabilities. Still, I tell ya, he's a bloody amateur,' Rob says casually as Louisa joins him to sit in the dirt and lean against the back fence.

'Race four already and bloody nothing.' He pulls a weed and casually wrings its neck.

Louisa sighs; she agrees but can't admit that the day will end like all the others, with the old man getting comprehensively pissed and aggro over anything. How can you allow that so early?

'Day's not over yet, it's only race four and he reckons to Mum he's got something special in the sixth, and you know the System doesn't just have to work on the trifecta.' Saying it she looks sad and somehow crushed as if she doesn't believe a word. The System can be independent of those races, she insists.

'Well, the trifecta's finished and that's where all the real bucks are, you know that,' says Rob, the bitter realist.

'Are not,' she says more fiercely than she feels.

'Are so,' Rob says and quickly sneaks in with, 'are so to infinity,' then he snickers, his shoulders moving with pleasure. Louisa says nothing, knowing he's right, and in frustration digs her big toe into the dirt.

The sun is a lemon and she can feel it tightening her skin, hatching hot freckles. Rob's in the same shorts, always looking a bit undersized because although he's small for his age, his clothes look small too. He wears a checked western shirt with some red in it, short sleeves too high on his arms and his greyish hair is crew-cut.

Louisa's dress is navy polyester/rayon/nylon with bobbles like warts strewn over the pattern of flowers that will never fade. She stretches the dress over her knees into a tent. Emmett has seen to it that she has not yet cut her hair. He likes girls to have long hair. It seems purer. Though he doesn't know it, the truth of it is that Anne and Louisa conspire in this and about once a month Anne snips off Louisa's split ends with her dressmaker's scissors. Louisa's dark hair is plaited and secured at each end with rubber bands.

Occasionally she paints her face with their paintbrush tips. Hairs escape the plaits horizontally. She examines the constellation of freckles on her left forearm, noting again that it's the Southern Cross. This has to be a good omen.

Rob lets go a fart, a long fat bubble, in a peaceful kind of way and laughs at the sound of it. 'A bit more choke and you would have started,' Louisa says amiably as she leans away to avoid the blister of smell. She punches him lightly on the arm, calls him a pongy old dog.

He replies with 'cow' delivered in the same friendly way, and pushes her ankle with his foot. The sun soaks into them. The fart is absorbed by the still day. The air is loaded with the smell of the petrol station behind them on the main road and the rubbish bin not far up. Idly, she thinks again it's a good thing all the smokers are inside. That pasty dishevelled Irish Catholic dog, Francis Xavier O'Hooligan, snores and flinches on the concrete. They are suspended in the aspic of the day waiting for their father to make it rich.

11

Emmett has fixed the black Bakelite telephone to the sticky yellowing wall in a rare act of home improvement and hastily jotted phone numbers surge upwards and outwards from it like arteries leaving a heart. Cards from tow-truck drivers are shoved into the back of the phone and by now they're as light and curled as autumn leaves.

Towies are respected around Wolf Street. They're tattooed outlaws who carry with them the allure of those who get away with stuff. Rob is deeply attracted. He sees something of the Wild West and the cowboy in the way they show up out of nowhere, screaming to a halt in their loose creaky trucks and then set about plainly sorting things out, roping wrecks as if they're ornery bulls and dragging them off into the distance, all the time roaring with laughter at their private jokes.

When they show up, *Bonanza* comes to Footscray. Rob thinks about being a towie one day but never says anything because Emmett has other plans for the boy. He's already decided what each of them will do for a living. Rob is to be a scientist and Louisa, a doctor. The rest he isn't concerned with as long as they bring him credit. Privately he thinks; a man just can't stay innarested in all these bloody kids.

Whether or not he'd make it to being a scientist, Rob fancies himself an inky illustrated towie. He loves the way they are, every single thing about them: their lack of fear, their maleness, their answers to problems, their handlebar moustaches and especially their clothes, the rusty-looking jeans and thick belts with buckles the size of ashtrays. Dressed like that, he thinks, you'd have to be safe.

Fifty-five Wolf Street is on a blind corner with Murphy Street and small prangs are a constant. The accidents come at the cusp of the day when the traffic hots up. Following the screech of tyres and the smash comes the astonished stillness as drivers register the accident. The silence settles briefly and spreads out in circles until gradually, shocked or furious voices emerge from that muffled hollow.

Inside the house at the first sound of the screech, someone will yell, 'Quick! Ring the towies!' And kids pounce on the phone as if it's taking off. The number is dialled and the name Brown is delivered to the operator with a kind of formal solemnity and then the comfortable thought spreads through them like warm pee in a cold swimming pool: they might get the spotter's fee! But being resolute realists they know the fee still might go to one of the rotten neighbours.

Still, they live in hope and after a decent interval, they amble outside to inspect the damage, looking real casual and sporadically concerned, though never greatly so because there's seldom blood.

*

Outside, the last rags of the day are pulling away from the clenched little pub. And inside the air is layered with shelves of smoke. Rafts of it surround the men like low cloud but they don't even notice. It's not far off six now and the swill is in full swing.

Emmett is drinking in a school of five and each of the five has five glasses lined up before them on the sawdust floor.

Their legs make pillars of support for the beer and though they spit and joke and laugh, they don't spill a drop. It's just another afternoon at the Station Hotel in Paisley Street.

And then a little salesman named Jimmy Collins comes in flogging encyclopaedias and gets the royal treatment from the blokes. 'Look at the little runt poofta,' someone says casually and Emmett turns a lazy eye toward the newcomer.

Jimmy pushes his little wire glasses up his nose and tries out a smile. He's wearing a thin, knitted tie and a tweed jacket, aimed at making him look intelligent. He's a law student working part-time at selling. He carries a leather satchel and a red sample book. Emmett notices the book straight away even though he's well into a diatribe against governments, all of them. 'Only people you can ever trust,' he declares, 'are union boys like us.' And he raises his glass, smiling, remembering something fine about unity.

Smoke trails from his fag. His audience agrees with every word he's saying and that's as it should be but still, there's something about the salesman bloke with the books. Something niggles.

Jimmy, hunched at the bar, is thinking about pushing off, pubs are never very productive anyway and this one looks hopeless, but what do you expect in Footscray? he asks himself. Plus he can hardly breathe with all the smoke in here and he hawks unproductively a couple of times, trying to dredge his sinuses. He's had a cold for weeks now and it's wearing him out.

'Gimme a look at that mate, will ya?' Emmett yells and Jimmy smiles and hands over the encyclopaedia, half expecting this bloke to spread beer over the sample or even rip it and wipe his arse on it, all for a bit of a joke. Still, better the book than me, he thinks resignedly.

Emmett puts his beer down on the floor, parks the fag

between his lips and squinting through the smoke, he cracks open the pages to the story of the oak tree. As he scans it, he knows he will buy it for the kids. Doesn't matter how much. 'What you asking for these books? How many of the bastards are there anyway?'

The salesman tells him a figure but Emmett's not listening, he's reading and thinking about showing the books to the kids. This is the answer. The idea of knowledge makes him feel different. His bloody kids will *be* different. They *will* have the lot, the whole fucking shebang, and they won't end up like this poor excuse for a mob.

He doesn't want to close the book but he hands it back to the little bloke. 'I'll sign up.' The others in the school pretend not to have heard. They reckon Brown's well on the verge of the loony bin anyway, talks way too much about any bloody thing and he's always had knobs on himself. And through the whole transaction they drink as though they are holding back the tide.

A book arrives every two months till there are ten of them but the hire purchase agreement takes years to complete. Emmett pays for it all himself. Every penny. When he tells Louisa to come and hear a story or to do some investi-gate-ing in these here books, she feels the difference in him. Here he is, she thinks. Dad is here, the real one.

The *Arthur Mee's Children's Encyclopaedia* is red leatherette. Shining gold words on the front. He hands a book to her and she holds it and believes in possibility. They all come to have favourite volumes. Nine years old and there are some truths she knows that aren't in any book.

12

The music of words draws Emmett towards poetry, which he knows in his heart with a searing clarity is the highest art form. He believes that the great poets Henry Lawson and Banjo Paterson can make anyone weep and this, he believes, is the greatest skill. These blokes weave actual beauty with the skill of angels.

On the league table of Art and Beauty his second art form has to be music. Few, he reckons, come close to the big two, Beethoven and Tchaikovsky. He plays the *1812 Overture* on an LP on the old red velvet-fronted radiogram in the front room and it leaves him speechless and shaken. 'Listen to this kids!' he roars over the soaring music. 'This is what life is about!'

Caprice Italien is called for when his mood is elevated and then the music bounds out of the room and waves itself like big flags from the windows of the little house.

And when he's really up, Tchaikovsky is Chockers and Beethoven is the Big B. 'Kids . . . cop a load of this! You bloody beauty Chockers!' he cheers and their hearts sink because there's much to fear when *Caprice Italien* goes on. No mood that wheels so high can remain in flight.

The thin wooden walls squeeze in and out and the music surges forth, dissolving in circles of distance. Across the road, the Quails, a family of one mother, five boys and a collie named Wedge, flinch at the onslaught of Emmett's music.

*

One night sitting on the swaying train coming home from work, Emmett reads a story about Rudolf Nureyev and a new production of *The Nutcracker Suite* and with a gathering resolve, decides this is something for him. He's long had a bit of a soft spot for Russians (he deeply approves of the Russian Revolution) and since the music was written by one Russian and performed by another, he determines that this Nureyev bastard will have to be seen.

He decides to take the two big kids because they need something decent to remember when they're old. They're getting older by the day and there isn't that much that defines their childhood, he thinks. (He excludes himself from the definition even though Emmett will be the only thing they will ever remember with any clarity.) To his mind, the things you can talk about when you're older are seen at the footy and cricket. For instance, he's always barracked for North Melbourne, the mighty Shinboners, and he remembers with a shining reverence Saturdays at Arden Street with thousands of others. Could never play himself, just born bloody clumsy, much to his own bitter disappointment, because he always felt he should have been brilliant. Would have been good at being brilliant.

The really sad part though is that the kids missed out on Bradman and this is a tragedy, pure and simple. All they have is Bill Lawry and true, he is a Victorian, but sadly, and he believes Bill would be the first to agree, he's no Bradman.

Emmett had never seen Bradman himself because he spent most of his young life working or stuck in orphanages and then there was the question of finances — tickets to the cricket cost money and he had zero. But at his Nana's, when he could, he listened to the radio all through the long winter nights when the Australians played the Poms in England. Listened to every last ball.

But he is prepared to concede that there's more to life than cricket and footy. He'll take these kids of his to see this Russian cove and Margot Fonteyn, who he's heard is also pretty damn spectacular even if she is an ageing Pommy prima ballerina.

It's winter and in the unremembered night, the weather hurls itself upon the house. The following morning, a Saturday, Emmett calls them into the kitchen to tell them they will go to Her Majesty's Theatre in the city to a matinee this very afternoon. Football will be given up for one week.

Rob squirts a little sideways look at Louisa but says nothing. It's final. 'And you will enjoy this!' Emmett booms at them.

After much scrounging through the clean-washing pile, Anne finds a cardigan to go with Louisa's best dress. Rob wears shorts and the duck-egg blue jumper that is imprinted in Louisa's memory as the only one the boys own. Anne, Daniel and Peter wave goodbye and off they set, both wearing school shoes and striding after Emmett, who sets a cracking pace, to the train station.

It is an intermittently bright, cold day and the roads are all slick after the night rain and Emmett is wearing the khaki coat he brought into the marriage. The sky is massed with heavy towering clouds, charcoal and indigo and the deep green of storms at sea. Sometimes it rains, but they walk through it as if they were waterproof, as if they were pilgrims unconcerned with the everyday.

Emmett sits opposite Rob and Louisa on the train and looks both menacing and handsome. There is to be no mucking around. In his low grainy voice as though he were imparting a secret, he says, 'This is your big chance to witness something important here. Now I want best behaviour, that certainly goes without saying.' He leans in and fixes them with his dark eyes, 'But you can have a bit of fun too, it's the theatre and that's what people do when they go out, they enjoy themselves.

'You,' and he glares at Rob who seems to shrink under the hot beam, 'will have to concentrate bloody hard. Are you with me?' He leans further forward and taps the boy on his bare mottled knee, 'because I don't want to have to say anything to you.'

He sits back quickly with his hands deep in his pockets and flaps his coat up around his legs. Rob says evenly, 'Yes Dad,' and Louisa pushes her gaze out the window towards the stacks of containers so she can't catch his eye. The sky continues to be iron grey and dense with rain but occasionally the sun shoots through the clouds like a cannonball.

While she's excited, Louisa isn't feeling optimistic about the ballet. Rob will mess this up, she thinks solidly, the habit of gloom already long ingrained.

Emmett continues the lecture. 'Now this Rudolf Nureyev bloke we are going to see, and old Mrs Fonteyn too, they are very special. Rob, pay particular attention to the leaps, they're as good as anything you'll see down at the football ground. Don't be put off by the tights son, that is not important.

'This is about the blending of music and the human body. This is an art. Right, we're off at the next stop,' he says, and bounds to his feet and pushes the door open before the train has fully stopped. The wind whips his hair about and his coat-flaps stream and he's riding into the station like a valkyrie.

In the city Emmett strides along the wet street with the children nearly running to keep up. Rob does try to trip Louisa at one point (he deliberately stands on her loose shoelace and she knows it was deliberate because he laughs) and she staggers forward and grabs Emmett's coat but he isn't mad, he flicks a small smile at her.

Louisa considers kicking Rob but common sense gets the better of her. Rob smirks. By the time they get to the theatre, excitement is pulsing through the puffing, sweaty children.

Emmett strides over to the ticket box to buy the tickets. The kids perch on a round red buttoned seat in the foyer, eyes swallowing the magic of the place. People cluster and chat, laugh and gossip and the kids are entranced.

It soon becomes clear, however, that something is wrong. Here comes that underwater moment when you begin to drown and your legs work like engines but can't save you. No matter how hard they try to pretend that everything is all right, it isn't. Something right here in this shining theatre is going all wrong. Emmett is taking too long and the kids know with sickly sinking hearts that there's a major stuff-up underway and when he strides back to them his face is a thundercloud.

'I'm short by two quid,' he says curtly, quietly, and it dawns on the kids that he doesn't have enough money to buy the tickets. Isn't it always the case? Money holds the keys to the game.

'Could you sell your wallet Dad, since it's empty?' Rob ventures helpfully.

Emmett looks at him as if he might snap him in half, and then he withdraws his eyes from the boy and says wearily, 'Shut up Robert,' and slumps on the round seat. He leans his head back and closes his eyes. His grey face sags.

The kids look at each other warily. They have not often encountered a defeated Emmett. Usually he shields himself from the reality of defeat with anger. This is very bad, they think simultaneously. Will there be an explosion? In public? Right here? They look around like mice in a room full of cats.

In a while, when most of the well-heeled have drifted into the theatre, Emmett gets up and the kids follow a few steps behind, heads down, shuffling like Japanese ladies. Emmett decides he'll at least buy them some Fantales, and standing in front of the lolly counter, he feels around for his wallet.

Then for some reason he pushes his hand into the inner breast pocket of his coat and amazingly, he pulls out a ten-pound note. He holds up the money as if it were a miracle from God, which it possibly is, and he laughs and whoops and roars, 'By God, the Browns are going to the bloody ballet!'

He buys the tickets *and* the Fantales and they go inside, only a little bit late, to watch Nureyev and Fonteyn fly across the stage like angels.

On the train home Emmett can see old Rudolf as a very plausible full forward for North and he and Rob rave about this for a while. Emmett doesn't tell them the music made him weep because he thinks this is beyond the pale. But Louisa saw him wiping his eyes and was astonished. She files it away to discuss with Rob later.

Louisa and Rob remember the train ride home. Sealed in there with him in the red rattler, shaking across the flat industrial acres and looking out from the dark windows, they can still see that leaping Russian and hear the music that spoke of otherness.

Near to Middle Footscray Station Emmett leans across to Louisa and whispers, 'You understand beauty, young Louie, and beauty will always console you.' Louisa smiles and doesn't know what to say to her father so she says, 'I'd like to be a dancer like Nureyev or even be like old Mrs Fonteyn, that wouldn't be too bad.' The sheer delight of having all this good attention from him is making her dizzy. Emmett nods sagely and sitting back on the vandalised train seat says, 'Anything is possible.'

He looks reflective as he watches the light bounce off the blocks of containers outside. 'Nureyev is very good but if you want a real artist, look no further than Frank Sinatra, a Yank, true, but what an artist. And of course, there's always Banjo.' He sits back and grins and Louisa thinks she sees happiness in him. The rarest thing in the world.

Soon, they're at their station and he's bustling them off the train with 'Get a move on, Robert, you dilatory boy!' And then the train is gone and they're walking in his footsteps, following him home through the thin, darkly shining streets.

13

To some, Australia is Europe distilled, but to Emmett Brown, it's just distance. And that is its strength. The Browns emerged from the round-shouldered question mark British Isles about 180 years ago and settled into the width of Australia, bringing every single one of their bad habits with them.

The small Scottish island in the chilly North Sea was steep with rocks and rich in sky and they stepped onto the great southern land with many reservations.

For one thing, the vastness really bothered them. The scale was all wrong. Everything was way too big. The sky and the sea and even the fish were huge. And it must be admitted that the trees with their tattered drooping leaves were a sore disappointment, though it was also true that back on the island their own trees had long since been felled for warmth and money.

Puzzled, amazed and isolated, not one of them expected to love this country but there was nothing left in Scotland – the highland clearances had seen to that. They had been turfed out of their own country by their English landlords and replaced with sheep.

They expected to tolerate this place, to eat and maybe even to make some money (they never did manage that) but then, somehow, love grew in their bones like a secret, at first quietly and then wildly and randomly it grew within each of their hearts until it reached Emmett Brown and in him, love of place culminated. Australia is his first belief.

'Wouldn't mind going over to Pommy land one day,' Emmett declares one evening stretching back on the chair and balancing lightly, a long man lounging on a small chair in a narrow room. 'Just to check up on those bastards who wanted to get rid of us so bad they kicked us out of their puny little runt of an island. Bloody Poms, can you credit them?' He laughs, comes upright with a thud and takes a pull of his tall golden beer. There's an art to pouring a beer and the Brown kids know it. They poured this one to perfection, a small head and the beer, the aspic clear of amber.

Tonight he's in a positive mood and possibly a reflective one, even on the subject of politics. The children are gathered again and know they must keep the mood where it is. Must not let it drop. They are the audience to his life and while not the ones he would have chosen, they'll do. Louisa is caught dithering in the kitchen and is frozen there, not knowing when or if to move.

Emmett is explaining to the kids that he doesn't actually hate many people he knows but there are exceptions among those he doesn't — the Poms, well, the toffs anyway, and then, chiefly anyone associated with the Liberal Party, particularly that old bastard Menzies and the low-life, Bolte. Both eternally unforgiven.

Louisa edges over. Rob sees her and gives a small mean smile. Emmett is rocking again and slams the chair down. 'What the fuck are you up to Louisa? Sneaking and skulking around. Get over here now.'

He reaches her and pushes her and she skids into the table and bangs her head on the corner. She finds her seat and sits down, the room seems to have shifted and she's having trouble seeing. She ought to have gone to the toilet and the knowledge of the pressing fullness of her bladder inches into her. Her mother, holding a smiling Daniel, reaches over and pats her arm. Rob stifles a laugh.

Emmett continues telling them that he hates snobs of any sort. Though they also know that he can be contrary because he admires people he thinks are classy. He's not mad on people who drive newer cars than his and he hates all bosses, but that's a matter of course, a simple routine hate, one most people would go along with.

He hates *World of Sport*, a Sunday afternoon football program and a universal favourite, a show where footballers are encouraged to act like idiots and give out hams and bottles of orange juice to other, younger footballers; but again this isn't a major hate, it's more of a niggle really.

Louisa wants to lay her throbbing head down but that would be fatal. She fears she might be sick. The need to wee grows. She holds on hard.

Her father's big hates, he declares, are reserved for Joseph Stalin and Mao Tse Tung because they got communism off the rails and ruined a perfectly good idea. The Vietnam War is a bad mistake because the Yanks went poking their noses in where they did not belong. 'Helpful Joneses,' he ruminates, falling back on one of his favourite negatives, 'ought to leave bloody people alone.' Still, he has a soft spot for that American bloke Kennedy even though he really got them into the Vietnam War with his meddling but then the poor bugger got his head blown off, so there you go.

Around the table the kids and Anne listen to Emmett. They smile and think of dashing for the door. No one dares, not even Rob.

On the wall behind Emmett is a pale map of Australia and each state is a pastel colour. He's been to all of them but can most easily be encouraged to rave about Western Australia. The ochre deserts and the scrub alive with wildlife and the engulfing sky and the white white sand and even the sea which is vastly superior to any other sea in the world. It's definitely bluer. Yep, there's something sacred about the west.

That Australia is God's Own Country has been explained to them many times. They know it. And when he tells them in detail about the high country in Victoria with snowgums the colour of bones and wallabies the size of cats, they feel proud. But the wonders have not ended. In Queensland there are houses built on stilts to catch the low cool air as it drifts and eddies under them like the currents of the sea. Could you credit that?

Emmett's love for Australia is based on the idea that this is the country for the worker, and so the fairest place in the world for the ordinary man. He believes you don't need to be rich to live well here and rejoices that there's no poxy aristocracy. He applauds free education and hospitals, and that he believes there should be more and better of both is neither here nor there. A quibble.

Louisa is sitting very straight and listening hard, holding the wee in but now she feels it happening before she can stop it. Oh no, she realises in an emptying moment, she's wetting herself. She feels betrayed, because it started so slow and then sneakily gathered hot speed. She cannot believe it. She's too old for this. Far too old. Shame has her in its sticky grip. Rob has noticed and checked out the puddle beneath her and she thinks wildly, overwhelmed by disgust for herself and aiming it straight at her brother, that he'd just better watch out. Suddenly she's had it with him and his smirking ways.

'And speaking of dead leaders,' says Emmett, oblivious to Louisa's puddle, 'when Harold Holt the Australian Prime Minister disappeared swimming off a rough beach in Victoria I knew immediately what had happened. Shark,' he announces as if he's top brass and takes a tug at his beer. 'No bloody doubt about it. Great White, I dare say. Still, he wouldn't have felt a damn thing.'

Sharks are always an attention-grabber around the table. Each of the kids has a deep-seated terror of them although none has ever seen one. The thought of the suddenness of a shark attack, and the power of it, works through them.

'Excuse me Dad, have you ever seen one, a shark?' Daniel asks, his eyes luminous.

'I have my boy, many a time, but mostly when they are swinging by their tails on the pier,' he says and roars laughing. 'The shark is a short-sighted creature and he senses movement in the water. Nothing personal when a shark takes you, he's just cleaning up.'

Why do sharks take people rather than eat them? Rob wonders, but it's best not to interrupt. Louisa squirms. The warmth has left the piss and the cold stinging has begun on her poor red legs. She prays no one else notices the puddle. Rob picks some snot from his nose, rolls it sneakily on his leg and flicks it at her under the table and it sticks to her leg. She wearily brushes it away.

Emmett often pauses in his stories and waits and scans the kids individually like a conductor eyeing the orchestra. He uses time to make sure they are paying the correct amount of attention and then, after holding the pause for longer than you'd think he could, he begins. Sometimes he seems full of life and happiness. This is when their hearts really sink. The story of the Balts is one where he shows himself off.

'I was there at twenty or so, helping out the Balts in the reffo camps in WA. The Balts were the poor old refugee bastards who'd been kicked out of Europe after a war; truth is, they're always having one war or another over there.

'They are all mad in Europe, let me tell you that for nothing, bloody stark raving mad, but that's the Europeans for you, hopeless, that's why they have to come here to get some peace and bloody quiet in this wide brown land of ours. This is the best country on earth,' he says sternly, 'and don't ever let anyone tell you anything else.

'Anyway the reffos, they were nice people. One of them taught me how to cook, she was a woman named Rina, and she was from somewhere Baltic, somewhere cold and grey, coastal lands, I think, by the sea.

'The strange thing was that they all spoke German as well as their own personal language. They taught me a few words of it and I picked it up pretty damn fast, "Sehr Gut", you know what that means?' he bellows and burps and sounds exactly like Sergeant Shultz on tele. They say nothing.

He thinks it's weak of the kids to be ignorant but he lets it pass. 'I cooked their tucker; they liked lots of sausage and potato. I liked it too. There was a woman who was very nice to me, I told you about her though, didn't I?'

Emmett stares off a bit and the kids know that this is just a ruse, that he's concentrating on the story and on them and should they lapse in their listening, things can change fast, the shark can rise from the depths. They stay tuned in to the story.

'One night they sent me over to get a start on tea for them in the big kitchen and I did, started sweating off some onions and garlic and I just got going. Initiative, that's what you need in life kids, I'm telling you.

'Simple initiative and I had it, piles of it. Trouble is, the pot I'd picked turned out to be lead-based and I damn-near killed nine Balts. How was I to bloody know it was lead? They weren't very forgiving and I lost the job in the camps. Came home not long after that and met your mother not much further along the road. So it all worked out for the best.'

He takes a deep swig and sighs. 'Things work out, usually, they work right out . . .'

They've heard this story so many times before. Still, they sit listening, holding onto the relief of the story. This is a good night with Emmett. Good nights come and they go, but while you are in a good one, you try to stretch it.

The map of Australia tilts on the wall as if it too is drunk. The light in the room is beer-stained yellow and there is a furry film of dust clinging to the sweaty wall and the smell of Louisa's puddle of piss is becoming unmissable.

She focuses on green Tasmania, the diamond island, and a place away from here.

She's always known that time is elastic. Bad times take so long but the good times slip away like a piece of wind and here it is again.

The change from good to bad can be instant because bad things happen faster. Rob usually messes it up. He will tonight, that much is clear. He is already not paying enough attention and teasing her about the pee and if you want to keep Emmett going, keep him in the good zone, telling the good stories, you have to pay attention. Is it so hard?

She pinches Rob on the thigh, just to warn him, to get him to focus, but she must have pinched too hard, she does have a mean streak, everyone says so, and here it is again, revealed.

It turns out the pinch is the wrong thing to do and Rob belts her and Emmett slams the table and the knives and forks (which are still on the table even after tea because there is no clearing away when he is in the good zone) scatter, and here it is, everysinglething spoiled. Ruined by Louisa herself and, she thinks, fuming, also by Rob. Always Rob.

They jump up in unison, rise as if they are levitating. 'If you little bastards can't concentrate, then you can bloody leave the table right now!'

He leans towards them and the trick is to escape the moment without being hooked on it and stopped. Louisa gets up but the mess is there and she's caught in the fear of the puddle.

She thinks she's being meek but she mustn't be meek enough because he smacks her face and her teeth cut the inside of her cheek and a tide of salty blood rises in her mouth and then she slips on the pool of urine. The twins are running everywhere and Anne is saying, 'No. Please, please.'

Rob cops a belt that sends him staggering into the wall. 'I'll give you ungrateful little smart-arses a taste of manners!'

Emmett hates them now. His voice has snagged on itself. His eyes are narrow. In his hand still resting on the table he grips the glass. A wave of beer slops forward like an amber sea and spills and this makes him worse. Louisa has slipped again and is under the table, hiding.

He's gone from being dark on them to insanely angry in a sentence. 'When I was a kid! . . .' he yells, swiping and grabbing at them, 'you have no idea what pain is . . . !' Louisa crawls out. He wants to go after the three boys as they back away from him. Time has stopped.

Bravely she dashes forward, covering her head with her hands, legs red from the piss, and catches up to the boys. Tears and blood. Later, she decides that the rules you have to follow to live this life are many and complicated but the first rule is head down.

Maybe if she were smarter, but there it is, plain to see, she's just not smart enough. They keep the sound of their tears down because they don't want things getting worse. Emmett throws his glass at the wall and at this moment they run away to the hedge.

The twins sleep in her bed that night. They hear their father slamming around in the kitchen for a long time. Is their mother all right? The sounds of the night.

14

Walking to the primary school down the long bluestone lanes that run behind their houses, they stretch their steps to land on the highest blocks. Mostly they stick to the lanes.

People's back fences always tell better stories than their neat front fences and it feels safer in the lane and even the weather feels better, cooler in summer and warmer in winter. The lanes are their highways. Full of old bike tyres and knots of rubbish that can yield anything, including the occasional rat.

But the Browns don't often walk together and sometimes they even seem to hate each other. Maybe they remind each other of their old man. Their life at Wolf Street is the weight behind everything. When they are out, by accord, they pretend home doesn't exist. They know other kids' fathers are rough and some are alcos too but they think the world believes that their own is normal and they want to keep the illusion going.

Still, down the lanes they walk, laced with the sense of each other being close by, if not too close. They spread out with Frank the dog in the lead, then comes Rob and Louisa, and the twins, together even when they're stepping around dog turds and under passionfruit vines, straggle along behind.

One day Louisa is coming last in the little procession down the lane. There's been yet another fight with Rob over his treatment of the twins. Strange, she thinks, how they make up with him more easily, even though she's been the one protecting them, and while she's mulling over this strangeness, Louisa is confronted by a man looming before her.

His mouth is open, his pants are down around his ankles and he's pulling at his white stalk of a thing, his red footy socks glowing. In that moment, it seems he wants something from her and she is stunned and she realises the lapse has come again, the moment between action and inaction, and she stands there shocked, waiting to be released from her own fear.

When the moment comes, she gets past him as fast as all speed but the laughing man with the big open mouth and the loose eyes haunts her. And as she runs all the way to school, she sees that whatever this is, it's not personal, it has nothing to do with who she is, it's just *what* she is that matters.

Though he's wildly fascinated, Rob pretends not to believe a word she says. 'Tell me again about the socks and about his dick, about his eyes,' he says, sitting on the back step that hot afternoon and when she does, and he laughs so much, she thinks he might choke. He loves such stories about anything seamy and enjoys seeing her embarrassed. It's not that funny but who else is there to tell?

When it rains, the troughs in the middle of the lanes run with grey water. The kids straddle them casually. Sometimes other kids push out into the lane from flimsy gates and join them on their way. Rarely a car might want to pass.

Frank sometimes deliberately stops to rouse up dogs behind fences and their fits of barking get him a nudge in the guts and a warning to get moving. 'Get on Frankie, get on,' they'll say as they move forward like shepherds towards a paddock.

When Peter, with a stick in his hand and a bag on his back, remarks to Louisa that he wishes he could just go somewhere else. 'I want to live where no one can get you,' he says. 'Where is that Lou? Where can no one get you? Is it London?'

She looks at his lightly freckled face. Like Daniel's but not identical, she always thinks he's smarter than Dan. She's holding Daniel's hand which is red with chilblains and she says, 'There's nowhere Pete that I can think of that's safe except maybe being a grown-up, reckon that might be where you get safe, but that's not really a place is it, little mate?'

Homewards the journey is much the same. Frank waits outside Mr Hessian's shop. This is where, if there's any money, they call in to buy a Redskin or some other durable lolly. When they see each other in the street or at Hessian's they act casual, as if they are strangers, and they never share lollies though they might swap, sometimes even generously, if the mood takes them, and if it doesn't, it's no skin off anyone's nose. Walking home, they stretch out, watch the cobalt sky with clouds like trailing smoke, chew their Redskins and take as long getting there as they can. No one ever wants to be first home.

Frank walks on ahead, carelessly leaps low fences and craps on scraps of lawn. When he does, the kids don't know him. Up the sideway into the fernery is the worst part and their scalps tighten as the alertness locks in. When they get there, they suss the joint out. Is he home? Second one home always whispers the same question, what's the mood? The answer varies.

He might be there and then, how will he be that day? Quietly, they take their bags and hope to pass through into the passageway that leads to the bedroom. Even after all these years, smoke from the fire still clothes the passage walls. Leftover smoke that can never bear to leave this home of theirs.

They pray the mood is good because when Emmett needs to be alone not much will save them. Wander past and they risk a swipe that will leave them bruised.

The Browns are hidden children. Mostly good at school though Rob teeters on the edge of delinquency. How far can you go? he wonders. The differences between home and school taunt him. It's amazing how daring a boy can be at school compared to home. How far can he go? Pretty damned far, it seems.

He touches his teacher Miss Summer's bum as she bends over in front of him one day and is strapped for it, both at school and by Emmett, which is far worse. But while they regularly refer to him as insolent in the staffroom, not many of the staff think about pushing things further. The boy often has a subdued quality that seems against his nature. There's something strange there, something broken.

Louisa, Daniel and Peter are quiet, attentive and grateful to be at school; like children of a cult, they are sworn to secrecy. They are no trouble, eyes guarding privacy and always keeping the distance between other people and themselves.

They walk the world with secrets nailed to their hearts. Images of their mother being slammed into a wall and of seeing her head held above a boiling pot of food are seared into them. Crying is a matter of course in their house. Things they do not want others to know determine the way they are.

And they hide the truth of Emmett carefully. Sometimes other kids at school notice, perhaps they see the bruise on Rob's neck where he'd picked him up ... there are always clues and other kids understand without words.

Ronnie Whitehead, a pale boy with honey eyes, sits beside Louisa during lunch for a week after her face and eye are bruised. Ronnie's kindness feels like a life raft, or pieces of bread left out in a fairy story. He gives her a way to not feel alone. He shares his geography book when she leaves hers at home, doesn't say anything, just pushes it between them.

The ones whose fathers terrorise them are a club. And though they hug the secret of themselves tight, they don't need to feel ashamed because all this cruelty, well it's just tradition. Just fathers handing on the past.

15

Mysteries bother Louisa. The first is a simple thing really, but it makes so much difference to them. How does he get home so early? The answer is that at work he bluffs and sulks and is occasionally brilliant and he knows exactly when to lay low. He survives for years on this strategy. He nicks off early and arrives home before the kids as if he doesn't know they'll be there, as if he expects them to have cleared off. He often gets there just in time to greet them.

Anne is always later than Emmett because she doesn't leave until five o'clock and it takes her twenty minutes to walk home. Louisa never works out how he gets home in time to plague them but sometimes when he's boozing he doesn't come home at all and these are times to relish. It's only when he has no money that he drinks at home.

The other mystery that plagues her with its tangling stickiness is why their mother doesn't take them away from the old man. But she never works out the answer to this one either, except that her mother is busy, too busy to be leaving anyone. She works all day sewing fine clothes for wealthy women up at the big green factory.

Some days Louisa combines her two questions and after she's put the potatoes on and cleaned the kitchen, she sets off to walk to her mother's work considering that she might miss the old man and mulling over the idea that maybe Mum will leave him one day. She stretches out her skinny knock-kneed legs along Wolf Street, hoping that she's got the time right so she doesn't miss Mum.

On days when she's mixed up the times she'll still be sitting on the step waiting for Anne when all the other workers file past her, a laughing stream of women released from their machines.

Her mum's Maltese friend, Maria, with her wild curly hair and chocolate eyes, stops and pats her back and picks up her chin and holds her face and smiles and says, 'Darling girl, your mama, she go. She first to leave tonight. You miss her.' Louisa jumps up and hides the tears rushing at her over the kindness of Maria and the missing of her mother, and takes off towards the footy ground. This is the way Anne walks. Louisa knows it.

Some days she catches Anne striding down the street in her high heels and the joy of finding her mother alone explodes within her. Anne can make her feel more alive than anyone in the world, just by the way she says, 'Louie, darling,' and spending time alone with her is like walking into a green sanctuary.

Other days, in that forlorn stretch between five and six, Louisa will miss her and trail into the house to find the spuds she's prepared either burned black and stinking of seared metal or not yet on. Both bad scenarios.

Louisa is always careful to be very, very good but still, she gets it wrong sometimes. She recalls her face near Emmett's knees, the belt coming down again and again, and looking up, seeing the white crust of sweat circling his armpit on his shirt and smelling the animal of him, like meat. She never understands why they all don't just run away but she could never run anywhere without the rest of them, so she's stuck.

16

Anne is beautiful in a way her daughter will never be. A brown-haired blue-eyed girl whose quietness Emmett believes is his own private haven. He needs the healing she offers and by degrees she becomes the mother he never had, whether she wants that or not.

At first she doesn't understand there's something wrong with him and later she puts his rages down to worries at work, thinks that if she gives him no reason to be upset, then the smoothness of life will continue.

It takes a year or so for that unquiet feeling she first had about him to re-emerge. She will never forget that day with Marge and Ray down at the beach when he had the tantrum because his foot got wet; but why, she wonders, did she go ahead with him after that? What was wrong with her? She had the chance to get away and missed it.

She's in bed next to Emmett listening to him snore. He sounds like a rusty gate caught in the wind and he takes up all the air. The booze makes him snore. She's lucky to have a small corner of the bed.

She remembers when he didn't snore, in the days when he was tender and when he seemed the cleverest man. It slips her mind that he was handsome, but she knows he must have been. Handsome. Never remembers this because it might lead to the idea that she loved him. Truth is, if there was good sex, it went away so fast it might have been imagined. Now, the best you can say about it is that it's fast. These days Anne thinks of sex with pure revulsion. And anyway, is Emmett still within that snoring man? Is this really Emmett sawing at the air beside her? Can that really be him? No, she thinks, it cannot be.

Anne doesn't believe in crying, doesn't indulge in what she thinks of as weakness. She just moves her face forward onto the cool cotton of the pillow. But whether she believes in weeping or not, tears seep down the pillow to make a pocket of rain.

The rhythm in Emmett's snoring drones on and then all of a sudden she realises with a stab of panic that she has to be at work by eight-fifteen. Work, thuds her heart in the language she most understands, work. Must sleep, she thinks. Must not let the sawing cut into her head.

And then, in a moment of clarity as clear as light, she cannot be in the same room as this man another second. She pushes herself up and with the practised habit of a ghost, puts her hand on her dressing gown, shrugs it on in the dark and quietly moves to her babies, drawn to them as though they hold every answer.

The relief of sleeping with the babies is a consolation she can't live without. Settling in around their soft warm limbs and feeling their small breaths, she believes there's no comparison to the purity of her children and their perfection is her blessing.

She tries to drift off but her mind is stuck in the groove of how she let Emmett into her life. Maybe she said yes to him because he was smart, smarter than anyone she'd ever met, and she wanted brains for her children.

She's stroking Peter's small head absently as a way of settling herself. She had wanted her kids to be cleverer than the others and cleverer than herself. Can that have been wrong? And if it was, who will know?

Anne sometimes remembers that she was beautiful in a way that made her look like the young Queen of England, refined and poised and somehow vulnerable, with her wide smiling mouth and innocent eyes. She could've married Des Peck, the gawky young plumber, and lived happily ever after in Newport but then Emmett called her Bambi. He saw the purity.

Her father never liked Emmett, he thought he was strange and dangerous and told her so. She never knew what her mother thought because they never discussed it.

At first she loved him so deeply it amazed her and she was his willing pupil. He read books to her while they were in bed on the weekends before Louisa was born. The girl who left school at fourteen to become an apprentice dressmaker was thrilled with what he knew and how he'd taught himself so much. He spoke about writing with reverence. He read *The Grapes of Wrath* to her and they were both in tears. Such a book. Then they tore through all of Jules Verne because the future appealed to Emmett. He loved the idea that it would be better then, that people wouldn't be slaves in factories, that their kids would be educated and if they were educated then they'd be rich and if they were rich, they'd be happy.

She doesn't think about what went wrong and doesn't allow herself the time to be disappointed. Anyway, all the women she knows are smarter and better than their husbands, that's just the way it is, and most of them take a belting now and then. She just gets on. She has only enough money to make it each week and it seems there are just so many kids.

She has to work, that's all there is, but she thanks God for it because without work she would be lost.

17

July seventeen was a mid-winter's night and the air in the fernery was frosty and nearly visible. The killing of Daniel was not intentional; it just happened that Daniel slipped over that bad night. You can't run that fast at five and you have to know how to behave. Daniel forgot and he panicked. Poor little bugger with his cow's lick and his matchbox car collection.

Daniel had been five years old for just four days when he died. He was already a schoolboy at four-and-a-half and he was as bright and shiny as the silver stars the teacher put on his drawings. He was proud of Rob's old school bag and he barracked for the Dogs and dreamed of playing cricket for Australia.

Louisa often wonders whose fault it was and finally decides it might have been hers. She never discusses this with Rob or with anyone else. That cold night when Anne knelt beside Daniel and picked him up in her arms she knew he was dead but the idea seemed too immense to be real. The hospital would bring him back to them because that's what they did. She knelt over him on the lino, holding and rocking him in her arms for a longest ache of time. When the ambulance came she had to be forced to let go of the child.

Emmett didn't think the hospital would help because he knew in that deep secret way that this was the truth that he would always live with. So Emmett was distraught and it didn't help at all. Anne looked at him as he settled into the horror of the knowledge and thought briefly, how many people can you look after in your life? And her weeping was silent and endless and then Daniel claimed her attention forever. Daniel in her arms stilled. The child who went away.

The ambulance men took him to hospital and there he was pronounced dead, his mother standing beside him holding his hand, lost and broken.

Later it occurs to her that Emmett always hated the kids just because they are kids. That he wants their place. Wants to always be the child, the eternal child. Is jealous of their time in the place of children. That's the why of it but it doesn't help, not at all. The reality is that the taste of sorrow lasts long and is bitter and heavy and never leaves you. Its sourness takes over and handles everything.

*

Rob and Louisa reckon Emmett ended up killing Daniel just the same as if he'd taken down the old Browning shotgun wrapped in the ragged grey blanket on top of the wardrobe and shot him.

Rob also thinks it's got a lot to do with him. If that sounds like rubbish, tough . . . it was his job to keep his brothers and sister safe and he failed. He could've stopped him, somehow diverted him you know, changed the mood or even made it worse so it would be aimed square at himself. He knows it. The world, he believes, knows it too. Daniel, he reckons, probably knew it, but all that knowing doesn't change a single bloody thing.

The way Rob sees it, the old man scared the boy to death; he'd done this before, to all of them. Daniel was running from him, but this time he slipped and his head hit the corner of the wall and blood came from his ear and his mouth and he just died. Doesn't take long to die.

Louisa had charged out there in the instant she heard Daniel hit the wall. She saw Emmett go berserk that night. He'd thrown his plate at the wall again, the curly tails of the chops snuggled into themselves, the peas scattering. Mashed potatoes making hills like clouds. Just crazy again for no reason, but the difference was that Daniel was outside in the toilet when Emmett got home and couldn't get back in.

He waited and waited and then he thought it was all right but his timing was all wrong because he was only a little kid and he couldn't get past Emmett, the wild beast in the kitchen fuming about 'bloody rats of kids always under your bloody feet when you're trying to get some tea for yourself because your useless wife hasn't done it for you. Bloody little bastards and who knows whose they are anyway, who knows?'

Strangest thing is, Rob concedes, there had been much worse times and none of them had died. And then there's this small moment and it catches Dan forever. How do you work it out? Rob was in the bedroom reading *The Phantom*, keeping the other kids awake with the light and knowing it but not caring one bit, and then Daniel needed to go to the dunny and it was obvious that Rob should have taken him because he was scared of the dark but Rob didn't do it, did he?

Louisa sleeping in Nan's old room knew he'd gone out there and was waiting for him to come back. She'd heard him nick out and then heard Emmett come home and she knew the boy waited and waited till he thought it was safe to run past. Louisa still says she should have gone out to get him.

'How'd ya know the old man would go off?' Rob asks her later when they talk it over in the shed. With the flatness of old knowledge, she says, 'Bad things just happen around here and you've got to expect it. Be mental not to.'

Rob wonders where his mother was and he's always wondered that. He decides she was probably hiding in the front room watching *IMT*. Graham Kennedy, the man with the bug eyes, was her hero and if she didn't concede that he was funny, then he sure was naughty. Best not to go near the old man after a night at the pub and she'd already put the kids to bed.

Emmett didn't go to gaol for killing Daniel. At the hospital a wide, pale man named Dr Steele listened to the story that Daniel was running around the corner after going to the toilet because he thought he'd get into trouble for being out of bed at nine-thirty at night and slipped and hit his head on the wall. Signed the death certificate and said it was an unfortunate accident.

Emmett wept when the police interviewed him, but it was all just a formality. The constables lifted their big shoes softly in the little kitchen and scratched down the details with their restive ballpoints, keen to get away from a place burdened with such sadness.

And the pain of Daniel's death goes on and on like something alive and growing in all of them. Rob doesn't believe that Daniel actually died that night. Maybe he just ran away. Daniel is withdrawn from them like all hope.

Peter is left trailing around after the big kids, lost and halved. He takes Daniel's school bag every day. He aches with a nameless pain. He keeps his eyes down. He will not hold Louisa's hand on the way to school. He drops back and Frank walks with him. He throws stones at anything that moves and takes no pleasure when he hits something. Once he hits a white cat and it limps away and he cries again. Every single thing is wrong. Every night Rob hears him crying. There doesn't seem to be anything to say. Yet the little boy keeps going. In the end he decides he wants to be a fisherman because Daniel liked the sea so much.

And Louisa finds it only gets worse after Daniel's death. Her silence is loud, but then she never spoke much anyway. Rob calls her Sourpuss Sally to get her going, get her mad.

Once he dares her to break an egg on his head and when goaded by taunts that she's weak and pathetic she does it, breaks the egg and feels shocked at herself. He remembers the shiny egg slipping over the cliff of his forehead. He laughs so much he inhales raw egg but Louisa doesn't laugh. She walks away and leaves the mess for him. It is as if nothing matters anymore. Daniel is between everyone.

Emmett is never home much now, he comes in drunk late after they are all in bed and even he is quieter, and the peace of that time is Daniel's legacy. Anne just keeps working away sewing all day, making food and cleaning, washing and seeing to the kids.

In time, Rob and Peter talk at night of ghosts and of Emmett. And later Peter tells Rob about his nice teacher Miss Wood, who smells somehow buttery, and that he follows her around when she's on yard duty, staying back so she won't notice.

One school night they're in bed waiting for sleep. They hear the shadowy canned laughter track steal away in waves from the tele in the lounge. Then Peter strangely announces, as a kind of declaration of intent, 'I like fishing best in the whole world. All I want to do is walk into the sea and stay there with the fish.'

Rob burrows into the bed and punches the pillow a bit. 'Oh yeah,' he says deeply unimpressed and beginning to wish he had his own room. 'Why's that?'

'Because that's the safest place you could be. Under the water nothing can get you.'

'What about air, mate, breathing, you know? Humans like air.' There's a silence between them for a bit.

'I won't have to breathe. It'll be special. I'll be like the fish, I'll be able to.'

Rob sighs, moves a leg to the cold bit of the bed. 'What about the sharks then, what about that?'

Peter is quiet. The full moon illuminates the room and makes crosses on the wall from the checks in the curtains. 'Sharks won't want me anymore. I'll be safe. Daniel will stop them. Daniel won't let things hurt me.'

Rob hears Peter's breathing become regular. He looks up into the soft dark and waits for it to take him.

18

Anne keeps the new pregnancy to herself for most of it and then with three months to go, Emmett reveals all with a guess. One night in the kitchen he grabs her, puts his hand on her slightly swollen abdomen and with a leer declares, 'I think you're hiding a baby in there, I think you are,' and laughs as if he's funny.

Anne swats his hand away and keeps on doing the dishes. 'I reckon you're about six months gone,' he says standing at the kitchen bench as if he's in a bar, 'definitely. No ifs or buts.' He knocks back half the glass and comes up for air.

The kids are cleaning up the table after tea and Rob is gobsmacked by the revelation. Can't stop looking at his mother, stands at the bin scraping his plate for ages. Louisa can't look at her at all. Peter doesn't seem bothered.

Outside playing cricket with a tennis ball in the mean little backyard in the width of the summer evening, they talk it over. 'Why do we have to have another kid?' Rob says outraged but keeping his voice down. 'God Almighty! Just another bloody mouth to feed.'

'I can't believe she'd let this happen,' Louisa hisses back through clenched teeth. The ball thuds into the house when she misses it. They all turn to look through the fernery to see if Emmett will charge out like a bull elephant because the ball's hit the house but no, he can't be stuffed tonight. She picks up the ball and hurls it at Rob harder than need be. 'It's bloody insane.'

'Watch it dickhead,' he says, stepping aside to avoid the arrowing throw.

Pete's batting. 'I don't care,' he says while Rob searches for the ball in the weeds down by the shed, 'what difference does it make anyway? We used to have Daniel remember?'

They ignore him. 'You're just a little shit anyway,' Rob says, grabbing the bat and chucking the ball at Lou. 'What would you know anyway? You little midget. And bowl properly Louisa, no grubbers.'

In the privacy of Louisa's room, they drop the front. 'What's going on? This is just mad. Why would anyone want to have another kid in this family?' Rob says, keeping his voice down. Sitting on Lou's bedroom floor, they lean on the bed, their legs straight out before them. Louisa feels a bank of anger welling in her. Textbooks spread out around them. She pushes the door shut with her foot.

Above them the light shade moves in the breeze from the window, an illuminated rice-paper planet. It seems Rob is so affronted by the idea of the baby that his hair stands up and his eyes seem huge. 'We are shit here and nothing works,' he says. 'It's all fucked up, you know it is. Mum's never here, always out working to support us and he's a pig and we're gonna have to look after it. You know it's true.' Louisa is looking down at the grey floor. Things, it seems, have turned on them again.

Her voice is not like her when she says, 'We got no choice Rob. None. We have to help her.' She's peeling away at the edge of her ruler with her thumbnail.

'Jesus,' he says, laying his head against the wall. There's so much he doesn't get. Stuff it, he thinks, I can't bloody fix it.

In the next few weeks he starts swearing more and it makes him feel older. Louisa is strangely ashamed about the pregnancy. She's old enough to be the baby's mother. She tells no one at school.

*

The baby, when it comes, is sickly, a small whitish droplet prone to rashes. Her eyes are as pale as a dawn sky and her small hands remind Peter of hermit crabs when they move and starfish when they're still. She even carries a whiff of the sea about her. She's not yet a Brown but an ocean creature come to stay. She does not open her mouth unless it is to cry and then the thinness of the cry reminds them of wire.

She stays in hospital a month after she's born to get her weight up. Anne and the kids visit her once a week on a Saturday morning. They dress up and take the bus because Emmett might need the car but it seems a bit like visiting a cemetery, a place where there's reverence for life but no joy. At each visit Anne holds the baby briefly while the kids look on.

As the baby stays on there, eventually leaving her becomes hard for all of them. Pete gets to pick her name out of Rose or Jessie; he goes for Jessie just because he likes it. He cries the second time they leave. In her dense plastic lens of a cradle, she's as alone as a small planet. They stand beside her lined up like the kids from *The Sound of Music* and silently wish her well.

And then it's determined that Jessie needs an operation on her stomach and things, it seems, just get worse. The sallow quality of her skin has something to do with her immature liver. The Brown kids stream out the hospital feeling like an endangered species.

But after a few more weeks, little Jessie comes home to a house that's almost forgotten she's been born. In Louisa's room, a cradle has been tucked behind the door and she's been throwing her clothes over it for a while.

The first night Jessie cries for what seems to Louisa to be the whole night. She rocks the cradle and waits for her mother to come and get the child. She tries to turn the baby over. She picks her up and pats her back. Tries to hear the rain on the tin roof. She can hear nothing but Jessie protesting with the searing cries of the newborn. She can see why: she'd complain too if she ended up here. The years yawn between them.

Anne's back at work and sits at the industrial sewing machine in the kitchen, her back hooked, and sews plastic suits for fat women to wear while they exercise. The radio is tuned in loud to the doom of commercial talkback. The baby lies on a quilt in a cardboard box at her mother's feet.

When they come home from school, the kids take over the baby and carry her around, give her a bottle and talk to her. Quieten her. It's as if they are workers or parents rather than kids. They do what their mother can't do. They wash nappies in the red bucket until they want to cry but there's absolutely no point in that.

Jessie's in with Louisa until they build the sleep-out for the boys. They all try to keep her quiet because of Emmett. He craves peace even while he's the greatest obstacle to it. He sits in the jaundiced light of the kitchen with his beer in the evenings on his own, weeping and laughing in turns, cornering them if they pass. He cannot relax because his life is lived on a wire. The loss of Daniel will not retreat.

Some days though he can be joyful with Jessie and he might pick up the baby in her holey singlet and sagging nappy and dance to a song on the radio, the baby soaring and laughing in his arms. When this happens, the kids stand a respectful distance with small smiles, feeling shy of this good father throwing the cackling baby in the air. Happiness is always worth watching even if it raises questions. Did he love them once too? Louisa's not fooled. No, she thinks with her stagnant heart. Or he wouldn't act like he does.

Rob and Louisa try not to like Jessie but it doesn't work. Rob ends up loving the little bugger while Louisa holds out longer. Pete likes her well enough from the first day he sees her. 'She looks,' he says as they all stand around the bassinet, 'just like a potato.' And they laugh with an unnamed relief that he seems happy.

Even when she's older and she thinks back on Jessie as a baby, Louisa recalls that time exactly. She can smell the petrol station behind them and the fumes from the tankers edging into the kitchen and the tap dripping into the sink and Anne wiping the table in big arcs with the battered pink wettex catching crumbs with the cup of her hand and always, always there's her ghost smile.

And she knows that things began to change then. That Rob started to go feral and the gap between them widened because Rob started to pick on Peter, always teasing him over something, and Louisa had to stop it. She doesn't understand even now how you can become the thing you most hate.

'Why do you torment Pete?' she screams at Rob one afternoon when they've both retired bloody. 'How could you even want to hurt someone younger than you? Hasn't there been enough of this shit in this house to last forever?'

He smirks, holds up his middle finger and slams out the door.

19

Peter walks across the main road behind the house after tea
one night when tangerine clouds are stretched out like string.
He's been thinking about fishing for a while now.

Getting away from the others, and from the bully Rob has
become and always from the looming Emmett. Yeah, he's
cutting out, going fishing, but first he's got to wait for the bus
to Williamstown. He sits down in the gutter with Danny's old
bag beside him.

The tin flag of the bus-stop sign holds itself in the air and
he edges up a bit towards it on the gutter so he's looking at the
back of his own house across the road.

The houses opposite remind him of teeth. The service
station makes a gap like a missing one and standing out boldly
is the back of number fifty-five. He can see most of the yard.
And there's something hanging on the clothesline. Looks
like Emmett's second work pants. Legs kick up in the breeze
now and then. From this distance, the house looks small and
exhausted from the effort of containing the Browns under the
harsh eye of Emmett, and watching the house makes the boy
uneasy. He feels like an animal separated from the herd.

He chews the inside of his cheek, a habit he's gotten into
lately. There's something about it that reminds you that
you're here. Then he peels a couple of flakes of dry skin off his

lips, seeing how long he can get them. Draws a bead of blood. He chews on the skin around his cuticles and there's not much left of his small white nails. In a while an old red bus lumbers into view and grinds to a halt before him. Inside, he balances like a surfer as it takes off grudgingly, all gears straining. He pays the driver, and then weighed down by the frozen bait he makes his way down.

The bus is tight with people coming home from work. Like most of the grown-ups he knows, they're pretty sour. His rod pokes them a bit and they scowl. He pulls it back and hangs on in the middle of the bus. He's not that tall yet but he sees out the window okay. He imagines that the houses they pass pull themselves back from the line of the road. He likes the look of most houses. Likes the safety he reckons he sees there.

Peter has the same crew-cut as Rob's but his skin is paler and he's still prone to little skirmishes of hives. He's bigger than Rob at this age and this makes make him popular with Emmett. But it isn't just his size that Emmett likes. There's something about Pete that everyone likes. A kind of stillness. A listening. Pete doesn't ever talk much but he's got something that Louisa thinks of as kindness; but then you can't say that about boys.

20

By the time he gets down to the pier at Williamstown it's getting late and it doesn't seem so much like spring anymore. He hurries to the fenced-in part of the foreshore and beyond it he can see the pier. He'll have to go over the top. He makes his way past the colossal petrol tanks with ladders up the sides and AMPOL and MOBIL printed in car-sized letters all over them. He climbs the cyclone fence and at the top drops his bag onto the sandy dirt on the other side. It skids.

The pier stretches out in front of him, a wooden road over still water. The place smells of seaweed and petrol. Love that smell, he thinks, smiling. The sea shimmers like beaten tin and far away the city rises out of the haze. The sky is verging on white and a string of seabirds pulls across it. He takes a deep breath. This is the only place he can hear himself. Everything ebbs away.

He's brought both his jumpers, Rob's old blue and white stripe and the green one he's wearing. He's got a singlet on plus his school shorts. So he reckons he's right. In the washhouse he found a bit of blanket, it's pinkness fading to memory, and stuffed it in the bag.

He gets out the blanket and spreads it on the wooden boards. It smells musty like the washhouse and that reminds him of his mum and a wave of tears pushes into him but he says 'no', and roughly drags his sleeve across his eyes.

When Peter starts to fish the world around him retreats. In the distance, fishing boats push through all that water and behind them tankers the size of buildings move towards Port Melbourne. He fishes with a determination he didn't know he had. Nothing else matters. Snags and knots and bait-loss are part of everything. He keeps at it, untangling, refixing bait. Even a cat's cradle of knots has a rhythm to it.

He fishes to catch something but really he fishes for the sake of being there. To be connected with the sea and the sky and he already knows that he's most himself when he's alone.

The bay is a pond tonight. He plops his tackle within a circle of where he stands time and again with the certainty of clockwork. The seagulls perch companionably beside him and when they see there's no food they leave, flapping into the evening like white rags. The sun falls away and night is revealed in the pearly sky. There's even a bit of moon.

He's forgotten his torch. He hasn't meant to stay the night but he doesn't have a watch to know what the time is. Knows it's getting late though and by the time he sees the lighted tube of the last bus hurtling around the corner, it's way too late to even move – he's missed the thing.

Doesn't matter. He feels safe and comfortable down here on his own. Free to talk to Daniel right out loud. Tells him about the fishing, about the others, about how Rob's a pain. 'Picks on me all the time. Dunno what I've done. Lou keeps him off me but she gets sick of it. She's not there anyway all the time these day, she reads books a lot and she's mad 'cos she has to look after Jess.' The relief of being with Daniel has him smiling. He can even see his brother sitting beside him on the pier cross-legged, with his crew-cut and his big eyes.

Peter keeps fishing until he has trouble keeping his eyes open; all the time chatting away to Dan telling him about Emmett and his moods and the fighting. About the last big one where Emmett nearly got the trifecta but the kids had been making a noise out the back and he couldn't hear the last race, so he didn't know.

That was the worst thing for Emmett. 'He was so mad he picked Rob up by his neck and then threw him down and smacked Louisa in the face. Her nose was bleeding all over the place.'

He speaks just loud enough for Daniel to hear. Then when it gets late and the pale moon looks down upon the boy, he succumbs to the weight of the day. He's not scared. Emmett is the most terrifying thing he can think of and he's not here. The fence keeps out stray idiots. He lies down under his bit of blanket, puts the bag under his head and sleeps. He keeps the rod in the drink all night though, his hand on it lightly.

21

By the time Peter's home, Anne and Emmett have left for work without noticing he's missing. He slips in the back door using his foot to stop the flywire door smacking shut just in case Emmett's around. You never know.

Rob, pulling his socks on while he sits on top of the radiator, is waking up slowly aided by the stupefying orange heat that will soon have him shifting. He knew his brother had gone fishing but didn't say anything, couldn't see the point. Why would you volunteer any information in this house?

Louisa is eating a bowl of cereal when Pete comes in. He sees she's got the blue bowl she likes, she carries on if the others get it first. And she's doing that weird thing where she concentrates on not spilling milk. The trick is keeping her head still.

Pete is convinced he has the weirdest sister in the world. The other sister sits beside her having a nibble at her vegemite toast and Frank helpfully eats anything Jessie can't manage. She smiles at Pete and he ruffles her silky hair as he passes.

'Where ya bin?' Louisa asks scraping milk up her chin with the spoon and looking straight ahead. 'Gelli Pier,' he says, voice low and husky from his night in the open. He gets the sharp knife out of the drawer.

Louisa goes back to the newspaper spread out in front of her like a map of the world. She doesn't keep going with questions. She's got to get ready for school, there's a history test today and she's planning to get the best mark. She earnestly wishes she'd spent more time on European kings. But Emmett got home from the pub earlier than he should have last night and she turned her light off so he wouldn't know she was awake.

She lay in her bed as still as a branch waiting for which way the sounds of night would go. Would something upset him? Or would he just get stuck into his cold tea sitting on a plate on the pot. Scoff it down standing there like a wolf who stole into the wrong house?

It took about ten minutes to know and things were quiet enough last night but the cost was in European kings. Pity there's such a bloody lot of them, she thought, seems like every second European was a damned king.

In the yawning mouth of the gully trap, Peter cleans his fish under the tap, enjoying the business of turning them into food. When the others are gone, he delicately fries the small fillets in a bit of butter in the old frying pan, the one Emmett reckons is well-seasoned whatever that means, and then with a sprinkle of salt, has them for his breakfast.

He knows he won't be going to school today. He also knows he'll have to be careful with this wagging it business. Not too much. He sits himself down in Emmett's chair at the head of the table. After he's eaten his little feed of fish, he pushes his plate back from where he's been sitting and starts working out what he'll need for his next trip to the pier.

22

Emmett starts them off on football with all his stories about North and his mates and about how bloody good they were. About the glory days of the league. About the high flying. The marks that defy death in the goal square, the big men flying. Strange thing is, he never goes anymore, just trails off and confines himself to horses and to the radio. Before that though, he and Louisa go down to the football ground. It was never planned, it just happened like the flu happens, right out of the blue.

It's a Saturday afternoon and she's walking down Willy Road towards the Western Oval, home of Footscray Football Club, the Bulldogs. Frank is with her but behind, caught, leg way up, taking a very long piss on a quiet corner. And suddenly there's Emmett, looming before her like a brick wall. Doesn't even seem that drunk and he's friendly. 'G'day Bugalugs,' he says, rocking on his heels. 'What's new?'

As ever she's speechless, so he speaks more sternly. 'Where ya going Louisa Jane Brown?' And he clamps his hand onto her shoulder and looks down at her.

'To the footy. Collingwood are versing us,' she blurts and reddens, immediately guilty and not knowing why. 'You get in for free at three-quarter time.' Her voice is squeaky and unfamiliar. Standing there in the road looking down, he seems as elemental as the sky. Frank has caught up by now and, allegiances switched instantly, he props at Emmett's feet.

And like a change in the weather, Emmett is suddenly irritated. 'Louisa. *Don't* say "versing", it's not a bloody verb. For God's sake.' He sucks his teeth to calm himself and then, after a small pause, declares that he may as well come with her, keep her out of trouble.

Though this feels harsh to the girl, she smiles crookedly and Emmett adds, bright and sunny and even enthused now, 'You reckon it's free to get in? Well, I love a bargain, always have liked a bar-bloody-gain.' And the girl's stomach flutters as they set off together, the very image of a father and a daughter.

He wears work boots, the jacket with the leather sleeves, his work strides and a blue shirt that makes his eyes seem bluer. Walking towards the football ground, the noise swells at them in low circles and the crowd lifts her from the oppression of being alone with her father.

He walks quietly with his hands in his pockets. Seems to be thinking. Doesn't speak. His hair is longer than usual and threaded with grey but he still looks a bit like Clark Gable and these days he even has the moustache. When Frank gets too close, a quiet 'Piss off, Francis' moves him.

Then he says, 'What's your favourite word?' and doesn't wait. 'I'll tell you about mine. Mine is "phenomenal". Well *today* it's "phenomenal", that's a word and a half. But you should always look at the roots of a word before you make up your mind on it. "Phenomenal" comes from the Greek and originally means something that can be seen. Now, these days it means remarkable. How about that? What d'ya reckon?' He pauses without expectation and she stays quiet, musing on her mental old man.

'But the greatest word of them all is "onomatopoeia". And what, Miss Louisa Jane, does this word mean?' It's the second time he's called her by her middle name, something he rarely does though she knows she's named after Jane Austen, one of his favourite writers. Louisa comes from Henry Lawson's mother, Louisa, also a writer. She feels a swamp of confusion get her. The quicksand is everywhere. What does all this mean?

She tries to concentrate on what he's saying instead of stretching her head with thoughts about writers but he's caught her right out. So she takes a stab. 'Something to do with rhyming?'

They've passed the railway station and people mill around on the platforms and beneath them the pewter tracks ribbon away and the thought flashes by, what if someone stepped off right at the wrong moment?

Emmett laughs. He's not mad at her for being a dill and she understands then in a flash that he's better when the other kids aren't there. The dog heads off home when they get to the station and she watches the thread of Frank moving out like a fish on a line.

But Emmett is still telling her something. 'Onomatopoeia is a poet's word and it means the formation of a name or a word by an imitation of the sound associated with the thing or action designated. Thwack is the sound you make whacking a ball and it has onomatopoeia!'

'Gee,' she says evenly and wonders if he's so smart, why doesn't he stop drinking beer and acting like an idiot? But she smiles and listens and the talk carries her forward. He says, 'There are other words I'm particularly fond of. "Branch", as you know, is an old favourite. But "ludicrous" for instance, what do you think of that one?'

He stops and cups his two hands around her face. His eyes are lighter this afternoon, pure blue circles of sky. 'Because that's what I am. Ludicrous.' He smiles and lets go of her face but holds onto her plait for longer than she thinks he should until she feels like a rabbit in a trap.

Just under Mount Mistake down at the ground, the big wire gates stand wide open and inside the bitumen terraces look like bad teeth. Green beer cans and knots of people are everywhere. Footscray is playing Collingwood. A cold wind crouches over the oval and harries them and Footscray's premiership flag from 1954 hoisted up on the grandstand flagpole snaps and sags. The best team in the league against the worst. Perversely, Louisa has a soft spot for Collingwood.

Footscray is routinely flogged and here it is again today, so Louisa has a go at making stilts out of discarded beer cans but she's clumsy and falls and she senses that it begins to annoy him and he shouts roughly. 'Come 'ere Lou, anyone'd think you were your idiot brother, behaving like that. Settle down.' When he gets mad his nostrils flare and he reminds her of an eagle. He can't be that mad though because he buys her a pie and for himself a beer and they stand on the iron grey terraces and cheer on the poor old Dogs.

When the players come close, their effort is shocking and the mud and sweat stuns and silences them. He explains the finer points of the rules, round-the-neck, holding-the-ball, in-the-back, man-on-the-mark, all stuff she believes she's always known, in fact was born knowing, but even so, when he talks she's listening.

'This game is special to us, special to this city right here. It was invented by a couple of toffs who went to fancy schools over the other side. But despite this, as you know, there never was a better game in all the world. That's a plain fact.' He pauses, aware of some kind of betrayal and adds as though he will be held accountable, 'But I am more than fond of cricket as you well know.'

Nearby, a Collingwood supporter, his bald head sitting

above a swathe of black and white scarf, hawks loudly and spits and a great island of yellow phlegm lands an inch from Louisa's school shoe. Oh no, thinks Louisa, the cold silence of anticipation creeping through her. Emmett pauses with his can to his lips and asks the man a question, loud but casual. 'You'd be a complete dickhead, wouldn't you mate?' Heads swivel. Louisa manages to hiss a strangled, 'Please Dad' and he puts his spare hand on her head and the panic drops away. She's amazed when he ceases hostilities.

They move down to the fence and he leans in to her and says, 'Never mind mate, it's only a bush oyster', and they laugh. 'You reckon?' she says. 'Pretty damn big oyster.' She's still full of lightheaded relief that he didn't spit the dummy and she sneaks a look at Emmett sipping on his can of VB and the innards of the boiling pie run between her fingers and scald a vee, and she burns her tongue cleaning it up, but everything is all right now.

'You see Lou, what this game has is the marking, the big men bloody flying. That bloke over there must be six-foot-four, can you credit how high he gets? And the man has no fear. Ah, makes your heart sing.' They are standing on the wing and when players thunder by, dots of black mud spray them and Emmett smiles and wipes his face.

Louisa listens and eats on, not at all worried about a bit of mud. 'You know, I took your mother to see North play when we first met and I got myself all overexcited when that Mopsy Fraser bastard from Richmond dropped one of our boys behind the play. Fair dinkum, felt like an assault on the family and there he was out there grinning like a shot fox. Smug as all get-out. Well, I just went berserk. I admit it.

'And soon enough there they were the bloody rozzers. As you know, cops have no respect for a passionate supporter and without wanting to big note, I *was* a bit of a lair in those days and possibly not even the full quid. Well anyway, the coppers escorted me from the ground, chucked me out the gates and I come a bloody massive gutser too. Grazes up and down me arms and all over the shop from the bitumen.

'Your poor old mum, who as you know hates footy anyway, did not have a clue what to do. She was stuck there till the game ended. I waited outside for her. She was not happy. In my defence, I will say that Mopsy Fraser went on to break Ted Whitten's jaw, so the bloke was always unreliable.'

He's smiling at the memory of his young self and shaking his head indulgently. He looks around at the wide sky so open above the ground, then gives his attention to a skirmish in the play. He's finished his beer and chucked it into the rolling tide of cans. The Dogs are going down by at least twelve goals and it may even get to twenty.

'You know, Louie,' he says after a while, 'sometimes there's not that much difference between winning and losing. It's all academic in the long run.' At that, something slips in her and it feels okay to disagree, as if some unspoken law has been relaxed. 'It's not the same though Dad, winning and losing aren't really the same thing.'

He grabs her plait again and shakes it. 'Good for you, that's the way, you take the bastards on Louie.' She wonders again what it was that has made him so weird, so alone and explosive, but doesn't even consider asking that one because she knows it's all beyond her anyway. She flings the pie crust into the rubbish, wipes her hands on her skirt, pulls up her socks. Even covered in oily mud, the footballers are too much to think about, the pure force of their maleness is a mystery to be deferred, so she waits for Emmett to be ready. But he's in no hurry and when almost everyone else has drained out of the ground he says, 'Let's go.'

A bit past the station, Frank is propped on the footpath waiting, people passing him as though he's a dog statue.

Frank always shows up, nearly always finding them in the web of streets; it's not even noticed much any more. Today he watches them approach with the patience of a fisherman. 'Frankie,' Louisa says dropping her hand on his head, 'you're late again boy.' Frank's heard it before and he nudges her and turns to lead them home.

As they walk through the end of the afternoon, Emmett puts his arm round Louisa's shoulder and despite herself and the good day, she flinches. 'Louie,' he says low and quiet like he's telling her a secret, 'I'm only a battler,' and then he drops his arm and like a small soldier, she walks beside him all the way. She thinks about trying to hold his hand but she's too busy at the moment, silently measuring her steps against his and being surprised that they aren't much different from hers.

*

In the winter, Peter's centre-half forward for West Footscray. He's fast and courageous and his skills are okay too. There's talk that he'll go all the way, play for the Dogs one day.

When they win the Under 13 grand final, the boy in the worst footy boots gets Best on Ground and the team drape themselves over each other, all caked in mud and grinning. Photographs are taken and Pete's head seems huge. His hair is wild and high but his eyes are calm. As the kids cool off, they suck their stomachs in away from the wet jumpers and by now Peter's skin is rough with goose pimples and he's shivering like a machine.

As the mud tightens on him he walks stiff-legged over to Anne and hugs her around the neck. 'Hey there Mum,' he says, still pretty hoarse from the game. She knows he's thinking of Daniel but with all the people laughing and patting each other on the back, it's not possible to say anything. She breathes in the mud of him and thinks about holding onto this moment forever.

He gives up footy not long after the big win. The next year a big kid lands hard on his neck after a thwarted tap down. A squad of his mates carry Peter to the car and then he's forwarded on to the hospital. He remembers the press of arms carrying him and that he can't move his neck and that the red pillow of his heart feels too big for his chest.

The doctors think the neck may well be broken. Anne comes to see him before and after work. She wants to keep him hoping, so for something to talk about she tells him about the ladies at work. Emmett stays away.

Louisa believes fervently and tragically that Peter will never walk again and weeps hard and long, settled into the dirt in the old shed. She leans against the broken washing machine and puts her face in her hands and says, she knew it. That she had a premonition and it was right. Rob doesn't believe any of it and says Louisa's cracked.

'That wasn't a premonition, you were just dizzy, you bloody idiot. It had nothing to do with anything. You are not part of every-bloody-thing Louisa. You can't fix things and you don't cause them.' But he's upset himself now and tears slide onto his jumper. He slams out of the shed. Jessie is too young for such stories to take hold but sitting beside Louisa, she mashes her doll's face into the dirt.

The swelling must go down before they know for sure. Lying in the children's ward, anchored to sandbags and stretched out in the slice of bed, Peter registers that time passes by the light from the window. And by the meals and by the number of times they change his wee bottle.

From the whispering, it seems he won't be walking again. He thinks about fishing. The pier. Rob and Louisa sit so quietly without bickering or punching or giving Chinese burns, they make him nervous. The only one he really wants is Anne, but her time is rationed by work.

Then one night, straight from a counter tea at the pub, Emmett strides into the ward, pissed and booming. His clothes, his hair and even his skin hold the reek of countless cigarettes and the sweat of blokes and the slaughterhouse smell of pubs.

On his face tonight, Emmett's got the look. It brooks no argument. He's got it all sorted RIGHT out. Peter can't see much, given he can't move his head, but hearing is more than enough. He wonders what the other kids in the ward will make of this.

Emmett gets up close. 'Listen mate, don't worry,' he whispers real loud leaning in to the boy, placing his big hard hand on Peter's bandaged head. A coil of nicotine circles two fingers. 'It will be all right. I've had a word to the big bloke about you. Upstairs. Told him I wanted my son to walk. We worked it right out. Said he'd fix it.' It takes some time for Peter to realise that Emmett must be talking about God.

Emmett's all stubble and bloodshot eyes. The newspaper, as ever, is folded to the form guide and stands straight up in his pocket. Hot beer fumes fan out from him and the boy actually breathes them in gratefully. Today he doesn't mind them, they smell familiar, remind him of home.

Emmett sits beside him, awkward on the little chair. He crosses his legs, the steel-capped boots incongruous and baleful on the shining hospital floor. He's uncomfortable and hot in his bulky work jacket with its squeaky leather sleeves. The newspaper slips to the floor. He retrieves it absently.

He remembers when he was in hospital as a child. How he liked that it was all so clean. Whiteness surrounded everything and the nurses smiled. It was real nice.

He drifts for a minute then something occurs to him and he brightens with the idea. Leans forward. He asks the boy if he's eating. His voice lowers gravely. 'Because you know boy, there's only one rule in life and you know what that is. You don't eat, you don't shit! You don't shit – you die! Simple rule boy. Remember that one.'

He's pleased with having recalled the rule. Not a bad rule, he thinks, off the top of me head, not bad at all, and success relaxes him. Some of the other kids in the ward are tittering at Emmett but he doesn't notice.

And then, in the pause between acts, some of the air seems to leave him and he sags with all these efforts he must make. It's as if he's not inflated anymore, not so hard, and Pete, though he can't see his face, feels it again, the mouldy sadness that circles the old man.

*

No one else seems to be in on Emmett's God-bothering. The doctors skirt around the bed reading charts and the nurses whisper to each other. They don't seem to have been told that Emmett has fixed it. For days they wait for the swelling to subside with Peter not moving. Days coming and going with other children enduring pain in the ward. Louisa, Rob, Anne and Jess visit and shuffle by his bed like some kind of lost tribe.

But it turns out that Peter's neck is all right and he is discharged. Brokenly, walking slow and careful as something newborn, he gets from the hospital to the Holden. In the car, safe from prying ears, Emmett changes the gears and claims credit. Peter shifts his fledgling legs and prepares to listen.

'Makes a difference a little chat with the big bloke,' he says with a nod. Peter can turn his head a bit now. The streets move past them as though they're on a conveyor belt. He sees his father in profile eternal against the landscape. 'Yeah Dad, it's a good thing you sorted it out,' he says, closing his eyes and leaning his head gently back on the car seat.

23

On the night of the first school dance Louisa is in a state of grim excitement. Never the most popular girl at school, she's smart and secretive, a watcher with ambition, but tonight she is determined to go to the dance, damned if she isn't. She's going. And she is going to enjoy it. She's just turned sixteen.

Anne brings home a crepe jersey dress the pale blue of eyelids. It's an old order left hanging on a rail in the storeroom for some time. Anne gets it for nothing which makes Louisa happy and it looks nice enough. It's long and swishes on the floor when she turns and it ties her up in the back like a present. Louisa washes her hair the night before. It's long and dark and shiny. She's all ready, she's just got to do tea.

Emmett's in the kitchen when she pushes through the fly-wire door into the kitchen. This doesn't look great. She carefully puts her bag down by the door. 'Get the fuck out of here, can't you see I'm busy,' he says almost casually and turns away, dismissing her.

She reads the mood off the map of his voice, not too bad tonight, might be able to move past it and get done the things that need doing without a brawl. And that's what might have happened, but for the smell of beer. The smell of it is a net, capturing and forcing itself upon her. She fights the urge to gag.

Emmett is pouring himself what he loves to refer to as a cleansing ale in the hub of the kitchen and she's the girl at the edges with things to do. But tonight is different. Tonight, the future begins. Louisa will not be diverted from her task. She needs to be busy and yet here again blocking her is beer, the old enemy with its yeasty yellowness tearing at her nostrils. The smell that means chaos.

She has a little time up her sleeve, she believes she will be right with time, even allowing for being careful of the old man's mood and yet, there it is, the strangest thing, tonight of all nights, she feels like pushing at the boundary.

Even years later she will not want to name the thing that pushed her to take Emmett on, but now it's a secret she can't open. Truth is, sometimes Louisa wants to serve herself up to the big thing, to just *have it done*, to finish it. This is the coward within speaking and should not be encouraged but the hero within, tired of heeding the moods of the monster, also needs restraint.

Some things are better left unnamed but if she named it, she'd call it the suicide impulse and it will always be a force inside her. And if she's feeling kindly toward herself when she thinks about the night of the dance, she might say that perhaps she was just being brave, that she had a heart as full of courage as a soldier facing the enemy in a muddy trench. The soldier heading into death. The ones they build statues for. But she doesn't often feel kindly.

Still, Emmett, it must be said, was pretty mild in his greeting so she knows he's not in the war zone yet, the zone of no return. Louisa reckons she can read him like she can read the battered barometer by the front door. Go a bit further, push it kid, the hero says.

So she pushes in behind him and drags the spuds out of the cupboard near his knees standing at the kitchen bench as if he's at the pub. And she plonks them on the bench behind him. He turns to her, knees just bent, glass in hand, as slow and as watchful as a big cat.

'I thought I told you to fuck off,' he says quietly, raising the menace a notch. He's surly now and broody, aiming his anger squarely at her, a warning because this is when he's most dangerous. In the beginning.

Still, for some mad reason she pushes on, thinking she has space and time but really she's crossing the tracks with the train bearing down. His eyes become darker when the storm is rising within, but it doesn't seem this way yet. She still reckons there's a bit of give there and believes, foolish confident girl, that she's correctly reading the mood. She has time to stop and to listen, even to back off and be compliant. And yet she does not do that.

It's time to stop listening. Time to think of Daniel and of where he went, of what the loss of him has done to them. Time to let the rage out. Time to lift her head, to watch the rhino charge. Take it head on. It's her job to prepare the tea and she'll bloody well do it, put the potatoes on and get the meat ready. Get things underway for the meal, for yet another bog standard meal.

Will it be one of those meals where silence folds over the kitchen and, heads bowed as if in prayer, they push the food into their mouths fast and stare at the scraps on the blue plates? All the kids have counted the cracks on those plates and can tell anyone who wants to know the average number on each (between thirty and fifty).

But tonight will be different because suddenly Emmett is coming at her and she's not moving. She will not be bullied. Something has spilled within her and something has been released. Louisa is coming out.

He tells her to wait 'til he's bloody-well ready and calls her a fucking little bitch and again says, 'Fuck off Louisa, just fuck off.' And she says, barely troubled it seems, 'No. No. I'm going out tonight. Now, I'm doing my jobs. You have to move.'

And the words slip out of her mouth as easy as a breath and she's amazed at herself because she just keeps going when she should have stopped but there it is, loud and clear in her bumpy schoolgirl voice and she says, 'Fuck off yourself, why don't you? You bloody great bully . . .'

Words you might say to anyone if you're mad enough but not words to speak to Emmett Brown. Though she doesn't fear, her body fears for her and her scalp prickles and her heart thumps and sweat starts up but she pays no attention to these details because she's entirely ready.

When he punches her face, it's almost a relief. She feels his knuckle meet her teeth and both lips split and swell. Bright blood rains down on her school dress and this takes no time, but to Louisa the moment has grace. She seems to be recording each instant and then, in that heavy space, she rips into him like an animal, grunting with sheer effort.

She hates touching him, it feels too personal and his skin is like scales, crusty and brown to the tide mark of the shirt that she rips open. She sees that the skin underneath is fish-white and that his eyes are yellow from years of grog and neglect. She sees it all in close-up, like she's never seen him before.

He stinks of sour sweat and his hair is long and stringy, but still dark enough to make him seem young. But if she has to, she will touch him, she will. She will be free of him even if she has to kill him. It's become so simple.

So, she enters into the roaring, the ripping and the spitting blood. Enters the arena with the old man and remembers the taste of blood and notes with the usual amazement that it tastes of salt, and while the thought passes through her that we are made of the sea, he beats the shit out of her.

There's no deciding. There's nothing, it's just a fight and she gives it every bit of herself, shovels into him like a boxer and he hits her over and over and while she loses the fight, she knows she's won.

He rips out a clump of her hair. She thinks she's doing no damage but she must be because he lurches back like a bear shambling across the room. He rests one hand on the table and looks shocked. They're both breathing hard. Blood runs from her swollen mouth like a stream.

And then, in a pause that might have been in a spotlight, they step away from each other in the kitchen where the light filters through the lattice that braces the fernery where the plants are mostly dead, where a tarp flaps in the corner, where the washhouse barely contains piles of dirty clothes and the lazy copper sits roundly waiting for someone to take charge. Surrounded by all of these normal things.

But here in the kitchen, their hearts beat hard and she watches him intently. She's astonished to see that she's dragged his watch from his wrist and she holds it in her hand and it swings like a scalp. He stands back, abashed. She puts the watch on the bench and notices that her hands are shaking so much they seem to be levitating and then, strangest of all . . . he's leaving.

He grabs a tea towel and holds it to the rakes her short nails have made on his arm and then he limps away up the passage to his bedroom. She wipes her mouth with her hand and then wipes the blood on her torn school dress even as she knows torn school dresses don't matter anymore.

She returns to the bench to do her work. Her hands are trembling but she peels the five potatoes and manages to cut them and put them in the pot. Then she goes to her room. She doesn't cry. She is elated. She reckons she's killed him in her heart. There's a curious calm. And a lightness.

Outside in the sideway between their house and Stan's next door where the moss inches along the fence, the mauve light is absorbing the day. She lays the watery blue dress out on the bed and thinks it looks like the person she will become, calm and clear and clean.

She sits down on the floor and rests her back on the bed. When she touches her mouth, it's huge and no longer hers. The lace curtain lifts with the scraps of wind that make it through her window.

At the dance that night she wears the blue dress. Her face is much noted by the other kids but not to her. No one asks her to dance, though she hasn't expected that. Why would anyone ask the dour serious girl to dance? The girl whose long dark hair falls forward and covers much of her face. A girl who might even be pretty if she smiled.

Rob is there in another clump of kids, as popular and funny as ever. They steer themselves away from each other as if they're barely acquaintances.

At the entrance to the gym under a banner announcing *The Footscray High Senior Social*, her best friend, Gail Godwin, puts an arm around her shoulders and Louisa feels a rush of heat in her eyes and instantly it seems the salty tears bite into her lip. People being nice, thinks Louisa, will always get you.

Gail dances with Louisa's favourite boy, the darkly handsome Steve Christou, and tonight Louisa even gets pleasure from seeing them together. Such things as jealousy seem irrelevant now.

Bad Company belting out 'It's All Right Now' through the big square amps gets her moving tentatively on the boundary line of the gym on the yellow basketball lines. She allows herself to think that it's becoming all right now but Steve, the boy she has cultivated in her dreams, well, at this moment he seems so very young.

24

Louisa does have friends, mostly others like her, standing at the fringes. Gail 'Goddie' Godwin is not one of these. She's popular in a heart-swelling way, at least to Louisa. She loves watching kids swarm around Goddie. Makes her feel like something's going right. They sat next to each other at primary school on that first morning and have remained mates.

In the last year of school Louisa works Friday nights and Saturday mornings selling shoes in an arcade in the city she loves. She also loves the lights and the money and the shoes. She got the job when she was sixteen by walking up and down Bourke Street with Goddie asking every shop if they had a vacancy. Taking it in turns to be rejected, it was amazing how fast they got used to the word 'no'. Since she started working, she has not asked for money from her mother and this is a source of pride. Not a farthing, not a brass razoo, she tells Goddie with delight.

But now at seventeen she has another job. It's Louisa's responsibility to take Jessie to her crèche and to pick her up every day. She boards the bus with her two-year-old sister as women board buses laden with bags of groceries, sighing and feeling every atom of their weight.

She has given up trying to look cool for the boys on the

bus and now they are as distant as mountain ranges but just as appealing.

Each day she sits Jessie beside the window and sometimes she engages with the child; mostly though, she ignores her and tries to read some novel or another from the school library. She reads *The Catcher in the Rye* and wonders bitterly how Holden Caulfield would go looking after a two-year-old.

She reads *Slaughterhouse 5* and sometimes on the bus she looks up, seeing Footscray and thinking of Dresden. She reads a book on British rock and roll and pinches it from the library because she wants to be droll and knowledgeable like the author, Nik Cohn.

Rainy days, she draws pictures of cats and dogs on the steamy windows for the child. She's almost always aware that she was delivered a burden when this child was born, but it takes too long to work out that it isn't the child's fault.

At the bus stop nearest to the school, the other kids streak ahead while she tows Jessie down Morrison Street. There are days when the weather opens itself upon them. The wind and the sun and the rain and the cold and high indigo skies, each of them shadows Louisa and Jessie.

In a thunderstorm one day with the bruised sky heaving from ocean-green to purple, Louisa pushes Jessie under her coat and runs through the lashing rain. Every drop that lands scalds as if it's boiling and they run all the long way to the crèche and Jessie loses a shoe.

Often though, if they're early, they nick across to the mangy paddock opposite where a raddled old swayback horse lives. They name the horse Chester because of his chestnut colour. Jessie loves him until he mistakes her fingers for grass and nips her with his great yellow teeth. Louisa holds the sobbing child and feels her distress in her own body.

At the crèche, Louisa deposits the rashy two-year-old – her

cheeks look like they've been sandpapered – with a goodbye kiss and a wave. Then she walks the last bit down towards the school, listening to the broadcast of Jessie's anguish for longer than she would believe possible.

Squatting at the end of the street, Footscray High is a pile of drab grey concrete bricks with a sagging tin roof and a gathering of scraggly shrubs making some kind of effort to be a garden.

She swings her bag over her shoulder and decides there will come a day when she will not have to look after babies. And a day when she will be free of her family. Free to be herself. But she always remembers acutely, as if pricked by a pin, that she has to collect Jessie at three-thirty sharp. Or else her mother will have to pay more – and this cannot be.

On the bus on the way home, the little girl is tired and wants her mum. Louisa holds the child's hand as if she is chained to her. At the service station, she gets off first and Jessie jumps down the big steps all on her own and into her sister's arms and Louisa swings her in a big arc that silently speaks of love.

25

Just because they're about the same size and both have long dark hair, people say that Goddie looks like Louisa. Some even call them twins. But they never notice that Goddie has brown eyes and a fringe and Louisa has blue eyes and no fringe. People, Louisa decides, are not very alert.

One dull summer morning at school Goddie slides in next to Lou. The surface of the desk has been carved with compasses then inked with so many names it feels like braille. The window allows in the muted breeze.

'Hey,' she says, not waiting for an answer, 'Louie, guess what Lou? This week at Festival Hall, oi, are you listenin'? On Friday, this Friday yeah, there's gonna be a grouse concert, all sorts, you know, Spectrum and Dingo and Daryl Braithwaite and tons of others. Come on, you gotta go out sometimes. You know you love your old Dazzling Dazza. Only three mingy bucks to get in . . .'

Louisa smiles, thinks Goddie's hair looks nice today swinging in its great fat ponytail, falling like a dark river. She has already decided she should get out more, and thanks to the shoe shop she has the dough.

'Yeah, I'd love to,' she says to Goddie's wide smile and they open their geography books. Today they're studying the structures of clouds and await the enervating Mr Champion with his whopping hooked nose and his soothing talk of cumulous and nimbus and stratus and the secrets of clouds, of the possibilities of all things.

Though Louisa is slow to trust, she trusts Gail because in primary school they bonded over theft. They nicked roses for the teacher from the big house with the garden. If the roses hung over the fence, Louisa reasoned, they were fair game. So she positioned Gail as lookout while she plundered the blooms.

But breaking the stems was harder than she thought and mostly Gail stood there guarding but sometimes, under pressure, she fled yelling, 'Look out, the lady's coming . . .' They stayed friends. Louisa would always forgive panic.

*

Friday night rolls by and it's a rainy one. They take the green bus to Festival Hall, passing through the lowlands between Footscray and North Melbourne, both seriously constricted by their jeans.

Gail reckons she knows one of the roadies who can get them up the front. Louisa doubts this but goes along with it anyway. They stand awkwardly round the back near the band entrance. Long needles of rain hit them and, damply, they edge closer to the wall. The roadies with their showy mullets and their astonishingly tight pants stream by like a chain of worker ants holding colossal speaker boxes above their heads.

Louisa isn't looking out and the corner of one of the speakers jags into her head. She's knocked backwards and Gail grabs her before she falls and says, 'God, mate. You all right?' Lou nods, but she's dazed and Gail peers at her for a bit and says, 'Carn, let's give this away and go up the front, I can't see the bloke I know anyway, bloody dill's not here.'

Gingerly, Louisa touches her torn scalp and following Gail she thinks, not that much blood, not too much damage. They sit up the back next to a couple of blokes drinking VB from bottles in paper bags. The blokes offer them some and Gail goes ahead. Louisa wouldn't touch the stinking beer if you paid her but restrains herself from saying so. The singers move onto the stage and the sound engulfs her. Dazza, past his satin phase, is all the better for it and Dingo is unbelievable.

The rain has slowed after the concert and the stars are out and the night feels as clean as tomorrow. With their ears full of music, they talk way too loud. They wait ages for the bus, in the flawless night raving away about the concert, and in the end they climb up into the empty bus and are transported back to the music by the static that still hums around them.

By Monday morning, Louisa's head is as tight as a drum and there's a throbbing red lump where the speaker corner got her. Time to show her mother. She's in her school uniform, bending her head over her mother's knee when Emmett walks in. 'Show me,' he demands and she says, 'It's all right Dad, it's nothing at all really.'

'Well,' he declares primly, standing back from the wound with some distaste, 'it's obvious you've got yourself into some strife here. Someone's probably raped you as well as bashed you.'

Louisa always suspected Emmett was nuts and now here again is solid proof. Anne says, 'Hang on a minute Emmett, Louisa's told you what happened.' But he keeps going, winding himself tighter and tighter. 'You'd better be honest with us now girl, or there'll be consequences.' By now he's turning scarlet and the pulse in his neck is throbbing and she notices that his hands are so fat, his fingers look like sausages. She forces herself to concentrate on yet another bizarre scene in the kitchen. But her head hurts.

She examines him through her long-seasoned bitterness and her eyes narrow and this is the moment, the real moment, when she knows there's nothing to fear here anymore. Her father is insane and that's it. That's all this is. 'You're cracked Dad, you know that? You are completely cracked. You should be in a bloody mental home. Do us all a favour and for God's sake, find one.' She has her hand on her head, holding the sore spot.

But Emmett isn't all that riled. 'Piss off then,' he sneers nastily, stepping back from her. 'If you're not worried about getting your bloody silly self raped, then neither am I.' She sees his big ugly face but knows that since the fight he's damned wary of her. Knows without any doubt that she will go for him.

Anne is once again furiously silenced and Louisa knows the dance is just about done. She slams out the back door, head throbbing like an engine. Not much longer to go, she tells herself on the way to school, hauling little Jessie behind her like a boat.

All day she thinks there must be a way of getting out of this. In the library at lunchtime her English teacher, Miss Burton, a woman with cat's-eye glasses and a halo of curls, takes the chair next to her. Miss B has a passion for the novels of Jean Rhys, and Louisa has been stuck on the same page of *Wide Sargasso Sea* for a while now, unable to think of anything but her head. Miss B asks if anything is wrong. 'Louisa my dear, you know you can always ask me for anything.'

And it's as if there's a drummer inside her head thumping away. She can't concentrate on the book, and though she can hardly bear to touch her head, that's all her hand wants to do. She hesitates and says to herself, you gotta know when you need help and here is a good, kind woman who will help.

She bends her head down toward the teacher and parts her hair tenderly away from the swollen infected lump. And then she looks up into the teacher's eyes and hoping it's trust she sees there, says, 'Dad thinks I was raped and that I won't own up to it. It's not true of course. A speaker box got me on the head,' and this sounds so silly she laughs, but then she feels heavily sad and pushes away a loose tear and says, 'I think my father's mad,' and it's a relief to speak of such things.

Miss Burton doesn't say anything but her face is a picture of sorrow. She pats Louisa's arm and leans in close and whispers, 'Come to my desk after school, my dear, I know a good doctor.'

The teacher takes Louisa out to her green sports car and they drive past the packs of kids surging through the gate like shoals of sardines. Miss Burton waits while Louisa picks up Jessie from the crèche and the child perches on her knee in the car in a startled state of suspended excitement, little white hands grabbing fistfulls of her uniform and mouth sucking in all that whooshing air.

The doctor says there's a cyst underneath the swelling that was caused by the gouge but not to worry, everything will heal. She prescribes antibiotics and Miss Burton pays for them and even buys Jessie a little ragdoll in a patchwork pinafore at the chemist.

When she drops Louisa and Jess off at Wolf Street the teacher pats her shoulder. 'You know, dear girl, it won't last forever.' Louisa and Jessie stand outside the gate for a time watching the sports car disappear down the winter-dark, rail-thin street.

26

In the last year of high school Louisa decides she might as well become a journalist. It's all a bit of a scramble driven by Miss Burton. Louisa wonders if a journalist is the same thing as a reporter. She's heard of Clark Kent and Lois Lane so reckons she's probably well on the way. If she'd known the Pommy author Nik Cohn was one, she would have jumped at it.

'You've got a good deal of curiousity in you, young Louisa,' Miss B says, beaming. It's lunchtime on a windy day in early summer. A knot of teenage girls gathers on the next bench. They're using their knees as plates and carefully laying potato chips on buttered white breadrolls then stuffing the chip bags into crevices in the seats. Some bags escape and lift across the yard in the wind like wonky stray birds.

Louisa's on her own under a worn-out gum, hidden by a long fringe of leaves and consuming *Catch 22*. The chattering girls might not even be there. When Miss Burton slides in beside her, glasses glinting in the bright day, Louisa, always easily startled, gasps as if she's been attacked and the teacher tries to recover from fright to friendliness. The scabby grey bitumen stretches around their feet.

'Journalism,' Miss Burton announces enthusiastically, still breathless from striding out to find Louisa. She likes this word.

This is a special word. 'They're looking for cadets now in the city. You could *do* this, my girl. It's a job for a special girl.' And smiling, she passes a square of newspaper ad to her and her smile feels like love.

Louisa holds the little square of grey print and it flutters like a living thing. Sounds as good as anything and she'd like to please Miss Burton seeing as how she thinks she might love her. She puts the ad inside the book. Later, walking to the bus with Jessie's small hand in hers, she wonders, 'How do you get to be like Miss Burton?'

Jessie is babbling about seeing the horsie but by now they're well past the horse in the thistly paddock and they head towards the red bus that seems to stream up and down the big road endlessly, and today the world seems all blue sky with a raft of passing cloud.

One of the clouds has slipped from the others and is forming a ladder and this makes her smile. Could it be the ladder leading her out of here? Rubbish, she scolds herself, as if the sky's got anything to do with anything.

She touches her sister's baby head for comfort and realises that university is the only way to climb out of here to become like Miss Burton. But then seldom do journalists go to university. Ah, you don't always get what you want and a job is what you need, she tells herself.

Jessie has been at swimming lessons and the metal smell of chlorine folds around her. 'Did you have a good swim today Jess?' Louisa asks as they sit on the bus. 'Nah,' says Jess staring out the window holding onto her bag of wet towel, 'I want Mum.'

Lou touches her head again and thinks, I know you do, and she wipes Jessie's trailing nose with the corner of her school dress. 'Carn little Jess, you're all right matey,' she says and rests her arm around the child's slight shoulders. If she ever has children, Louisa decides, she will be with them every bloody minute of every bloody day.

*

Nothing can be real about her possible life as a journalist until she tells Anne. In the kitchen that night before her mum gets home, she goes about her chores. The louvre windows are open and she can see into next door's yard where white sheets flap on the line.

She begins to feel a sense of portent and when this happens her right wrist prickles. It prickles now and she feels change is moving towards her and even though she wants it, it scares her rigid. She decides to delay telling her mother because she knows that when she tells this part of her story, it will happen in short time and then she will be gone and the time of Emmett will be over and the newness, what will it be?

She sets the blue laminex table with knives and forks and salt and pepper. Rob stumbles up the fernery steps and bursts into the kitchen. The day has dredged away and the gloom says maybe it will rain. He flicks a switch and the stick of light on the ceiling blinks on reluctantly.

'God, Louisa, you're fooling around in the dark here, always sitting in the dark, what's the bloody matter with you?' He slides his bag up the passage out of the way.

'Get stuffed Robert,' she says casually and gets herself a bit of bread, holds it in her palm and forces a small river of tomato sauce onto it and eats it before the sauce can escape.

Rob can tell Emmett isn't around because she's relaxed. There's not much sign of Emmett these days. They have entered into an island of time when he's always at the pub.

Rob wrenches the fridge door open and stands there gazing in as if it will answer everything. 'What's for tea?' he asks, lulled by the bright void and stilled by the cool air.

'Chops,' Louisa says, poking at them, curled and spitting in the pan, 'It's always bloody chops, dill boy. Haven't you noticed?'

He grabs three slices of bread from the plastic bag on the bench, wads them up and stuffs them into his mouth and heads out to the sleep-out. 'How long?' she hears the words exiting past the bread but doesn't bother replying.

Later that night after tea, the others scatter to enjoy the lounge room and the tele in the absence of Emmett. They could get used to this. Telling Anne, the idea of herself as a journalist takes hold and begins to grow. She's drying the dishes. 'Miss Burton thinks I'd be good at it,' she finds herself saying, getting stuttery at the idea. 'Newspapers, you know, you can be a sort of a writer.'

Anne draws in a long breath. She's got a smoke going beside her in the mosaic ashtray Louisa made in grade four. The smoke is drawn upward as if by a genie. Anne smiles her beautiful smile. 'Write to them Lou. Write them a good long letter all about yourself,' she says, her hands in the sink moving in and out of the grey water, passing out plates and knives and forks.

She finishes up and dries her hands on the tea towel Louisa is holding and picks up the ad from the bench, squinting as she scrutinises it. She grabs her smoke and takes a long contented drag. 'Write all about everything,' she says, still smiling and handing it back. 'They will not be able to resist you.'

LORETO KIRRIBILLI LIBRARY

27

Ten cadets are hired by the national newspaper *The Antipo-dean* because apparently, they want new blood. When Louisa realises she's the only girl, she tells herself it's no great sign of anything. Must have needed one and I showed up, she thinks, but still, there's a creeping sense of unease.

Louisa's first sin as a journalist is that she's inclined to be slow on the uptake and her second is paralysing shyness, two big disadvantages. Hiding both brings certain challenges. On a tour of where they will work, she's startled by the typewriter that will be hers. Oh dear, she thinks recoiling, never reckoned on typing, but at least the shyness keeps her quiet.

And being the only girl in the office puts her into an uncomfortable place. If she stretches her arms out above her head, men dart looks at her. If she stands up to get copy paper, their magnet eyes follow.

At first she thinks they must be bored, or maybe they're kind and they want to help. It takes a while for her to see that to men she's just ripe fruit, and to realise that the men watch all women with the same ardent intent. The secretaries know all about it.

Even men with families do it but they look at her sadly, as if remembering something. Louisa, never slow to rile where men are concerned, would really like to kill them. These men who are never satisfied, they have their lives, so what's she got to do with them? And what's with all the perving? Apart from the hang-dog looks, there's something about them that reminds her of Emmett, but maybe it's just their evident seeping dissatisfaction with their lives. Does *he* look at women like this? She finds the answer without strenuous research and recalls that, yeah, Emmett always did have trouble with women.

It became apparent to her when she was about twelve. He called her into his room. She'd heard his voice down the tunnel of the passageway and been shocked that he would call her.

Though she felt guilty that she must have done something wrong and now would be found out, she went straight towards the door anyway like the condemned. She knocked on it. Opened it to a surly 'enter'.

The big desk stretched before him and the blinds cut into the hot light pouring through the window and though Louisa was subdued, a steady tremor ran through her and she held her hands behind her back to still them. Her bowels felt loose, her mouth was a desert and the dizziness was there yet again.

'I've called you in here, young Louisa,' her father began, leaning back on the chair until it cracked and strained before he snapped it back up, 'to tell you something important. Are you ready to hear something important?' His voice lifted with every word.

'Yes Dad,' she said, her heart sinking.

'This thing I have to tell you is about . . .' and he leaned towards her as if he might whisper or bite but decided instead to shout, '. . . BLOOD.' At the word, she flinched and her skin prickled. He paused and drank some beer to settle himself and then he launched into it again.

'The fact is that pretty soon you will find that there is blood coming from between your legs. You are already twelve or so. Each time it comes it won't last for long but, and remember this, Louisa, this is nothing to worry about. Do you hear me?' His megaphone voice hummed through her.

Louisa was looking hard at the floor. Possibly he was trying to comfort her, but why was he talking about such a thing? She tried to block him out. What had she done to deserve this? He drained his last inch of beer and continued. 'All women have it. Some make a great big deal about it. But YOU will not do that.

'Some women spend their lives whingeing about such things. That's all they do. They are nothing more than bitches. They seem to like to make people unhappy,' he said with a kind of sad bitterness, leaning back again on the creaking chair into the stale, stinking bedroom.

'But that's another matter. The blood, well, that just means you're growing up. And sadly Lou, we all have to do that. So just to recap: blood – when it shows up, don't panic. Now, off you go.'

Like a zombie, Louisa reached for the door handle but knew it would be a mistake not to show appreciation. 'Thanks Dad,' she mumbled in a small voice.

'My pleasure. Anytime. Shut the door. Properly.'

28

By the time she gets her first serious pay cheque, the job has really achieved something for her mother and herself. Louisa is able to leave Wolf Street and Anne will have her room.

Louisa finds a place in Windsor with Gary Turner, one of the other cadets. The flat is across the river, it's full of nooks and looks down onto a road full of unceasing traffic. Gary's looking to move from way out in Nunawading where he's number four in a family of eight kids.

He's short and gingery with speckled skin, a pinched face and pale eyes and he picks her up from home with her boxes and watches her saying her goodbyes to Anne and the kids. Says nothing while she weeps in the car all the way there.

In the flat, there's a scungy old mattress on the floor, a chest of drawers and a sideboard. A tree scratches the window. 'You haven't got a bed, have you?' Gary asks after they put down the boxes in her room.

'Nah,' she says, 'not yet, can't afford it yet. You?'

'Yeah,' he says, 'I'm taking the one from home.'

So she gets the mattress and that night they get Chinese food and eat sitting on the mattress but even the dim sims taste different from Footscray dimmies and she loses her appetite; and though he tells her about each of his brothers and sisters in long detail, she can't even begin to speak of her family.

The first night the tree taps on the window and wakes her. She's not scared, only relieved that she's finally free of Emmett. The kind of peace she feels within her is so profound, it's as if she's stepped into another universe where you're allowed to breathe deeply; but when she thinks of her mother and the boys and Jess she realises that guilt is the price of freedom. She's abandoned them and knowing it doesn't help, so most nights she runs down to the phone box on the corner to ring them but they can't talk when Emmett's home.

'Hi Mum,' she says the first night they do talk. It's raining and the windows are waterfalls and she's wet and shivering. 'I'm good yeah, I miss you. I'm learning shorthand. Not very good yet. Gary's great, says to say hi. I got a new Joni Mitchell record. I'll take the train over on Saturday.'

Jessie clamours at the phone and says, 'Hello Louie' and then clams up and won't let go of the phone and then, when it's about to be snatched away, she says, 'Frank's good,' and Anne takes the phone back and the child's bitter crying engulfs everything until Louisa is weeping too. She manages to make out that Pete's gone fishing and Rob's not home either.

She wants to ask Anne if Emmett's hit her lately, but she can't bring herself to come out and say this and Anne would never tell her off her own bat so the question sits between them like a ghost. That night, she weeps, running all the way home down the dark street, passing through pods of light from the street lamps, the spare coins leaving circles in her hand.

*

With Gary she enters into a life of perfection. She imagines living with him and her mum and Jess and the boys and then things really would be perfect. They cook cannelloni and soak beans for stews with chicken and green olives. They listen to so much Dylan they are word-perfect. They read e.e. cummings and Virginia Woolf and every single newspaper they can find while they compete for by-lines. And keep tally. And they travel to work on the train looking over the pages of *The Ant* at each other.

She only discovers he's gay one Saturday when he comes out and says it when they are building a bookshelf out of big grey bricks and planks hauled to the flat strapped precariously to the roof of his Beetle. It's been going so well up until now. 'Gay?' she says, astonished, but retying her ponytail to gain time.

'Yeah,' he smiles, 'I like boys, you know, better than girls.'

Louisa's eyes are stretched wide. 'But how do you know?'

He reaches his hand over to hers and says, 'Louie, I've always known.'

She finds this impossible to believe. He looks abashed or something, she thinks, but then he's laughing and she's at least smiling because the truth is that Louisa is stunned at the very idea of people being gay. This has never been discussed at home but then she knows she didn't learn much of use at home apart from how to spell ornithorhynchus (the biological name for platypus), what hedges are best for and how to stay clear of Emmett.

And she has harboured such strong notions about young Gary Turner that it feels awfully foolish to have missed something like this. Still, she must not show it. 'But Rhett,' she says grinning and bunging on a lame, syrupy Southern accent, 'you still love me don't you?' And he smiles, relieved that she's laughing and grabs her in a headlock, 'Always, my dear, always.'

They talk all day with the planks and the books scattered around them and understanding settles into them and she reckons she could get addicted to peace. She might marry him whether or not he's gay, not give him any damn say at all.

They finish the bookcase late in the afternoon and he goes off to the kitchen to make soup while she settles down to read about Gerald Durrell growing up in Corfu. Later, in the evening, they eat minestrone soup from blue bowls as the little birds settle into the tree outside the window.

On the train one morning, he calls her Mrs Turner and she calls him Mrs Brown. 'You wish,' he laughs and she finds herself thinking that yeah, she really does wish.

29

At work a reporter named Wayne Goade spends much time caressing her with his eyes. He's got a high thready voice and he looks a bit like Van Morrison, pudgy with fairish hair and smudgy little granny glasses. Pity he doesn't make music like Van Morrison.

He's married and lives outside the city at a distant muddy place with his wife, Jan, and two little girls named Star and Venus. Louisa meets them when he brings them in to work. They seem to be sick a lot. They cough constantly and straw-coloured sludge edges from their noses. She shrinks away from them and goes back to thinking about by-lines, her favourite subject. How can she get more? Or even any would be good.

Wayne looks for gaps in her day and employing stealth and cunning, pounces on her. He sits on the edge of her desk and tries to make her laugh. Drinks in the freckle above the left corner of her lip. Wonders about the pale scar that runs from her mouth.

It seems he longs to touch her and sometimes takes the opportunity when he's ushering her into the lift or towards the coffee machine, guiding her by the small of her back. These small touches last him weeks.

In that whole year, there's never a time when Louisa's not lighting up his life and it doesn't matter to him the slightest little bit that his feelings are not reciprocated. Louisa thinks Wayne is a creepy dork.

But the photographer Michael Abbey is something else. With his dark wavy hair and neatly clipped beard he reminds her of Queen Mary's lover Lord Darnley or at least the actor she saw playing him on a BBC production she watched with Turner.

If Wayne Goade had been a fly on the studio wall one wet Friday evening when Louisa and Michael Abbey are both rostered on for late stop, the unfolding action would have felled him. Mercifully, Wayne is spared the sight of Louisa losing her virginity to Michael Abbey.

Michael and Louisa are in the office on that quiet winter's evening, sitting around waiting for news that even if it happened they had little intention of using. A massacre might get a run in the big pages of *The Ant* (how many dead and who were they?), a bushfire (number of lives and houses) or perhaps a huge accident (say the Westgate falling down again). But not much else would get in this late.

Rain slides down the windows which look onto the side street and at the end of the lane homeless people huddle inside big boxes with sheets of sagging plastic draped like canopies over their camps. It briefly crosses Louisa's mind that Emmett will end up in a camp like this.

Near the jaws of the mighty black presses downstairs, mobs of printers play poker. From the office window she can see the slap of cards and the piles of money and the men laughing and the calling. From a distance, these men seem interesting. Their hands and faces are black and the cards flare and match the whites of their eyes and glow in the gloom. Sitting on milk crates, they roar and laugh and gamble and tease. More fun than sitting upstairs waiting for blasting phone calls from Mick Fan, the latest hack to be made night news editor just because he lives in Sydney.

Up here in the newsroom, nothing much is happening and that's fine by everyone but Sydney. Michael Abbey leans back on his chair with his feet up on Louisa's desk. He's Keeping Louisa Company while she knits a scarf of many blues.

But she can only knit straight, anything else is way beyond her, and she believes she's making progress purely because the thing is growing. Abbey watches for longer than she reckons would be interesting for anyone, let alone a man, and by degrees it makes her nervous. And then there it is, her wrist is prickling.

She drops a couple of stitches in a row trying to scratch the wrist and is curiously embarrassed. Her fingers grow sweaty, which tangles the yarn all the more. Finally, Abbey stands up and says, 'Come into the studio. I'll take a few pics of you.'

'What for?' she says and laughs, her fingers knotted in the blue wool.

In his measured, sensible voice he says, 'Well, there's nothing much else to do and you can't knit, my dear girl. That is very obvious.'

She feels her heart beat in its solid familiar way and it seems to her in a flashing moment that this is the time to change things. So she laughs and balls up the wool, spears it with the needles and follows him.

A radiator in the corner of the studio is sending out orange rays like a small sun. She wonders why the heater's already on and hovers in the doorway. She feels like a lamb with a wolf and there's that familiar feeling of finality. It reminds her of the feeling she got with Emmett sometimes, the sense that the thing, whatever it was, would happen and she would not be able to stop it. That another will would prevail. The fatalism of the everyday.

'Sit down on the couch, my dear, while I see to this.' He

gestures to the couch and then returns to fooling around with the camera, clicking and winding and polishing.

He moves the camera closer and takes many pictures of her face, coming over sometimes to turn her head or lift her hair and once he says, 'You are very beautiful, young Louisa Brown.'

'Come off it,' she says laughing and flushing scarlet, her wrist quivering away like a trapped bird.

'No, I won't come off it. These pictures will be perfect and they will show your beauty and you will always have them.' Then he sits down beside her and kisses her mouth slow and tender as if she were beloved and says, 'I could take some really lovely pictures of you if you would take your clothes off.'

She looks at him as if he's an alien and notices that his eyes are the green of leaves.

'No way in the wide world,' she says, and it comforts her that she can still think. She wonders why he reckons she's special and realises it's because he wants something of her; but still, this suggestion of beauty is engrossing. She should have left then but a feeling like concrete keeps her there. Beauty is a sticky, seductive notion.

He takes pictures for a long time while outside the rain falls dark and slow. Inside it is warm and Michael is thrilling, his eyes, his hands.

She never thinks of it as losing her virginity to Michael Abbey. She sees it more as a gift to herself and to someone who, for that moment, seems to care for her. He shows her how to hold him and he's tender. This is the most you can ever ask of men, she reasons, that they seem to care.

They clean up the bit of blood on the couch with copy paper. When tears appear he holds her and strokes her hair and then the phone rings and it's Mick Fan on the speaker screaming, 'What the fuck is going on down there? Where's the hourly update?' he also wonders whether it's a bloody morgue in Melbourne and Michael Abbey and Louisa, both half-dressed in the studio, have to laugh at that one.

After she assures Mick Fan that she will get his updates to him soon, she finds her tears have dried and that Michael is getting dressed and time is back in its envelope.

The next day Louisa feels the weight of a bruise within. Feels that her pelvis has carried something heavy. She knows she won't be the same and yet she's pleased about it, pleased that girl is folding into the wind. Now she is really an adult and that means she's further from home. She realises she could have made a more careful choice but what's done is done. Childhood is over. Let the future begin.

On Monday, Wayne's hanging around as usual and after taking a surreptitious peak, clears off briefly when Michael gives her the folio of pictures. Louisa remains friendly with Michael for years but they never make love again. He never offers to help with her knitting and he never offers to leave his girlfriend.

*

Louisa edges at her father with little squares of ten-paragraph stories cut from the paper and stuffed into a manila folder and later, with Abbey's photos. Perhaps she hopes that these things might tame him.

On the Saturday she takes the headshots home, she finds Emmett alone at the kitchen table, a glass of VB and the form guide open out before him. It's a glassy kind of day and she's enjoyed the walk from the station past all the houses she knows with a terrible intimacy. Every step is charted. And every inch of change noted.

Stepping into the kitchen is like walking back in time. She falters when she sees him looming at the table suddenly right there before her, absorbing all space. But today he recovers fast from this unexpected privacy theft. 'Louie, the baby girl come to visit the old man!' He sounds up but he looks old. The grey cardigan is strained across his stomach and the darkness of the years is disclosed under his eyes.

'Everyone's out mate,' he says gruffly, then remembers his manners, 'but I'm glad you dropped in. Bit of a chinwag eh? Would you like an ale?'

'No,' she snaps, appalled that he would offer her beer. 'Dad, it's ten-thirty!' she adds, with a kind of umpire's reason in her voice. She's surrounded by the stench of booze, the old rival but experience says shallow breathing will defeat it.

Briskly, she gets her coat off and puts the kettle on and soon a chaste mug of tea seethes before her and she asks, 'So how ya bin?' and he says well enough and looking her over brightly says, 'You look pretty swank today, Miss Louie.' Now that she's got money she dresses well and today she's got her new short brown boots under her Levis and a short tweed jacket and a long-sleeved white T-shirt with small pink roses all over it.

As ever, compliments leave her puzzled and silenced so she slides the folder across the table at him and it nudges the form guide and that's not a good thing, could annoy him. She decides to ignore it.

He straightens the newspaper carefully, even reverently, and then opens the folder and pushes the pictures out over the table. When he looks up he smiles like an old man. 'Hmmm. You know Lou, you look like a movie star,' he decides. 'Reckon I could have this one? Spare your old man one photo?'

She agrees and as he holds it, the alcoholic tremor works itself in him and a loose fragment of pity hits her and she thinks, you poor old quivery thing, and closes her eyes for a second to steady herself. Emmett, in his grey cardigan and unironed blue work shirt, collar up on one side, scans the photo like there might be an answer in it. 'I know!' he says, jubilant and clears his throat. 'I know who it is you look like. That little girl in *Romeo and Juliet* from the film, that's who you look like.' Louisa says nothing. It's Emmett she looks like, not some movie star.

So they fall back on book talk for a while and Emmett gets interested because he loves matching books and people. 'I tell you who you should read. D.H. Lawrence. A wonderful writer and a true voice for mine.' He's getting misty now as he often does about his special writers.

Louisa starts to bristle. She hasn't read much Lawrence but it's 1977 and the accepted thinking says that Lawrence is a male chauvinist pig. She decides to share this with her father even though her knowledge of Lawrence is extremely limited. She brushes her hair back with a hand, her voice lifts a notch and she heads into the breach. 'Come *off* it. He's nothing but a misogynist. Why on earth would I read that crap?' she demands. 'You must be joking.'

Emmett is astonished at the attack. Bloody kids, he thinks, a man's trying to be sociable and gets it wrong yet again. He has no wish for bloody tension today so he says, 'Don't do your block now Louie. Bit prickly today, eh? Strike me. You kids have got an answer to every bloody thing in the world.' He laughs, scratches his head, messing up his hair so he looks slightly crazy, and can't disguise a longing look over at the form guide.

He doesn't give up on the books though but when he suggests Mailer, Louisa stands up abruptly and with a haughty look snatches up all the pictures, including the one she's given him, and shoves them in the folder. She gets her coat and heads home, glad that home is no longer where he lives. It's two trains away and the pictures are balanced on her knees in the manila folder and all the way she can't decide whether she's a bitch or whether she hates her father. Both true she allows.

And on that departing train, she realises there's no going back. Whatever home was it's all finished and I don't know what I'm doing or where I'm going, she thinks, grabbing at her hair and pulling it over her shoulder.

On the dirty old Saturday train, a knot of leering youths is looking for trouble and a woman with almost no hair reads a fat pot-boiler. The shipping containers are low but they'll build up again. Things come and go. Life sucks and then it's fine. Emmett is disconcertingly pleasant and then he's a shit again. Stuff happens. She looks around the train and thinks, these people are all making it. Pretend you know what you're doing, and keep going. She holds that thought all the way to Flinders Street.

30

At work in the long days of learning about journalism, Louisa is well aware of John Keele. He's tall and lean and maybe, she thinks, he's kind. But mostly she likes his tanned face, his grey eyes, his full lips and wide smile. She forgives the slightly beaky nose and loves the straggly straw hair. Gary says he'd be right for her because there's some kind of symmetry going on, fair and dark, tall and not so tall; but then Gary reckons many men would be right for her, which is becoming annoying.

John works up the back of the newsroom in the sports department a few desks away and over time they become distantly connected through lust. Often, in any lull, they will glance towards each other then guiltily, hastily, look away. When he catches her looking, she feels a tilt in her heart. There's an old intent at work here and Louisa, even though she's wary, would be happy to look at John Keele all day.

And John even seems less threatening than other men. There are the smiles for one thing, and his surfer looks make him seem otherworldly in the office. He wears the same grey suit every day but this has been duly noted because little escapes trained observers like renowned luncher and Melbourne sports editor, Ralphie-boy Hobbs. It's often late in the afternoon when he puts on his little performance pieces and today, in a booming voice so everyone can hear, he asks Louisa,

'What is the difference between a journalist and a reporter?' Bit of theatre to cheer up the troops. But Louisa couldn't care less. She's about to make a phone call to the Lord Mayor to ask him about a councillor charged with something seamy involving council funds. She's nervous and she's written out her questions but as usual she's got the order all screwed up and the good questions end up at the bottom of the list and as the time appointed for the phone call looms, she re-numbers but her nerves are as taut as a kite string. 'Honestly, I would not know Ralphie,' she snaps, looking down at her messy list. 'I'm sorry, I'm still busy here you know.'

She's impatient, but Ralphie's pushing on with the joke. 'Never mind love, must be that time of the month.' Everyone laughs. 'Take young Mr Keele here,' he says and winks, 'he's a reporter because he's got one suit. Now if he had two, he'd be a journalist.'

Weak laughter wafts through the newsroom and copy paper is scrunched and hurled at Keele. It's that golden time of the afternoon when early deadlines have passed and the light sneaks in through the big smudgy windows and first thoughts of clearing off for the day arise. Today there's a game of cricket with a taped-up copy paper ball and a cardboard bat and the news editor's bin as stumps and sixes are carted all over the newsroom.

But Louisa still isn't finished so she keeps her head down behind the shield of the upturned typewriter and tosses the paper ball back without looking when it lands on her desk. She does the phone interview with the hostile Lord Mayor and he calls her impertinent and hangs up on her so all is not in vain. When she looks up, it's like coming up for air. She manages to read back her notes, which is unusual. Sydney wants five pars just to cover themselves so she files.

It shocks her later that night when John Keele is waiting

for her downstairs in the circle of light out the front. She steps back when she sees him, understanding instantly that the time of looks is over. 'Come for a drink Lou?' he asks, and in the bright light she sees his one suit is shiny and creased; but still, it is thrilling to be so close to him. This Keele person seems like someone I know, she thinks, someone I've always known.

In the corner of the drab smoky pub they sit on high stools at a round table away from the others from *The Ant* who are already running a shop on the likelihood of a match. John Keele talks about music and poetry.

He puts a glass of paint-stripper wine on the table before her and says, 'That'll put hairs on your chest,' and blushes then yanks opens a bag of chicken-flavoured chips way too hard and spills them over the sticky table like so many communion wafers. Louisa picks one up, eats it and smiles.

After a silence, acutely observed and snickered over by the comrades at the bar, John wants to know her favourite book. She surprises herself by saying *Alice in Wonderland* which is the truth but she instantly wishes she'd gone for something cooler. She smiles and sips wine.

He drinks Coopers beer from South Australia because that's where he's from. Men and beer, she thinks, and a mild wave of nausea catches her. John laughs at some of the things she says and thinks she's kidding when she describes her father as a psychopathic maniac. 'You are an absolute riot Louisa, who would have thought it,' he says, grinning like a happy schoolboy. She sips the turpentine wine and thinks, this is not going so well.

He talks about his poetry and then about his mother's heart disease and he seems caring and tender and, almost against her will, she finds herself noticing his fine hands, his wide wrists and his raw mouth; and then her heart is beating way too hard. This is no good. She gets up to leave, gathering bag and coat fast. 'Goodbye,' she says, brushing chip crumbs away, 'I've got to get home.' And she's gone, leaving the chorus of comrades smirking at John until he joins them with tales from the front.

Walking to the train, almost running, she tries to work out what has just happened. Whatever it is, this cannot be good because when he speaks to me, she thinks, I feel empty. Empty and full. As if I had so much room to hear him, as if listening were a whole new thing. What is it? she asks herself. What *is* this thing that's going on? Later, she will recognise that it was his kindness that got her.

The next day on her muddled desk with its fossilised phone numbers and addresses and mugs lined with mysterious festering layers, there's a small brown paper parcel tied with string. Her name is written gracefully in black ink. She smiles. Seeing her name in print always gives her a jolt, makes Louisa feel real, that if someone's written it down, there must be a person to match. Vain idiot, she mutters to herself, open the damn thing.

Still in her coat but slowly, to stretch the moment, she opens the parcel to find a very old copy of *Alice in Wonderland*. It can only be from John Keele. On the title page he's written a quote from *Alice*: 'He was part of my dream, of course . . . but then I was part of his dream too.'

31

Though she's out of there now, out of the daily round of it all, Louisa assumes that Emmett is much the same and no one tells her different because once you leave, the group closes around those who remain. She can see this.

But regardless of Emmett, change is on its perfect swooping course and not even a year after Louisa leaves, Anne decides she needs to be around more for Jessie.

The local rag has long been a solace for her. It means half an hour to herself and any child who interrupts her at it gets short shrift. She often gets a snack to go with her read and in summer it'll be a nice tomato cut up fine and dosed with a dash of vinegar, salt and white pepper. With her tomato diced in a dainty dish, she retires to the kitchen table for a detailed perusal of the local, and she always finishes with a smoke.

Today, a tiny speck of an ad says there's a shop for rent on the road to Footscray about a mile away backing onto the railway line; but still, people get used to trains. She pores over the ad. 'The House of Norma' has been on Williams Road in West Footscray for at least thirty years and now it's for sale. A ladies' frock salon, she reads, frocks, hmm yeah, I could sell frocks till the cows come home. This will do me, she thinks, I'll have my own income and I'll be there for Jessie. Two birds, with one stone.

LORETO KIRRIBILLI LIBRARY

When it's time to tell Emmett, she's hollowed by fear but he stuns her by being sensible. It's one of his reversals when he behaves just like a normal person. 'Reckon you can make a go of it, do ya?' he asks quietly, even reverently. They're sitting on the back step after tea. 'Time to change,' he says, 'best for all of us.'

That late summer night as Emmett and Anne talk, the crickets sing in the hard grey dirt of the yard and they catch a glimpse of a pocket of indigo sky tucked between their roof and next door's. She explains her strategy slowly to Emmett and the possibilities reveal themselves one at a time like emerging stars.

They could strike it rich here, he thinks, feeling heat in the idea, she's a bloody handy dressmaker, can talk to anyone and she's got a business head on her shoulders. Could definitely be a goer. 'I'll be in it,' he declares, 'definitely.' They shake hands and respectfully, he kisses her cheek.

They decide he will stay on at Wolf Street with Peter while they sell up and Anne will go straight to the shop. After the sale of Wolf Street, they'll buy the shop and all live there. She'll get Jessie settled in at the state school down the road and get the shop going. All sorted.

Emmett's nearly fifty now and as dull as an old boxer. His hair is whispery grey and the circles under his eyes are muddy. Even the blue of his irises seems to have drained away and his fingernails are ridged and chalky. He drinks as much as he ever did, but it takes less to get to forgetting. He's drinking whisky now and only the dream of early retirement keeps him going. Five years to go, he thinks, just five rotten years.

Apart from working and drinking, he grows tomatoes and he's just about perfected a new feed for them which he calls rocket fuel. He soaks seaweed in the old yellow bucket until it's so ripe it feels like you're dicing with death just to breathe. Then he mixes in blood and bone. Labels the side of an old

LORETO KIRRIBILLI LIBRARY

cordial bottle and splashes it around liberally to produce Grosse Lisse tomatoes as big as bulls' hearts.

The afternoon they collect the kelp down at Willy back beach long stays in Anne's mind. She's living at the shop but comes back on the weekends to help keep Wolf Street decent. She has work to do but he wants her to come with him, and won't take no for an answer.

It's a wide open day and she can see at least three shades of blue in it, and the bay is as flat as a pan. She sits on the bluestone wall watching him awkwardly stumbling around on the rocks collecting seaweed that looks like hessian strips and stuffing them into the yellow bucket. It's the one they made the Christmas pudding in all those years ago and each of the kids got a stir for luck and Emmett called Rob a stirrer and laughed and Rob threw the spoon at him and it all ended in tears. Time in a bucket.

Anne's not speaking to Emmett today. He might not be so rough anymore, she thinks, but he's still a pig and a bore and she lets her silence do the talking.

Yabbering on and on as he drove to the beach with the car slicing down the narrow road through this bluest day, Emmett told her over and again about his bloody seaweed stew.

'It's *the* best stuff, Annie,' he boasted and turned to her and his big face filled all space. 'Annie, you listening to me? This stuff is the goods, I'll give you the drum on that. Jim, the old wog bloke at work, the cleaner, you know old Jim, the one whose kids are so smart? I told you all about them. One of them's an engineer and the other I can't remember what he does, might be something at Holden over in Broadie. Anyway, he gets a new car every second year whatever he bloody does, lucky bastard . . . well anyway, this is his recipe. Swears by it. And you know these wogs, they can grow any bloody thing.'

He burbled on and on and who cares? thought Anne. What difference can any of it ever make? Raving on about tomatoes and other people and not about normal things like his own kids or fixing up the house or even cutting back on the grog.

He'd insisted she come down here to Willy. It's not as if she didn't have plenty of other things to do at the shop or even over in Wolf Street. The laundry there looks like a Chinese joss house and the ironing pile is starting to smell. Centipedes dart at you when you shake the clothes out. But even these days it's better not to say no flat out. Always keep your head down.

And then down there at the beach while she's having a quiet smoke, she sees him at a distance and he seems like a speck of a man and not much at all. There's a clarity that falls on you some days. You wait for it and when you wait, it doesn't show and then, here you are sitting at the beach not waiting and it's there. Just there, plain and beautiful. He's just a man and not much of a one at all really, a small man out there under the increasingly fleecy sky against the disc of bay.

She gets up from the bluestone fence and dashes out her smoke not even regretting that it's only halfway through and takes herself across the rocks, careful on her wafer-thin thongs, over to where Emmett is industriously loading up with seaweed, sighing and groaning and enjoying a sly fart into the wind. When she gets near enough he says in an injured tone, 'A man wouldn't mind a bloody chop-out now and then,' and he reminds her of each one of her children.

The sun is gentle and the wind whips her hair under her sunglasses and into her eyes. She lets it be. She grabs hold of a long strip of seaweed and he gets hold of the other end and he laughs, lets it fall to Anne and she picks up the rubbery strip and drops it into the bucket. And she smiles, but just to herself.

*

The days of Wolf Street are numbered. There's been a change in Emmett, a slow sagging decline that on good days Rob sees as a kind of apology that comes with a kind of ease. But Emmett is still as changeable as the future. And so there's no surprise when one day in this peaceful period, Robert must tell his father the truth.

It's been a happy Saturday afternoon, the sky outside holding the pearl light of winter and the moon already hanging like a white penny, while inside the Browns are laughing and talking. Rob is working these days at a factory where they recycle old car batteries that leak acid like dirty rivers. It's gruelling and filthy but he's getting strong, making some dough and starting to see himself as a man. 'You've got muscles on your muscles, Robbie boy,' Anne tells him one day after work and he allows himself a smile.

Dreams of science degrees have washed away with his childhood, but they weren't his dreams anyway. One day he will do his horticulture degree but now he just wants money so he can get away. The work at the factory is tough and it's made him hard. But he still needs more money for his trip so, a couple of nights a week, he serves drunks just like his father at The Standard, a dark ungainly triangle pub on the junction in Footscray. It's always filled with shoals of drunks. And he watches them with a cool reckoning. Human sponges, he thinks, sucking everyone in.

Even though lunchtime at Wolf Street is noon, hours later, in a little act of defiance, Jessie's making herself a sandwich. No one will notice her because no one ever does. From the barren old fridge, she's wrangled a slice of Stras and now she's after the tomato sauce. She's planning on meat with sauce, so she keeps her movements quiet and creeps around. She's nine and round as a speckled egg. The bread is stale, so she toasts it and knows the noise of the toaster will annoy her father. He darts a look at her every now and then, as if she were a blowfly he means to squash.

In the hub of the kitchen, Emmett is expansive. The footy drones out of the radio and is turned down because North is losing. All afternoon it's been one VB after another and, now that he's fully tanked, he reckons Jessie shouldn't be here. She's bloody infuriating, cramping his damn style with the boys who, now they are adults, are finally innaresting. She has her hand on the food, knife underneath, ready to cut it in half when he lets loose with, 'What the bloody hell are you doing over there? Why the fuck didn't you eat at lunchtime? Useless fool of a child. What is the matter with you? Bloody pest of a girl, always have been. Go on. Get out of there, bloody idiot child . . .' He flicks his wrist at her as if she were a dog while he drinks with the other hand. And, over the glass with his practised hard look, for good measure he hisses, 'Piss off outta here now. Consider yourself warned.'

In the scheme of things, it isn't much. There's been worse. But for Rob at this moment, Jess and her little sandwich stand for everyone. He's been hearing this shit since the day he was born. The sediment of it is in his bones. And hearing the crap has poisoned him. So now he doesn't think. He pushes himself up and stands, leaning hard on the table to brace the shaking in his hands, in his heart, and quietly but loud enough says, 'I've had you, Dad. Had you forever. Just do us all a favour and shut your mouth for once. You don't care about us. You never loved any one of us, so why don't *you* just piss off and let us get on with our lives?' His eyes are wide, fists clenched and his heart is driving blood through him. It's as if he'd taken a lift to the next floor and now he's there.

Oh oh, thinks Jessie, pushing herself back into the corner between the stained cupboards and the dull sink with the scungy pink wettex neatly under the plug. Fear lifts in her but there is something else, and she doesn't know what it's called. When she's older she'll call it elation. Now she thinks with astonishment, 'someone stood up for me'. Her delight is short-lived.

The scene unfolds, Emmett comes charging at Rob and the chair falls behind him as he pushes forward. He roars, 'You fucking little dickhead. Who do you think you are? You are nothing, boy. Absolutely . . .' And Rob sees his broken father held by an eternity of defeat.

The old man shoves Rob in the chest but Rob, now grown tall, blocks him and Emmett staggers. Over in the corner, Jessie still holds the knife in the shadow of her hand so hard the bone handle prints into her palm. She's stopped breathing but she's utterly ready.

Emmett and Rob stare at each other for a second or two and that small slice of time burns away. Then Rob grabs the tea towel on the table and chucks it at his father, and the cloth lands on Emmett's head, checked and floppy as an Arab's headgear. Rob looks at the old man and, in that tiny moment of disgrace, a smile passes through his eyes and he says, 'Think you're bloody King Farouk, don't ya . . .' And then, screen door slamming, he's gone.

Jessie watches her brother leaving. Sees her father raising his glass to his lips, sees the amber of it and the shaking hand. Her heart is loud within her and her eyes are running with stealthy tears. She edges past Emmett, ducking down out into the yard, thinking, you're a bully, nothing more and you know what? Robbie's found out about you and you're finished. And she weeps till she doesn't know who she's weeping for. As she climbs the peppercorn tree, she pushes the bread and butter knife up her sleeve.

Up here she can see the Uncle Toby's silos. She's still shaking as the coldness of the day moves into her. There is, lurking within, the unusual idea of stabbing her father. The image of it is there, but not the reality, which she is glad of. She wonders what she would have done if he'd hurt her mum or either one of her brothers or, she admits grudgingly, even Louisa, but she doubts she would ever have the guts to go through with it. And sitting there on the pitted branch of the raggy peppercorn tree, a goods train passes between the silos and the back fence and she watches it being absorbed into the cold cottony afternoon and still her tears fall and as she touches the dent in her palm left by the knife handle, it's then that Jessie realises who she is and who she loves, and this gives her hope. She wipes her eyes and has a go at carving the letter 'R' into the gnarled tree limb and after a while, she realises this is not a knife to have done damage to anyone.

32

Demand for weatherboard box houses in skinny streets in West Footscray is slow, and selling takes months. Emmett's trying to take it easy and cut back once again on the grog. But it's not easy. He can't get a proper breath into his bloody lungs. And he cannot sleep. Not at all. Not one single bloody wink. Beer, that's the answer, he tells himself, good old beer never hurt anybody, it's practically medicine.

The new neighbours are wogs of some kind and the woman next door bellows the kid's name morning, noon and night. Sounds exactly like 'arsehole' to Emmett. One night over spaghetti puttanesca, Peter tells him that the kid's name is Tassos but this doesn't help. Emmett isn't mad on these spicy sauces either, or spaghetti really when it comes down to it, but the kid's made an effort, so what can you say? These days there's not much of an audience for his tantrums. And tantrums really take it out of you. He often finds he has to take a sickie the next day.

One afternoon, Emmett, home early as ever, finds Peter herded out by the estate agent into the backyard under the clothesline on the crate picking out 'Wish You Were Here' on the guitar. The tomatoes have gone all leggy and smell ripped and tight, with a few as red as rubies and getting redder.

A family of six is poking around inside with the air of owners. Emmett comes upon a grandmother sitting in his chair in the lounge room and for one white second he nearly explodes. Instead he storms out, alarmed and ready to riot, but for some reason he keeps his voice down. There *is* money involved, he reasons, and a deener is still a deener.

He heads straight for Pete in the yard and hisses pretty loud, 'What the fuck is going on? Who are those bastards telling a man what to do in his own house? And there's a bloody old wog sheila sitting in a man's chair. Fair bloody dinkum mate, this is it. We have reached the dizzy fucking limit!'

Pete explains that the agent wants one last go at selling the joint. 'Apparently they're fair dinkum,' he says, and Emmett's eyebrows rise and the peerless blue sky swims around them. The light's so clean today, Pete thinks, that even here in Footscray, you feel the planet moving through space. Not such a bad day. He manages a smile at the old man.

Emmett turns to the hose for comfort and waters his remaining tomatoes. A small child detaches itself from the party looking at the house and comes to stand beside Emmett. 'What's your name?' says the child.

Emmett can't bring himself to speak to the boy and briefly considers hosing him, could do with a good drenching, he reckons, but decides against it and just says quietly, 'You better choof off now young man, your mother wants you.'

Peter goes up to talk to the agent and it seems the Greeks do want the house and have even made an offer there and then on the front verandah with a solid brick of cash to back it up. The agent holds it like it might fly away and grins nervously.

The years at Wolf Street tower before Peter. This house is at the heart of every single thing he's ever known. He walks down the passage out to the kitchen. He stands on the step and looks over at Emmett watering in the yard and the idea of leaving slams into him.

How can we possibly not live in this shit-hole? he thinks.

All the pain. And Daniel. In his mind Pete sees the corner of the kitchen where Daniel hit his head.

When Peter walks over Emmett, feeling philosophical, says, 'Agent piss off then? So much for fair dinkum with those blokes. Would *not* know the meaning of the word.'

'Growing things, Peter. This is what it's all about mate. You grow something and it does what you want. It's obedient and quiet and you can eat the bastards.' And Peter understands that his father clearly prefers tomatoes to kids and his wife, which is no surprise. He looks back at the house, steadfastly refusing to praise the tomatoes.

'Come on Pete, look at this beauty. They are works of bloody art, for Key-Ryst's sake mate, you've got to admit.' So inevitably Peter slides his eyes towards the tomatoes and says, 'Yeah, they look great Dad. What do you want for tea? Tomato soup?' He'll tell Emmett about the sale after tea. Tell him before, and he'll only get himself all worked up and ruin another good meal.

Silence follows and Pete moves into the kitchen to produce a dinner that since Louisa has started teaching him about food always has something special: yoghurt and mint sauce with the chops or a glistening salad and a good vinaigrette. At last Emmett has the cook of his dreams working for him.

*

Emmett takes to Louisa's John Keele with an ease that astounds everyone. The man who hates outsiders, who trusts no man, well, it turns out, he doesn't mind John Keele at all.

The first time Louisa brings him over he says politely to John dithering at the screen door, 'Come in, young fellow, what the *hell* are you waiting for?' and gives him a quick once over. 'Hair's very light. One of them Scandinavian mob are you?' he wonders out loud, not waiting for an answer.

He turns to Pete and bellows, 'For God's sake Pete, get this bloke a bloody beer. Quick smart! Can't you see a man's dying a thirst here?'

Pete goes to the fridge and swoops in, grabs one and hands it to John who smiles his thanks. Emmett's grinning away at John like the Cheshire cat but Louisa thinks, I'm the invisible one. Unfolding plainly before her is something she's long suspected, her father prefers men. Women, she thinks bitterly, he sees no sense in us at all. You need a penis to be real around here.

Still, she gives a thin little smile, glad enough that Emmett likes John. Relieved that the night is full with Emmett's bounty. Pete leans back against the wall and they settle in for Emmett's performance. He launches into a few poems starting with Banjo and moving on to Lawson and C.J. Dennis and John keeps smiling.

Louisa doesn't know whether to be horrified or to laugh. She thinks she loves this man, but having Emmett in full flight is bound to put anyone off. How do you stop Emmett Brown? And what if it turns? But John seems to be happy. He's laughing and joking with Emmett and even reading a few poems. What's going on?

Then the mood shifts with the light outside the window. Anne says they should be thinking about tea. 'What about Chinese,' she suggests, 'celebrate meeting John?'

Emmett puts up ten bucks and Louisa and John nip down to Poons to pick it up and leaning on the wall in the restaurant under the giant chopsticks clock, he remarks, 'Your dad has quite a strong personality, doesn't he?' The understatement of the century, she thinks, and that she might start laughing and never stop.

'Yeah, he does,' she says, struggling to stay calm. And later, stopping at the traffic lights, they kiss and she feels she has had a reprieve from something, that John has been spared for her.

33

In possibly the smallest house in North Melbourne live Louisa Brown and John Keele. When John stands out the front with his arms outstretched, he touches both walls. But in that narrow width they are happy.

The house is in Leaf Street and even the name makes Louisa smile, but then she's in love and smiling comes easy. In Leaf Street they make love whenever and wherever they want and they want to often. They smile at each other and make each other cups of tea just how they like it, they read books to and with each other while they sip wine. They throw dinner parties for other journalists who gossip with a kind of feverish mania about anything, and they love having people round to their little place.

They make coq au vin and bouillabaisse from old recipes from his French mother. They walk to the market first thing most Saturday mornings and she believes life is as good as it can be. She puts her face close to his shoulder as they walk and she thinks they are just like Dylan and Suze on the cover of the *Freewheelin' Bob Dylan*.

She treats John's poetry ambitions with complete seriousness and reads every transcript of his poems, encouraging each draft. When he does a reading (he calls them gigs) she sits up the front and claps embarrassingly loud and she brings Rob and Peter along to boost the audience. The brothers seem so clean with their combed hair and washed jeans and they listen politely, sipping their beers and sneaking looks at their watches, wondering when it'll be all right to nick off.

At work John gets promoted more quickly than Louisa despite having lousy shorthand, but this is common ('it's not all about note-taking, Louisa') and soon she's a C-grade and he's a B. Louisa is very good at shorthand and does much court reporting. It's soothing to watch justice at work.

John's hair has faded to a dirty blond and she begins to wonder whether he'd been bleaching it. She never asks though, it seems too personal. He cuts it shorter and soon it settles into mouse-brown with barely a glance back at blond.

His special skill is ghost-writing columns for ex-footballers. He likes the time he spends with them and says getting something out of them is like emptying the sock drawer looking for pairs. Their thoughts are rambling and unmatched. When he says such things she loves him.

Though Louisa is wary of gambling, they go once to the races. John is persuasive, tells her he operates only on tips and doesn't bet if he doesn't get any and he never even mentions probabilities. With John's tips they do all right but still, it feels strange being there. There's a tightening in her chest and a sorrowful feeling that she's given something away but then since she can't name it, she thinks it isn't that important anyway. In the last few months she has started to bite her nails though, and this is unnerving too. Maybe, she thinks, she's losing the way.

She's conscious of the similarities between John and her father — poetry and racing are both impossible quests — but she tries not to think too deeply.

And then at the races in her blue dress she does something strange. Going down the grandstand stairs at Flemington to watch a race, she puts her hand on John's arm and almost in a trance state says, 'I'd like to marry you, if you'd like to marry me.' And John is utterly shocked. His eyes, it seems, become transparent.

In the long pause Louisa laughs far too hard with a kind of terror bursting through her. Why on earth, she wonders incredulously, would you say such a thing? And from the look on his face, he's embarrassed. My God, she thinks, I've read the whole thing wrong.

'Just a joke,' she says cracking up, trying to save herself, and he laughs too, his hard barking laugh. Trouble is, she's been thinking of children, his children. She believes she's old enough now to make a good mother. She often thinks about Jess. Something there needs to be repaired. Some shame in the way she behaved that needs to be erased.

John Keele stops a second on the step and then grabs her hand and keeps heading downstairs. 'Jeez Weeza,' he says, using his pet name for her, 'you caught me by surprise there. Wasn't thinking about marriage, just thinking about the next race.' He bark-laughs again. 'Anyway, thought you didn't believe in marriage.' She doesn't answer, just keeps laughing lightly, though nothing seems the least bit funny. She blames it all on going to the races. The poison of it. Your own fault, she says again and again to herself.

The horses, sleek as seals, are moving towards the barrier. Phil Dwyer, a pimply- faced streak not that much older than Louisa, joins them. She knew him when they were cadets and now he works for the little paper. He's always curious about what's going on at other newspapers. 'You on today Keelie? Business and pleasure,' he says, eyeing off Louisa, but doesn't listen when John replies that he's mostly doing football these days. Then Dwyer gets to the point and nods towards Louisa, 'See you brought along the little filly.'

Louisa bristles because Dwyer knows her, knows she's a journo, not some fancy bloody piece. Just what she needs today, a nasty little shit who thinks he's God just because he's got a dick. She wants to tear his head off or to run home, just run, but she flicks her hair back harder than she means to and snaps caustically, 'And what are you Johnny? A stallion?' Then, quite pleased with that one even though she thinks she might cry because she got it so wrong with John, she turns to see the horses better.

'Ho, feisty!' Dwyer replies with a smirk, 'I love 'em feisty.' And Louisa imagines killing him slowly with something heavy.

John pats Dwyer's shoulder to shut him up. Then the moment of the race begins and they watch intently and are hypnotised by the cacophony of hooves, the beautiful humming. The strain and the spatter and the rawness of these divine animals striving to win for someone else stirs Louisa, brings tears for them and for herself, for the foolish racing endeavours of her father, for all those years, and for the pure spectacular futility that is gambling.

While the jockeys are turning back, Louisa turns to John, 'We'd better get going, we've got dinner with Jules and George tonight,' she says brightly, trying not to show that she's been moved or that she knows she's been rejected and they walk away, uneasily holding hands. Halfway to the grandstand, he stops her and says, 'Listen. I want to say something to you . . . Yes, I'd love to marry you Weezey, you know I would.' And so, with those words, the world has righted itself. Smiling and kissing John's perfect mouth, she is elated. All she must do now is shake off the ghost of his hesitation.

*

That night they lie close on the tiny high old bed she bought when she first moved out, and the airy curtains fall in and out with the breeze until she gets up to shut the window. At first the billowing seemed romantic and then it just got annoying – like so many things, Louisa thinks grimly.

She can't sleep, so she goes into the lounge room and gets a sheaf of his poems from the drawer in the dresser. She hasn't read any for a while, and the second one is new. Look here. It's about a woman with brown eyes. Well, she concludes, staggered, and right then her heart is clamped and towed away.

On the couch, in a funnel of chalky lamp light, she wonders whether there is anyone in the world you can trust. Anyone you know. And she completely doubts it. She puts the poems back and goes to bed, and the dark closes around her like the night sky.

*

Louisa Brown and John Keele are married at the registry office one Wednesday lunchtime in May. Their witnesses are two subeditors. Round old Harry Marks gave her sound advice when she began. 'Just start at the beginning love, and the rest will follow,' Harry said, the pen in his spotted hands hovering over her copy. The other witness is the very wrinkly Alfie Jordon, whose hairy ears are elephantine and who wears spotted bowties most days and always has three sugars in his tea.

They've known Louisa since she started work at *The Ant* and on her wedding day they wear suits with white carnations in their lapels as if it's a special occasion. Louisa wears the black dress with the tiny flowers, the one Emmett paid for after he won the double and, today, there's another echo of Emmett – her hands shake just like her father's.

But John is not the least bit nervous; if anything he seems heedlessly eager to tie the knot. 'Let's get going,' he says, rubbing his hands together as he strides up to Louisa and the two witnesses standing on the wide grey steps on this windy day. His hair, grown long and blond again, is moving in the breeze. Louisa's is streaming back from her face and today, she thinks, John looks shiny as though he were made of metal. She puts out her hand to hold his but he doesn't notice.

And when they come out arm in arm, they are married and it doesn't feel so different; the wind still pushes at them out there on the steps. Harry and Alfie wouldn't mind a drink but they're all due back at work. John kisses Louisa and hurries off to a sacked coach press conference (it's that time of the year) and she goes back to the office.

She rings Anne from her desk in the humming, gossipy newsroom and nestles into her corner to talk. Can't understand why she feels so shaky. 'Hi Mum, it's me,' she begins brightly as she always does and Anne, as usual, says, 'Hello you and what's happening in there today?' Louisa is hesitant, feeling ashamed, like she should weep and admit to all mistakes. But she swallows hard and pushes on and her voice is high and young.

'Nothing much. How ya going Mum? Good. Listen. Guess what? John and I got married today, yes at lunchtime. Because I wanted to. Well, I didn't want Dad there. Couldn't stand for him to mess it up and John didn't care either way. Mum, are you all right?' She presses the phone to her ear, seeking the rope of her mother's voice, the voice that steadies and holds her, pulls her from the deep.

Anne is stunned. She pulls out the stool from under the counter. It's a quiet day at the shop, there's time, there's no one around. Anne says, 'It's okay,' several times and truly means it.

Part of her is even relieved that she doesn't have to go through a wedding. It's true, as everyone knows, she does hate a fuss. And can you imagine Emmet at the wedding of his eldest child?

But then, something strikes her. 'You're not pregnant are you Lou?' In that silence, the question is answered.

'John knows,' Louisa says as if it makes a difference.

*

Harry and Alfie give their carnations to Louisa to press for her glory box. And though no one knows about the wedding, at Louisa's desk there's a bottle of French champagne with a ribbon and a card from Michael Abbey. Reading his name, she feels the electricity of him. Regret stirs her heart as she holds the bottle. She puts it in the bottom drawer and slams it and takes a sip from a glass of water with a skin of dust and begins work on a feature on hospital closures. She looks up and says 'hi' to a passing shaggy illustrator as if it's just another day and kicks off her shoes under the desk. First, she thinks, I've got to sort out these notes. And her gleaming gold wedding ring seems huge on her hand.

34

Rob is waiting for Louisa to have a cup of coffee with him. The weather's been patchy lately and he's had to cancel work because of storms; still, he thinks and allows himself a smile, it's swings and roundabouts with storms, there's plenty of work after they've done their worst. Insurance jobs are always the best kind, no doubt about that.

The café is in Linen Street, North Melbourne, near the market. It's halfway between both their houses and they meet there for convenience and maybe, if they'll only admit, for their father's sake. He lived in Linen Street as a child with his Nana and his uncles. In North Melbourne they feel the child their father once was, feel the possibility of his life before it was lost.

There's something Rob needs to say to Lou and it won't be easy. He orders a short black to give him strength and knocks it back in a hot speedy gulp. How do you say such a thing? he wonders, looking up at the sky. How do you tell your sister that you think it's a mistake for her to have children, for any of us to.

It gnaws at him and now she's gone and married this Keele bloke, something is bound to happen. There's something about her that says secrets and something just a little too happy for his liking.

The truth of it is, he reckons, after long thinking on the subject, that considering the childhood they survived, none of them can possibly become a decent, let alone an excellent, parent. And for Rob that is the only sort anyone should be: wonderful. But how're you supposed to get it right when you've got so little to go on?

He gears himself up for the talk. Knows she won't appreciate it. What woman would? he supposes. Though he will never really think of Louisa as a woman, she's a sister to her core, so that excludes her from the woman issue. Rob has his own complicated relationships to worry about, but one thing he's sure of: he will *never* have children. It wouldn't be fair. It would be gross irresponsibility.

He sees her striding down the street before she sees him. She's wearing a new cream coat and her dark hair is long and shiny. Okay, he decides, she looks well enough. Possibly, she even looks good. He likes the big brown boots but he won't tell her.

She kisses him and he seems to flinch so she punches his upper arm and ruffles his hair which he straightens immediately with both hands. 'You are a dag Robbie boy,' she says and orders a decaff cappuccino which would have given him a clue if he had truly been awake.

They try to catch up at least once a month at this café and when they do, eyes privately held behind sunglasses, they talk in snatches with their frothy coffee before them.

As usual, she starts, 'How are you then, how's things?' He stirs his second coffee for a long time and says they're fine and she thinks, oh dear, it's going to be one of those days when talking to him is like pulling teeth. Poplar trees whisper beside them and further along, plane trees line Linen Street like green soldiers. Traffic is orderly and cars slip by like ants heading inside before rain. The market isn't far and the occasional call of the stall-holders reaches them.

Emmett inevitably comes up. Louisa has heard from Anne that he's having blistering headaches. Shockers that keep him down for days. Rob's not impressed. 'Oh well,' he says, trying to make his face show some concern, 'bound to happen with the booze *plus* he's getting old and he's hardly a poster boy for taking care of yourself.'

And then flatly out of nowhere it seems, he snaps, 'You know Louie, I hate the old man and I will never feel any pity for him. I hate his fucking guts. He was a brutal bastard, the worst, the worst . . .' And Louisa thinks, No, not today, I don't want to hear it. Today is a clear good day.

Rob sips his coffee and though she agrees with him, Louisa tries to talk him out of the hate 'because hate just eats into you', she says like some American talkshow host. And so then, of course, the talking slows because just for once Rob would like to hear someone agree with him, just this one time would do. Not someone who tells him about their experience the minute he tells them of his own. No, he'd just really like to be heard.

'Say it,' he urges, leaning in, 'just say it, just say you know what I mean and don't try to talk me out of what I'm feeling. Give me some credit Lou.' Louisa doesn't feel like agreeing, so they grind to a halt. Rob peevishly scratches at the new beard he's grown because he can't be bothered shaving. It's bloody itchy and he decides it will have to go. The sun slides in and glints on the cups.

And then again, baldly out of nowhere, like an actor walking onto a stage for his big moment, Rob stretches his neck, lifts off his sunglasses and tosses them on the table and says, 'You know, I don't think it's a good idea to have children.' Louisa thinks it's payback time and looks at him. He lets the statement sit in the chasm between them and pauses, sipping busily at his coffee. There, he's said it, now he takes a big hot swallow. '*I for one,* would not be rushing into it.'

Louisa is already pregnant with Tom and while Anne has guessed, no one else has. She hadn't expected it, but John is enthusiastic, which seems a good thing. She feels the world of possibility expanding within her. She thinks for a moment she might say something to Rob but then she feels a boiling anger followed by a kind of pity. Still, she wouldn't mind sticking it to him. Thinks he knows it all, flashes through her but she takes hold of herself, smiles and says, 'Surely, Robert, it's got to be a personal decision. What are you going to do mate, have us all sterilised?'

'Ha!' he laughs far too loud, 'Ha! Good idea! Excellent! Yeah, I'll book us all in, there must be some doctor around here who'd be willing to give us a family rate.' And he keeps up the ruthless, biting laugh.

'You are such an idiot,' she says, leaning back in the chair to get a better look at him. 'One out of the box. Don't you realise we had a wonderful mother, not just an insane father?'

She's at the point in pregnancy when perfection is not only possible, it's likely and she places her hand across her stomach and holds it there, protecting the peanut that will become her child. The breeze picks up and the poplars begin to scatter their small gold leaves and some are cast in Rob's hair and rest there unheeded, like coins. Rob is too careful, she thinks, and what a damn shame he had to be male, he'll never know this feeling because this really is hope, and it's the best thing in the world.

And she realises that because he's male, the shadow of Emmett falls heavily on him while she's got Anne, a mother above all mothers. However you work it out, sadness follows them around like a faithful dog, she thinks. And Robert, poor Robert, could use a little mercy. She looks up from her coffee to smile at him but he's scanning the poplar with his clever eyes.

35

Settled in upstairs at the shop with her mum, it's not long before Jessie has trouble even remembering Wolf Street but she doesn't tell this to anyone because the girl can't afford to get left out of anything else, even memories. After settlement takes place at Wolf Street, Emmett and Peter move into the shop and that's something else to get used to. The bloody goods trains passing by the back fence whenever they like, shaking everyone up with their low sad horns, and sometimes, lying in their beds, the Browns can even hear the mournful sounds of cattle as the trains slow down. Living at the shop is a tight fit and they're on top of each other again, but thankfully Emmett is hardly ever there. The pub beckons.

Peter's doing some course or other but the truth is he's always out with his mates, the crazy Argentinians he met down at the angling club, having barbies at their place and cooking up massive meat feasts and playing music that forces people to dance. Before too long though, the crowding gets to him and he moves out with Rob to a terrace in North Melbourne. Twice a day he feeds rainbow lorikeets in the backyard. He loves to watch as the ball of dappled colour falls upon the old tin pie dish.

And then there's Jessie, the last survivor, stuck at the shop like a mouldy leftover that's slipped down the back of the fridge. Doesn't talk much at home, mainly because no one wants to hear what she has to say, and these days she doesn't care one way or another whether her mother's home or not.

It's much remarked upon that Jessie doesn't look like the rest of the Browns. Where's the olive skin, the dark waves of hair and the blue eyes? In the future, she'll dye her hair the colour of mahogany, get the freckles zapped and with the aid of make-up she'll look much like the other Browns, the ones she's not real keen on at the moment.

Now she's whippet-thin with pale freckled skin, red-gold hair and hands as small as a six-year-old's. Anne often wonders why Jessie is the only real rebel in the family. She'd worked so hard when the others were young and they'd all been reasonable, supportive and mostly obedient. Now, here she is giving Jessie all this attention and it's not working. The endless, involving mystery of kids.

'The House of Norma' is where the ladies of Footscray go to shop but given there aren't many ladies left around the place these days, it's gone a bit too quiet and no-sales days become regular landmarks in the takings book. Jess reckons Anne might as well not be there because she spends all her time out in the shop magging on to horrible old bats who never buy anything anyway and money is always in short supply and the truth is that the big shopping mall being built down the road is doing 'Norma' right in the eye. Plus interest rates are through the roof.

Jessie reckons won't be long now and they'll be broke again. And then soon enough Anne'll be back at the tannery. She took on that job when Jess was little because they paid women equal wages and she lasted six months, tanning hides. Carting buckets of dye and cleaning down the skins with brooms loaded with bleach.

Anne never told the kids she vomited most meal breaks at

the awful sight of the skinned animals. Didn't seem any point telling anyone, who would care anyway? And she didn't see it ever changing. In the end she went back to dressmaking even though it didn't pay as much. Maybe it was true, she thought, money isn't everything.

When Jess comes home from school down the shop sideway and sees Frank's old kennel leaning on the fence she always feels a pulse of loneliness because she reckons that scrappy, shaggy old dog with his scabs and his hidden brown eyes really was her mother and her father.

All the best things had Frank in them. The time Emmett and Jess went up to Clark's grocery to get his beer and Frank led the way and took a wrong turn in the shop and knocked down a stack of tins and people were slipping over and yelling and Frank was charging around barking and kids were laughing and someone asked Emmett if Frank was his dog and he said, 'Never seen him before mate,' and winked at Jess as he hefted his carton of beer up onto his shoulder. Outside in the drizzly morning Frank was calmly waiting for them, having a relaxed scratch.

And the Christmas morning he brought home a hot stuffed roast chook he'd pinched and laid it at Emmett's feet in the backyard, and Emmett gingerly cut the string from the oven-hot bird and took the rosemary out and gave the chook back to him. 'He's copped some poor old wog's Chrissie dinner.' Emmett roared with delight. And it seemed to Jess that this was a sign that things would be better and that, as Frank ate his stolen chook, it seemed a kind of happiness fell upon them and they knew it and held it.

But then in the end, Frank developed a cancer the size of a football on his side and the vet said it was over. He would have to be put down. Before that last trip to the vet, Emmett went down to the butcher shop and picked out a pale pork chop as round as a moon for the old dog. He heated up the barbie, lovingly standing around waiting for the right temperature, and then cooked the meat up nice and slow and cut it up and cooled it and then fed it to him slowly, by the mouthful.

Frank seemed to know what was coming and let them all say goodbye with the patience he had always shown. But when Emmett carried him to the car, even then Jessie wasn't impressed by her father's tenderness, she saw right through it. All fraud.

Still, she knelt beside Frank all through his last meal and she's practically crying now just thinking about it, but holds back when she remembers her recent application of mascara. That day Emmett had cried too, though it seemed to be by chance and no one mentioned the tears that slid straight down his face.

Emmett brought Frank's body back from the vet still wrapped in the striped towel Louisa won for being Most Improved Swimmer in Grade One. And even then Jessie thought, 'God, bloody Louisa, the Paragon has to be in every-thing.' Emmett buried the dog under the kennel and now Jessie sees that even his name is fading. She'd re-paint it if she was a good person, but since she isn't, that lets her off.

36

Emmett's been sleeping in the garage at the shop for a while now because he never could stand the cramped little rooms upstairs. Being up there felt exactly like he was choking. All of them jammed in there together, three little rooms in a row, exactly like a prison.

So he decided on the garage and hired a bloke to line the walls with ply and then painted them peacock blue himself (with help from Anne of course) and the big green desk was installed under the louvre window. He likes it out there and for Emmett, there's something about being able to piss outside your door onto the weeds that just lifts a man out of the mean little suburbs and takes him somewhere else. Gives him some dignity.

Retirement emerges from the misty future and he can almost taste it. Until that day arrives, he's waiting for every other to pass. They mean nothing until he tears them off. When he does retire, he knows it will set him free.

He plans to buy a little house somewhere deep in the bush, it doesn't matter where. Then, in the bush, things will right themselves. They will. He knows it. Just a bit of space, that's all a man wants. Anne will keep going with the shop but she'll visit him at his rural paradise. Sometimes, though, the days seem so long.

*

One Saturday morning Anne finds Emmett asleep in the backyard. The Browning shotgun is cradled in one arm and a whisky bottle stands by waiting for the next call on it. He's shot the weeds beside him and despite this, they look surprisingly alive, though the dirt could have been ploughed.

For a small tender second she thinks he's dead, that he's shot his head instead of the dirt and a kind of hot relief surges through her. But even when she's thinking it, she realises there's no blood, so it's not real. And when she kneels beside him, kindness, her old saboteur, takes over.

'Now Emmett,' she says patting his cheek, 'this is no good my poor old friend, we cannot have this.' When she does rouse him and gets him sitting up, the poor wretch he has become is evident and she is saddened. He dribbles like a baby. She half carries him into the kitchen and gets his scrambled frame onto a chair. Then she makes a cup of tea with lots of sugar and she calls her doctor and speaks of Emmett as if he's a child. He feels safe sitting in the kitchen despite the awful, unending sadness. His tea shakes as he sips it. Anne, he thinks, has become his mother. He's crying. He puts out his hand to touch hers but she's busy organising on the phone.

Emmett is admitted to Turramurra House for a six-week course of rehabilitation for alcoholism. He has many visitors. After week three, Jessie says to a fragile red-eyed Emmett, 'Well, I suppose I'll have to get to know you now Dad. I've never known you sober. You're probably a different person to the one I know.' He agreed and smiled but wariness would never leave Jess.

37

Working as a journalist begins to wear away at Louisa. Every day she feels she has to pull on another personality, to become someone who isn't herself. Someone bigger and grander and more decisive, even more competitive. Once, she'd enjoyed the swagger of ringing people and telling them she was calling from *The Ant*. Now it all exhausts her and she misses her young son, Tom, more than she would have believed possible.

Tom is two years old, grown too heavy for sitting on Louisa's left arm, as he did when he was younger and she made dinner after work. He was so round and peaceful sitting there like an owl that she didn't like to put him down. Eventually though, she found she wasn't able to close her left hand and went to the doctor who put it into a splint and told her she had carpal tunnel syndrome. She had to smile because at the time there was a rash of repetitive strain injuries among journalists, so she blended in. Once again, for the wrong reasons.

Now that Tom doesn't sit on her arm, he stands on a little stool beside her. He has a bowl cut and his hair is long and thick and shot with gold, and his cheeks are round as peaches. He is placid and funny. The first time he had a haircut, he fell asleep. He loves playgrounds and singing 'Kookaburra Sits in the Old Gum Tree' in the pusher. Louisa calls him Owl-Boy, and when he calls her 'Mum' she knows no one has ever called her anything better.

He is easily the most interesting person in Louisa's life. Tom made having a baby all right for her, she knows this and every night kissing him goodnight with his ragged bear, Bluey, she is aware that time is moving past her and that he is growing faster than she can believe.

The brightness of certainty has slipped in her. She's sitting at her desk as ever, shoes off, doodling, when she should be writing a feature about some ageing opera singer. She'd rather be with Tom. She's sick of asking people questions and hearing their pat answers and watching them check themselves in the mirror.

She's begun to think about Daniel again. Maybe it's having Tom, she doesn't know, but there is something about him that takes her back. We were all so utterly changed when he died, she thinks, it was as if the world had tilted too far, that anything could happen, that we might fall off.

She understands that she should have stopped the death because she was older. Everything, she has realised, changes you incrementally forever. She looks at the picture of the opera singer, so fat and such a voice, and she doesn't want to be here anymore.

She thinks maybe she's let the baby take over her special self, that's what Anne reckons, and maybe it's true, she keeps nothing for herself anymore, everything is about Tom. So it's no surprise she's seen John dimming. Men seem to crave every attention, she thinks. And soon there will be another child. Can she love anyone as much as she loves her first child? She has a feeling she can.

And children heal all things, they even begin to heal Daniel. Now, she thinks, with my children I get another chance. If your childhood was stolen, how do you make sure everyone else's is safe? How do you make sure it never happens again?

That's one for another day, she decides, taking a swig of cold coffee and getting on with the piece on the opera singer without mentioning the circumference of her neck.

One Friday afternoon she has an interview with an ageing rock star. He's lined and grouchy and reed thin and touchy about his lost looks. He directs the photographers caustically and exactingly to his approved side. She's three months pregnant with Beck and feeling delicate.

Once she'd thought this bloke was magic; now, dressed in black, holding court in the smallish stale hotel room as he chain-smokes, his pleated little mouth puckering with each intake, she's not so sure. He doesn't care to say more than three words in a row, or to take off his sunglasses. What a total wanker, she allows herself to think, knowing this approach won't get her a run.

It's clear from the clippings that he's flat broke, that's why he's out here inflicting himself on us. Australia is always the last stop for the formerly glorious but he still expects toadying. Who can be bothered? Flogging something – a book, a CD, a tour – always selling something. Louisa sighs as she checks her questions. And then it's her turn. 'Jack,' she starts out and smiles, 'the last time . . .' And that's as far as it gets.

'It's Jackie,' his PR hisses and Louisa says, 'Sorry, oh dear, off to a bad start.' She laughs, coughs and trails off, floundering. A waiter slides in with a tray of coffee to be ignored. She wonders . . . and before she can get the question out, that's it, the end of the interview. He flicks his hand at her. Doesn't feel like talking to her. She picks up her tape recorder and backs towards the door, barely able to believe the blunder and the consequences. Outside the suite, she holds the tape up to her heart, flicks it off and whispers, 'That's it. It's over now.'

Back at the office, they're understanding. 'He's always been a nasty prick,' the news editor, Eric Anderson, says soothingly. 'Don't worry Louie, we can pick it up from the wires or maybe we just won't run anything. He's just another Yank has-been.' Louisa thinks that's a good one, of course they'll run something, everyone else will have him. No choice. 'Lou,' he says kindly and lays his heavy hand on her shoulder, 'go home mate, take the rest of the day off, see the little bloke.' She doesn't need any more encouragement.

She gets her coat, and feeling like a girl let out of school early, she can't get out quickly enough. The day is bright and cold and the air might have been shaved from an iceberg. On the way to the station she walks past three or four rundown travel agencies in the scungy Greek part of town. Around Lonsdale Street, blue and white flags flutter patriotically and souvlaki shops seem to wait for evening when the feeding will begin. This is Greece for Australians.

She comes to the Mykonos Travel Agency and stops dead. A half-size replica of some ancient god stands naked and white on a mini-column by the door. In the window she sees an ad for a travel agent. 'Willing to train,' it says, 'part-time work available.' If she had money she would not work at all, she'd stay home with Tom, but this looks better than the long hours at *The Ant*.

She thinks of Tom currently at a crèche and the new baby, who will also need to be handed over to someone, and something rebels in her. She needs to make things more manageable. She stands at the window for a long time. The frigid, broken wind eddies around her. Finally she goes in.

She leaves *The Ant* with barely a backward glance and spends short days typing in destinations to faraway places, pleased that someone is going somewhere. And her boss, the very round Mr Christos Conti, is understanding of families. You even look a little bit Greek, he says and she smiles.

*

On Sundays, they go over to Anne's for a roast. No one does a roast like Anne, Pete reckons, her food tastes so clean and each flavour distinct. The irony of Louisa being a travel agent is not lost on anyone. Rob delights in reminding Pete, 'The joke is that she's the worst traveller, possibly on the face of the earth. Gets lost going to the shop to buy a bottle of milk and gets sick as soon as you start moving.'

Pete laughs. 'Yeah, remember all the times she got carsick? Well, she always did. You don't remember anything. That's why she got to sit next to the window. I thought it was an excellent strategy since I was stuck in the bloody middle and then, it got worse, I was always having to nurse Jessie. Sorry, Jess.'

And Jess, who is cutting bread, waves the bread knife at him in a friendly, forgiving way.

'Which time would that be?' Rob wonders. 'That time she heaved when we were going to Maryborough. She must have eaten corn. There was an awful lot of corn in it. Dad made her get out and he took a photo of her covered in sick.'

'Shut up Robert,' says Jessie plonking herself down.

'Pretty funny heh?' Pete says sourly and takes his plate over to the sink, washes it, then says he has to be off. He kisses Anne on the cheek and waves to the rest as if he barely knows them.

Rob won't be long heading off either. He's definitely off the family at the moment. There's something stilted these days that he can't put his finger on but then the rest of his life is not working out that well either. He's had two partners in eleven years, one a horticulturist and the other a hairdresser, and neither lasted.

Still, he thinks, you never know your luck in the big city. He swings by and rents a couple of political thrillers at the video shop and he's off home to his house behind the hedge. It's not a cypress, couldn't quite manage that, it's a lilly pilly, a native that ripens with purple berries that spurt.

38

Beckett Keele is born after a day and night of monumental struggle. A cap of fine dark hair hugs her small round head and her eyes are the midnight blue of memory. Louisa sees Emmett's eyes in them and, though the power of his reach lives in them, when she holds the child he is transformed into purity. If this is love, she thinks, then here it is again.

A few days after they get out of hospital, Peter buys a soft pink rabbit for Beck as a welcome for being born. He already has something for Tom. It's a blustery Saturday afternoon and the occasional leaf and stick brushes up against the window; it feels like the end of something though he realises his feelings are often early, long before the actual event, and even when it happens you're never sure whether that moment of recognition was about endings or beginnings.

Louisa's living room is cluttered with teetering stacks of folded nappies and impossibly small baby clothes. Tom's toys are strewn around carelessly. Last night's pizza box is open on the coffee table and Pete has a nibble at a crust that's a serious danger to teeth while Louisa tries to settle the baby. Maybe he should make a cup of tea, he considers. He would really like one but somehow the room is like an inertia trap that has taken him into itself, so he stays still and watches it all like a bemused spectator.

Outside, the choppy wind hurries through a clump of swaying gum trees down at the park and then the moaning begins. It seems there might be a storm. There's no sign of John even in the room, not a book or a coat, nothing.

'He's at a poetry reading,' Louisa says curtly. Having given up on putting the baby to bed, she's folding a nappy longways to place on Pete's shoulder — Beck spills after she's been fed. 'I'll get us a cup of tea,' she says but then sits down as if she's forgotten the next step in tea-making requires walking to the kettle.

Peter holds the baby gingerly, as if she might explode, and Tom is enticed away from his uncle's knee and over to his mother by the absence of that rotten baby and by the idea of showing Mum his new red matchbox car.

'One of Dan's,' Pete says and Louisa feels tears stabbing at her. 'Are you sure? No use keeping them for nothing, better to see young Tom enjoy them.' She tries a smile at her brother but it's not quite there because exhaustion has claimed her. People always say their babies are so good, they just sleep all night. How come hers never do? Typical, she thinks as she lays her head back on the couch and sees a tree outside bending before the convincing wind, the granite clouds huge behind it.

She closes her eyes but tears fall straight down her face anyway, at the thought of Daniel, at the hole John has left in her life, at this endless consuming weariness. The cat moseys on over and settles up against her leg. Tom waves the toy in her face, saying 'car Mummy car' over and over, and then Peter realises he's never seen anyone so tired. That you could even be so tired.

He gets up carefully and, with the gentlest movements he can manage, places the fragrant sleeping baby into her basket and mimes 'shoosh' to Tom. He pushes the snoozing cat down from beside Louisa and the cat stands, affronted by this startling displacement. Peter then puts an arm around his sister, who wakes instantly, and he says, 'Louisa, rest. I'll look after the kids.'

He steers her into the bedroom, finds a blanket piled on the floor, covers her with it and pulls the blind down then goes outside to Tom and Beck. 'Now young Thomas,' he says, 'dishes are our first priority.' At the sink with Tom beside him, he feels the strength of something beginning.

*

Mr Conti, Louisa's new boss, is as short and wide as a tram. His face is completely round. He is so short he can't reach the top shelf near his desk and he keeps a little wooden box for that purpose. He combs the last strands of his dark hair across his shiny brown scalp and, obediently, they stay put all day.

He calls her Luisa and it sounds exotic. He has no time for computers which are just starting to revolutionise the industry because he prefers the old methods of forms and phone calls. He thinks they should work civilised hours and that they should always take care to be accurate. His loyal clients come to him because of his old-fashioned ways.

He runs the family company like a benevolent dictator. Gives the staff access to every junket that comes in but never takes them for himself and neither does Louisa because of the kids. His wife, Eleni, with her dark eyes and her host of gold rings, shows up occasionally at the agency as do their three daughters, Paula, Maria and Kylie, so named when Eleni thought something more Australian was required. Kylie Conti has a thatch of dyed blonde hair with dark seeping through at the roots like soil.

The girls are always jetting off here and there. Jetlag is an excuse to stretch on the couch where the customers should sit. Louisa reckons this is the way work should be, plenty of giving and taking. You do your job and you get it right. There's no need to be the smartest or the rudest or the funniest and no need to have your copy dissected or spiked by ambitious dolts. No need to compete for favour with worn-out editors. Especially when everyone is better at most things than you are.

Stepping into the office in the mornings is like walking onto a Greek island. Greek coffee, hot and thick, becomes her favourite kind. She works hard and learns well, even picks up rudimentary Greek, and the girls are there to help her when she strays. Eleni brings her trays of moussaka and in time Louisa returns the favour; her own is declared almost as good. When she works on Saturday mornings, she brings Tom and Beck with her and the Greeks cherish them. How did she get so lucky?

Some days, she has lunch with Gary who's still at *The Ant*, he's on industrial relations now and she notices a certain hardness creeping into him. He always keeps her waiting because he's so busy and when he strides into their Malaysian restaurant, The Golden Noodle, he pecks her cheek rather than hugs her, which leaves her feeling cheated.

He asks after John but not Tom or Beck, even though he must see John at the office, and then launches into the current gossip (affairs and promotions) with a seriousness of intent as if journalists are the only people worth talking about.

Warren Silk, his new partner, is an arts journo on the local broadsheet and he reminds Louisa of Mel Gibson. She once interviewed Mel, and on arriving back declared to the office that 'men don't get more handsome than that'. And so it is with Woz.

'How's Woz?' she asks, thinking of Mel. Gary's hopping into a plate of lemony seafood noodles and says tersely, 'Haven't seen a lot of him. He works so much it's becoming a joke and then he plays water polo or he's off at gallery openings. There's always something going on.'

'You sound like the wife,' she laughs, trying to keep her voice light. She's diligently picking out the tasty bits from a seafood mee goreng but she's not hungry. 'For some men, there's always somewhere more interesting than home,' she adds, and pushes away a curly piece of squid that looks like elastic.

Though he agreed to be Tom's godfather, Gary is not fussed about even hearing the details of motherhood. He does his duty though and on each of Tom's birthdays he's arrived with a different children's classic carefully wrapped and ribboned. *The Lion, the Witch and the Wardrobe* when Tom was two and at three, *Kidnapped*.

Gary seems to regard being a parent as a diversion from Louisa's real life. She believes the colour in his eyes fades when she talks about her family. His own spare time goes into getting fit and these days he has biceps like Sylvester Stallone. Louisa could not believe they were real until she touched them one summer afternoon. 'Didn't know you had it in you,' she gaped, and he grinned like a boy.

He thought she was insane to leave journalism. 'How could you just chuck it all away?' he asked her incredulously. 'How?' He was honestly mystified. Journalists were his world and gossip was its fuel. He was cynical, funny, bitchy, very well-informed, and made you feel anything was possible; and she thought, he's definitely lost interest in me. Perhaps the price of admittance to his world was a press pass. Ah, Mr Turner, where have you gone?

Walking back to work after lunch, it seems to Louisa that Gary and maybe even John are being swept away from her. That she is here in the middle of a wide prairie, alone, tending to things, checking the walls of the house and trying to get things to grow. And growing her kids.

39

Beck is named for Samuel Beckett, her father's favourite play-wright. She grows into a dark-haired, olive-skinned plump little girl who loves water, is mostly grubby, and is very fond of her special penguin cap. Tom is a quiet boy with deep blue eyes who has the look of his uncles about him.

When Beck's eighteen months old, John opens the door to the bedroom and Louisa is reading in the lamplight. Once again, he's home late but at least he's still got his tie on. He drags it off absently, like a man letting go. He's been at a lot of poetry readings lately. He's out most nights. He's so busy. She's heard there are poetry groupies galore. Doesn't believe a word of it.

'Lou,' he says, standing in front of the chest of drawers with his back to her while he watches her in the mirror.

'Yeah,' she says, reading hard and resisting the current of her husband's attention.

'I've got something to tell you and you're not going to like hearing it.'

She seems to drag herself from the page, but really she hasn't absorbed a word since he walked in. She sits up straighter, arranges the covers and knows immediately that what he will say will change every single thing.

She's always expected that he will leave her, that it wasn't really love, and here is the truth. If you wait long enough, it comes. She wonders whether she might intervene, put up her hands and stop the words, put her mouth against his, but no, it doesn't seem so.

'You see, the thing is,' he says, stumbling forward with resolve and red eyes, 'I've fallen in love with someone else.' He seems to hope that she will show him a little mercy because he's in love. He hasn't planned it, you see, this thing has just befallen him.

'What did you say?' she asks thinly.

'I've fallen in love with someone else.'

'Fallen?'

'Yeah, fallen. I'll move out.'

'Who did you fall in love with?'

'Her name is irrelevant.'

'Not to me, mate, and I'm guessing her name is not irrelevant to you or you wouldn't be doing this.'

'Well, I don't want to get into that.' And then the rage is released.

'You unbelievable, you complete fucker,' she cries, and it feels exactly like her heart has been torn out.

The emotions that flash through her are as familiar as family. Fear returns like an old enemy who knows its way around, but there's a kind of release and she seems to be becoming Emmett and she runs at him stumbling from the bed in the ugly duckling pyjamas and hits him around the head but he holds her hands away from her until, sobbing like the girl she always held at bay, she sinks into the bed.

She cannot think. Nothing works. This pain has halved her. She lies there while he sits beside her, tentatively stroking her back with an involuntary kindness that even she can't stand. At each touch she feels a little more dead. She can see nothing, nothing but her children, and they are all there is.

It takes a while for her voice to remember how it works, but when it does, she says nastily, 'Well, fuck off then. We don't need you around here.' And that's all it takes. He packs a bag, stuffing in socks and underpants, his T-shirts and carrying his other stuff on hangers. And he leaves. In an effort to seem normal, Louisa switches off the light and gets into bed with Beck and there she stays, awake all night.

It takes many months for Louisa to recall who she is. Her mother and the babies are what get her through. Slowly, she comes to see that she will survive John Keele but it takes longer to understand how she is changed.

*

'How come Louisa always gets on better with men than women?' Jessie asks Anne one day while they're hanging out washing in the yard behind the shop. There's not that much washing anymore, and they're both aware of it. 'She drove her own husband away by never talking to him. Remember last Christmas? She barely looked at him. She spends more time talking to Rob than anyone else and Rob doesn't give a stuff, he just can't stand John, so anything that gets up his nose is fine by him. He's a stirrer, but what's her excuse? I tell you, I pity those kids.'

Anne cannot be expected to choose between her children. To her they are equal in every way. Ah, let's be honest a minute, she thinks and smiles to herself, Jessie was always the favourite of my heart, but that will go to the grave with me. And so it follows that she cannot let Louisa go undefended.

'Well as for Mr John Keele, he was no great shakes, nothing but a gutless wonder really,' she begins. 'He didn't even have the guts to try to work it out, no, he just kept up the little dalliances. He's long had a roving eye and it seems to me they were never really suited. Louisa had to do all the work with him. He's one of those men who wants a woman to do all the running. She has to come up with all the moves, but only after he approves. You know where the house will be, and she must keep the children happy and bring up all the topics they talk about. He will never contribute. Then she's got to entertain him and make a home for him, cook for him, bring in half the income, give him children and then keep them quiet so he can pursue his great dream and you know what? Louisa's a more talented person and a better one than he will ever be.' Anne savagely pegs a tea towel and it flutters, a stained and captured flag snagging occasionally on a brave red geranium that climbs the wall of the garage. Anne continues. This is a theme she's given much thought to.

'She got tired of it all and who can blame her? In the end, if you're doing everything, then you may as well do it on your own, that's the mistake I made, staying there under the thumb all those bloody years. Once there are children my girl, every single thing changes and some men do not cope well with the changes. And by the way, did you know Mr Keele used to dye his hair?'

Jess is not hugely bothered by any of this news, as far as she's concerned people can have whatever hair colour they like. Anyway, she still likes John Keele but she's got the sense to shut up about that and she always had a sneaking feeling that he liked her better than Lou and maybe he did. 'Oh,' she says limply, dropping a dry yellow towel into the dirt and Anne says impatiently, 'Give it to me, give it a good shake. And did you know if you fold it in half on the line, the fluffiness increases?' But Jess is lost to her, she's kicking away a pile of cat shit, shoulders slumped. Her mother grabs the towel and shakes it vigorously. Jess wishes she didn't have to hear any of this. Bugger Louisa, Mum's always on about her.

The truth is, Jess will always strive to find a way to feel left out because that's where she's comfortable, but now she wants her mother to agree that Louisa excludes her and always has. She strides over to the plastic seats and hurls herself into one so hard the leg buckles and has an adolescent sulk, years late.

Absently, Anne asks, 'What did she do love, what was it that upset you?' as she follows her back into the yard with the clothes basket on her hip, and a ripple of impatience shoots through her, though it's got nothing to do with her girls. It's those rotten little birds at it again, disturbed all her mulch, chucking it around willy-nilly.

Triumphantly, Jess believes she's finally captured her mother's attention. 'She just ignores me, she always has, and she seems to love the boys. What's so special about them? They're not fussed on her. She just bars you, that's all. Never asks a question, doesn't give a stuff what I'm doing. Looks through you. It's always only about herself. Doesn't even talk about the kids much. You have to drag it out of her.'

Anne wishes that Jessie could see past herself for just five minutes but she says, 'Louie and the boys have a special bond. Before you were born they were very close, especially after Daniel died, and I think if you look hard you'll see that it's not men she prefers, it's her brothers.'

Though it's true, Anne thinks, she's always been a bit on the odd side has our little Louie. She smiles and gets up to go in, that's enough now. Time for a cup of tea.

40

Louisa stays on in North Melbourne in the smallest, cheapest house going. It's a dusty old weatherboard in dire need of a paint, a single-fronter about as wide as a bus and sandwiched between four others. A milk bar on the corner seems to be collapsing onto itself. Only the signs hold it up.

The faded red of an old softdrink sign makes her think of Emmett. She hears him say, 'Lolly water, will rot your teeth, but look at ya, plenty of bloody teeth,' and laughs as if it's funny. Thinks of him waiting for retirement and trying out sobriety. She thinks of the only time he visited her here. Two babies and Emmett and how tenderly he nursed Beck. How he taught Tom to shake hands. Before he left, he slipped her a hundred dollars and kissed the babies as if he loved them and she wept into Beck's soft hair afterwards because she missed him, well, because she missed the him he was today.

Down the street where Tom plays cricket there's a park, dry now in the drought, the grass powdery and loose. The boy sleeps in the front room in a sweaty shrine to cricket. When Pete calls him the next captain of Australia, Tom's eyes shine. In the evening, he often sits on the verandah roof waiting for his mother to come home and, seeing her at a distance, stands up and yells 'Mum' until she sees him against the blue, a slim boy with dark hair and a shining face. She wonders at the beauty of him. As she gets closer he readies himself for the ritual of the throw.

Louisa prides herself on her ability to catch a tennis ball. She grew up believing that catching a ball was her one skill. So now the pressure is on Tom. Too close, he thinks, and it's cheating, too far and she'll miss. So when he lets the faded bare ball go sailing across to her, the onus is on himself to get it right. He usually does and Louisa carries the ball to him while he scrambles down from the roof and kisses his mother and takes her bags. And she is relieved again that he looks nothing like his father or her. He looks like himself, she thinks, and this makes her happy.

Beck has a tiny tacked-on cupboard of a room. Black hairpins are scattered across the floor like insects and posters of pouting boy singers in eye make-up and torn jeans line the walls. Louisa has the stuffy middle room with a paper blind and flimsy lace curtains losing the battle to clench back the western light from the rickety casement window. Even on dull days, the window is illuminated.

At the back, a pine-lined family-room and kitchen takes up the width of the house. A sage green leather three-seater and a matching chair were bargains from the Brotherhood shop. Mao, their grey tabby, named by Beck when she was two, seems to shed everywhere. The television dominates the room and it's always a relief when the kids aren't there so she can shut the damn thing off. It takes all her money to keep the family going.

She cooks the kids' dinner and most nights picks up something fresh on the way home. Then she helps with the homework and puts a load of washing through, does the bills and maybe, if it's a good night, watches a crime show on tele where some poor woman is murdered and avenged by cops while she nods off with a glass of cask wine in her hand and

Mao beside her purring. The comfort he offers is inestimable.

Jess sometimes rings way too late. She's a lawyer now, working at a women's refuge in Sunshine, and she needs to talk about some case or other. When the phone rings past nine-thirty Louisa treats it as if it can see her. She lets it ring until it leaves her alone or else she swoops on it to stop the attack of it. If it's Jess, the drama of her workday spills into the living room until Jess gives up and lets Louisa seek the refuge of her bed. 'I'm just so tired,' she hears herself saying again and hates herself for it.

This house sometimes reminds her of Wolf Street but the real difference is her beautiful garden. Louisa makes gardens grow with a kind of magic. Her herbs are bright and fragrant. Her roses flop and fold and smell like wine and when she cuts a bunch and puts them in Nan's vase on the table, for that single moment life is perfect.

Her kids don't see their father much because John Keele finds it unsettling but they don't seem to mind. His new partner, Katie Slattery, is a blonde PR person who looks after John as if he were a baby or a genius, which makes the kids uncomfortable. 'She puts salt on his food and gets him drinks and kisses him on the mouth,' Beck reveals in hushed tones after one visit. She pulls her mouth down, pretending to be sick, 'And she calls him babe.' Tom grabs his basketball and slams outside to punish the ring. Beck puts her hand on Louisa's shoulder.

John has moved to an arty part of the country and Katie visits on weekends to tend to him. In a shack up there he's writing poem cycles based on the *Iliad*. Apparently he's putting them into an Australian context. It's his life's work and he can't contribute financially to the kids because, well, this is art we're talking about here. 'Ha,' snorts Louisa when she reads this in his latest letters.

Some nights, Rob comes over after the kids are in bed and

they eat potato chips or chunks of apples and cheddar and talk with the TV muted and the world silently flying by on the screen. He tries never to talk about John but that's not possible. He believes that he alone, out of the whole family, saw through him but he doesn't want to say, 'I told you so.' What would be the point of that? Perhaps some kind of maturity is finding its way into Robert.

So these visits get off to a quiet start because all Louisa can think about is betrayal and she needs to work it out slowly as if it were a splinter. But there are many forms of betrayal and even if it begins without regard to him, most roads lead to Emmett. With Rob and Louisa it's as if everything is a hurdle till they can talk about the time of him.

So after his weekly dose of John Keele poison, Rob is slumped on the old green couch. His hair is still carrying sawdust from an elm he took down today, and his eyes are full of sighs. He doesn't recall anything tonight, he's tired, he'd rather just watch the news, catch up on other people's miseries, anyone's is better than their own.

But something about theft on the television takes them back to the time they were robbed. They'd put Anne's purse in the back of the billycart and taken it down to the shop for the milk and smokes. Some boys saw it and took the purse and the kids ran but couldn't catch up so they went home and Emmett put them in the car and took off after the thieves. 'Bloody cops and robbers. I was terrified when we went cross-country over those paddocks. What was the old bastard thinking?' says Rob, biting into his apple so hard Louisa is hit by a speck of juice and flinches.

'Yeah, scary. Then when he caught them. God, I thought he'd kill 'em, but he took them to the cop shop. It was fun too though, dontcha reckon?' Louisa says wiping off the apple ricochet with the back of her hand.

'S'pose . . . That's the weird thing.'

'Remember the story in the local paper, "Louts rob children"?' By now they are cackling with laughing and then it reaches the point of convulsion and Rob mixes up drinking with eating and manages to get a bit of apple stuck and needs to have his back thumped. Louisa is gulping with laughter but Rob is wiping away tears. 'Don't know how much more of this reminiscing I can take,' he says wheezy and red. 'Bloody dangerous.'

'And the time we got lost on the bus?' she continues, the energy of the laughter and of the memory lifting her. She's pouring a grassy, pale wine for them and it occurs to her it's as if she saves herself for talking to him.

Louisa will not be swayed from the past. 'Come *on*, this is a good story! You know,' she insists, 'we were coming home from the pictures on a Saturday morning, the pictures at the Grand, and Auntie Betty from next door was on the lolly counter. God, life could get no better, a free bag of lollies clutched in your filthy little hand as you tore through the dark picture theatre, utter bliss.'

And suddenly Rob is in. He gulps at the cold wine. 'Yeah,' he smiles, 'we caught the red bus after the pictures in Foot-scray, but it must have been the wrong red bus and we sat on up the back, bouncing along the wrong way but not sure. Nothing looked right, we were holding hands like Hansel and Gretel. By the time the driver turned into the depot, we were the only ones left in the bus.

'And when the bus driver saw us there, he walked down the back and asked where did we want to get off? And I started crying and you recited our address to him and he said, "Right," and then he drove us home. Remember? All the way in that big red bus. It was like a dinosaur turning around in the court. Mum was out the back doing the washing and she came out wiping her hand on a tea towel, I remember her standing there. Totally amazed.'

Caught in the web of memory, shaking their heads, they wonder how they could have been let out to catch buses on their own at that age. 'That's nothing,' says Louisa, 'they didn't know where I was for four Sundays in a row.'

'Bullshit,' Rob says calmly, 'Lying Louie. Always the liar.' Louisa flicks him, barely spilling a drop, and continues seamlessly.

'No, you idiot, I ran away and joined Sunday School, probably because Dad banned it. You didn't want to come, you never were big on religion.' They both grin at that one. 'And I would have been only six or seven because we still lived at the housing commission. I told them my name was Louisa Black. I loved all the stories, but really it was the food for morning tea. You know, saveloys and fairy bread. Never seen anything like it, but the Christmas party was the end. I made a total pig of myself with the party pies and then, to top it off, choked on the red lemonade and then it bloody well came back down through my nose all over my dress. Unbelievable mess. The end of my religious education, too ashamed to go back. But I learned something out of the whole shameful experience, you cannot snort red lemonade.'

She puts her hand on his shoulder and is glad he is her brother.

Sometimes the talk goes on too long until they can't pull out of the quicksand of it. So they must ration the past.

After the memories have closed down for the night, they sometimes read each other bits of things they love and Louisa these days goes for *The Hitchhiker's Guide to the Galaxy*. It makes them laugh and she loves the bits about Norway and reading it, she sees northern fields on long summer nights when the skies are pea-green curtains and stars are swirling.

And Rob, in a voice carrying weird echoes of Emmett, reads mostly from his trade journal, *The Arborialist*, so that Louisa braces herself for rambling descriptions of tree structure. Strong laterals are frequently mentioned, and she often nods off.

41

It takes years for Louisa to admit there's something wrong in the deepest part of herself, that the darkness she sees may be within her. Mostly she's okay, but then years later, she's not. One day it seems she isn't going to work, but she explains this to herself by deciding that she deserves a sickie here and there and that her boss will understand. Mr Conti is a prince among men, she thinks, a prince. Oh, to have such a father, calm and kind and fair.

When the darkness first comes, she just feels heavy and sadder, as though someone has turned her down and she can't see how. Sometimes she thinks about things that she hasn't meant to think about. For instance, about John and the kids and that it's become too hard. The kids are moving away from her and, while she wants this, she also wants them back. The intricacies of her children's lives, their fights and their dreams, are lost to her.

There is too much to do. Can't do everything. She wants to go away. She wonders where the tough girl she was has gone. The one who stood up to Emmett, who could stand up to anyone; but then she remembers she only stood up to the old bastard once and boy, did it cost her. Used it up, that's what I did, I used myself up, she decides.

Each morning, if she can, she makes the kids' lunches. Puts

a few little packets and a couple of pieces of dubious fruit into brown bags. Vegemite sandwich for Beck and peanut butter for Tom. She's having trouble remembering even that. Useless at work, she thinks. Utterly useless. She leaves the two lunches on the bench for them and goes to her room where the gloom and the stale air are comforting.

She sits on her mother's little wooden chair, and it feels like her mother has her arms around her. Nothing is the thing that most appeals. It's the mirror image of something. Emptiness swarms around her and when she gets tired of sitting she goes to the bed and lies down. She pulls her arms and legs in and becomes a lump.

She doesn't think there's anything wrong with this because it seems so natural, a slide into another reality. She's always been a bit like this, a bit of a loner, and now it's inescapable.

People have been telling Louisa she should get out more all her life. But she never knew what it meant and still doesn't. She'd still be herself wherever she was. There can be no escape.

If she's awake in the little room she stares at her summer-brown hands, the wedding ring still on the left hand, even after all this time; or she looks at the walls and tries to think about nothing. When thoughts come she sends them away. It isn't long before the most persistent thought is about death. Then comes ways that might get her there.

Food tastes like cardboard and nothing makes sense when she reads and nothing interests her. And in the end she can't talk much either. Words won't form. She's shutting down.

When the phone rings, she leaves it echoing throughout the house looking for attention, the ringing coming and going like a memory. If she picks it up, she can't get a word out anyway. One day she hears Mr Conti tell her to take some time off to fix herself up. He puts her on half pay for a few weeks and she doesn't think any further.

In the afternoon, the children let themselves into the house and scrounge around for something to eat, a stale Salada, an old apple. Once Beck knocks on the door of Louisa's room. She's about ten and her dark hair is in plaits, just like her mother's used to be. She knocks at the door with a picture of the world she made at school and when she hears nothing, she opens it. When Louisa sees Beck, she believes she's seeing herself. The child moves into the room bringing the stiff painting and stands beside her mother in the little chair and lays the world on her knee. She puts her hand on her mother's head and pats her hair while Tom is a shape in the doorway.

42

Rob often visits Louisa on Saturdays. They read the papers together, drink coffee, dunk biscuits and whinge about the conservative government, but really, all governments are entitled to their scorn. Lately, he's missed a few Saturdays because Lou doesn't seem entirely with it at the moment and he hasn't wanted to delve into why. Then, there's the kids and he's been helping a lot lately and if she starts to rely on him, he decides, it will end in tears because I am not to be relied upon.

This bright Saturday morning is different. Bizarrely, John Keele decided in advance that he wanted the kids for the weekend. His parents were interested in them or something. So today when Rob walks round the back, he finds things very quiet and he's surprised. Not that he's looking forward to seeing Tom and Beck, he's just forgotten they were at their father's.

Rob doesn't love them, actually he barely knows them, with their limbs like stalks and their eyes like a deer's. Kids! Who needs bloody kids, he wonders, getting the spare key out of the hide-a-rock that looks so pathetically plastic. Inside, he drops a swag of newspapers on the table, fills up the kettle, flicks it on with a glance at Beck's latest drawing on the fridge and sees with a strange rush of pleasure that she has drawn her Uncle Robert up a tree. He has a closer look. The girl has talent, he muses, then pushes on through the house looking for Louisa.

By now he's thinking that Lou must have nipped down the shops but he looks around anyway and pops his head into her room. When he opens the door, he sees she's on the bed and apologises, assuming she's asleep. But then something makes him look again, and he sees the empty bottle beside her and that she's unconscious on the sagging smelly bed with her mouth spilling white froth. He feels a wave burst within him and he drops beside his sister.

He cannot understand that she had wanted to be dead. His heart is pounding. He needs to wake her up now. 'Lou, LOUISA, WAKE UP,' he shouts way too loud, shaking her and he turns her on her side and then she's sick everywhere and there's so much white foam. He wipes her mouth with his hand. No, he thinks, this is not over Louisa.

'No, no,' he says to her softly and urgently, 'No, Louie it's all right, it's quiet now. It's really all right. The kids are with their father and they're all right. He will look after them. You'll be right, we'll get you better.' He just keeps talking because it seems the right thing. There's no telling how long she's been unconscious.

With shuddering fingers he grabs his mobile and rings an ambulance and runs to open the front door, ready for them. Louisa moans and Rob sits beside her. He puts a towel over the vomit and cleans up around her mouth with a wet face washer from the bathroom and while he's doing that, it crosses his mind that he's never cleaned anyone's face before and then, persistently, that Louisa looks like Emmett.

In an ambulance with the siren cutting through the bright morning like a sword the paramedics take her to the hospital and Rob goes with her. He sits up the front looking out on the shiny day with the kind of fear he hasn't felt since Daniel died. He finds he's crying and his breathing comes in swells.

At the hospital, they take her away from Rob and push a tube down her throat and pump charcoal into her and the nurses say things like, 'You'll be right love.' Between themselves they wonder lightly about the story of this one.

She can't speak because of the tube and she can't really hear because everything is clouded, but there's something she recalls and it's a sort of questioning from within that goes something like how could you even mess this up? Useless. Useless. Rob sits outside the swinging doors holding his arms to make himself be still.

He's in the ward when she's wheeled in on the narrow bed but she turns her head away from him to the window. Still, he sits there and without turning to him she says in her hoarse voice, her throat raw from the tube, 'Don't tell anyone.'

He puts his hand on her sweaty head, 'No one,' he says. 'Ever.'

She's transferred to a psychiatric hospital and ends up being there for six months. Clinical depression has her in its grip. She doesn't eat unless people stand over her. She doesn't talk unless she absolutely must. She stares. She's gone away. Rob moves into Louisa's house and the kids live with him because it suits everyone.

Louisa's children tell no one about their mother. They visit her with Rob on Saturdays and always come out wildly brushing away tears. Rob takes them for a medicinal burger afterwards. Kindness has caught him up in itself and the weeks pass by slowly as if they are all on a boat on a frozen glacier.

At first they look at Rob as though he's an alien, this gawky, skinny, jokey uncle who eats apples, core and all, and who puts tomato sauce on everything and who loves dim sims with a passion.

Peter and Jess bring dinner on Tuesday nights, but it's soon clear that Jess is hopeless at food so Pete does it all. He settles on lamb roasts and cooks them like Anne's, the flavours clean and separate and the gravy light and shiny. Jess and Rob help the kids with their homework while he cooks. And a kind of pattern emerges.

One night they start upon word definitions and Jess asks them to define 'cadaver'. Rob groans about 'my macabre little sister', but the kids love it and a dictionary is produced to clear up misunderstandings. Rob takes over as quiz master and their haul of words includes 'immense' and 'dogged' and 'going Dutch' and 'drop kick', as in 'What exactly is a drop kick, Peter?'

When the kids are in bed, they drink wine or tea and settle back into being together. One night Jess says, 'We've got to show the kids that they will survive this, that it's possible. We did. We knew we would. And they will too and so will Louisa.'

'Yeah,' say her brothers, each thinking how clever she is and not saying it and then Pete says, 'I didn't always know I'd survive. I have to say there were times when I thought I was gone but somehow you don't give up even when it seems obvious that you should. Even when you know the chances are that you are totally fucked. These kids have each other and that helped me, knowing you were all there going through it too.'

Rob laughs from the couch, 'You're glad we suffered too, are you? Little shit.' Later he says, 'You know, doing the homework with them tonight, it kind of reminded me of Emmett, and he was always a bastard but there is a real truth about him and it was that he wanted us to get an education, remember that? And I want these kids to get one too. It is crucial, but how do you get kids to know that?'

'I reckon they know,' Jess comments, 'they'll be right as long as Louisa is. Can you imagine what our lives would have been like without Mum?' she asks, tucking her feet under herself in the armchair. 'She was all that stood between us and the shit heap. Having her there and knowing she loved us, that was everything.'

There are murmurs from the brothers and then Peter stands up and says firmly, 'Let's not turn this into another Emmett session. Let's just not, I'm far too tired to enter into it,' and he makes a start on the dishes.

43

Over the months, four different drugs fail on Louisa and as they fail she spirals into another place and becomes a more wasted version of herself. So the hospital tries shock treatment. A buckling picture of a smiling dolphin looks down from the ceiling above the treatment table in the ECT suite. It's there to give patients something to linger on while they embrace the nightfall of anaesthesia. She knows she saw it and that's a comfort because, while it saved her, her memory never fully recovers from shock treatment.

In time she gets used to waking in the recovery room and hearing Rozzie, her favourite nurse, move around slowly and carefully, calling each patient by name, gently, like a mother.

'Louie are you there, my dear? Back with us yet?' and touches her cheek and rearranges the white cotton blanket and then floats away to tend to the others. She hums softly to the old hits playing low on a little radio. She sings for the lost ones who wash up here in the recovery room after ECT, the ones whose brains have badly let them down. Often on hearing her, Louisa wants to weep with joy, partly because after ECT she's so damned bright she's nearly normal, and partly because kindness, wherever you find it, is a visit from angels.

After the recovery room, she wakes up again later in a ward, one side of her hair stiff with the gel that conducts the shock, her doctor sitting in the chair beside her writing his notes. 'You're just having a snooze,' he tells her and, in a while, he's gone. In a day or two the treatment wears away and the slide begins again, the gradual tapering.

Emmett comes alone to the hospital one Wednesday afternoon. He's driving a white Commodore these days and he's rapt about finding a shady car park. Ah, the little things, he thinks. He walks fast through the brilliant day, not noticing the crepe myrtles in bloom, their redness like a memory of hearts. He's not interested. He's looking forward to the pub later. Tell the truth, he's not completely convinced about this depression business. Nothing a drink wouldn't fix, he reckons, hitching up his trousers and thinking about the counter lunch that awaits him at the North Star.

Emmett's nervous about this kind of place though and doubtful about the whole shebang and when he comes upon Louisa in room 602, he's thinking about telling her to get her act together. But then he sees her and something overcomes him and he kneels before her chair and wraps his arms around her and begins to weep on the top of her head. He can't make himself stop.

With her weary eyes and her slow blood, Louisa wonders what's going on here. Time is still so slow and having Emmett here is outside of everything. After a while, Emmett looks at her and remembers to wipe his face and with two hands out behind him staggers back to find the bed. He has called into her house on the way and picked a rose from the climber out the front and popped it in his shirt pocket where it has been a bit crushed. Thought she might like to see something of her own and he lays the pearly thing on her knee.

Though Louisa isn't talking, she still looks at people and now she studies him. He doesn't look like much but she still can't completely place him. She's not glad he's here. The thing about fathers is beyond her.

*

She'll always remember the day Rob and the kids came to get her at the hospital. Though there are many outpatient treatments to go, it still feels like a milestone. And that last day seeing Beck in her pretty dress and Tom looking serious with his hair all combed and Rob, the big goose, in his denim jacket with a bunch of straggly pink carnations for her, seeing them lifts her but not too high, she hopes. As they walk out to the carpark together, she's reminded precisely of what she almost lost. What nearly went away.

At home she walks inside the house gingerly as if she might break. But in time she finds she's able to talk more and even to eat again.

Mr Conti has helped where he can. One Friday night he thrusts an envelope with five hundred dollars at her. He stands at the front door, hand out, and says in his choppy accent, 'For you dear Luisa and for your babies,' and he kisses her hand and is gone. And then there's the dole.

She needs ECT as an outpatient, at first twice a week, and Rob, still sleeping on the couch in the battered pine family room, drives her to the hospital at six-thirty on Monday and Friday mornings and picks her up a few hours later. His business is floundering, but he is able to do a fair bit when she doesn't need him.

Louisa can't remember much about the trips to the hospital in the morning, but she never forgets the emptiness that surrounds her as she walks across the carpark at dawn and that void is always the most recognisable part of the experience.

And yet, even though she believes it will not end, in time she does recover. She has ECT once a week, then once a fortnight, then only when the doctor thinks she needs it. And now a new medication is working.

And the lifting is so gradual, she barely notices but there's a day when she's leaving the house to go to work and she sees the sky and it's as if it hadn't been there all that time, as if it had run away.

She never forgets the way the sky opens up over her that day. The structure of clouds, she thinks, and remembers geography lessons and how mastery over the names of clouds exalted her, that these are, well, alto-somethings. She smiles. She feels so new at being alive, as if even her skin is newborn.

To see the world again, to have her eyes working again after all this time is enough to last her forever. The small surrounding things make her feel alive. To think what she has missed, but she stops herself because that road, with blame hiding in every corner, will lead her the wrong way.

For part of that first day she feels she's come back but she keeps it a secret, even scared to smile outright at the force of it. It's okay, she reckons, they think I'm nuts anyway. She's been away and she's lucky to be back. Never wants to go there again. People climb mountains and sail solo around the world because they're looking for a challenge. Ha! she thinks, they ought to trying climbing back after such a depression but sponsorships would probably be out of the question, she speculates shrewdly.

44

Saturday morning and Jessie sips her tepid coffee, the thin blackness of it settling in around her mouth like a crust. Her translucent skin is fine and the lines around her mouth fall easily into a scowl, possibly from smoking. She doesn't wear make-up and she's very thin. Why, she thinks, should I wear make-up? Just to conform to gender stereotypes? Don't get her started.

She's lived with Warren David Davis, a secondary school English teacher, for eight years now. They live in a pale weatherboard house in Kensington on a street full of other houses much like it. Louisa used to call it Lifesaver Street because the houses sitting shoulder to shoulder are the colours of a packet of Lifesavers. Pink tea roses with bronze leaves nod at the picket fence. Jess and Warren have two small scruffy dogs, Bert and Podge, as well as a cat named Sacheverall or some other wacky thing. Louisa has always called it Puss just to shit Jess and that seems to work.

Jess met Warren at a party in Elwood on a rainy night and they bunched up in a corner of a leaky verandah with the smokers and got talking about their ideas for living.

These days they have an understanding, they each work hard at their own saving of the world and they let the other be. She used to call him Warren David when they were in the first phase of love, which has long since slipped away.

He wears his greying hair longish possibly, she thinks, because he believes it keeps him looking young. But Jess reckons he's just plain wrong. He's pin-thin like her with skin like creased linen.

Jessie realises there's something of Emmett in Warren's passion for words but she doesn't dwell on it. Besides, he's so different in every other way. He's enough for her. He's gentle, reliable and he's kind. Even does the washing properly and without arguments.

Though he believes he loves Jessie, Warren doesn't love Jessie's temper especially when it's aimed squarely at him. Or when anything that comes to hand gets thrown at him — picture frames, vases, bunches of keys. He loves her for her work but just as much for the sorrow she's seen because it's something deep and old, something he could really help with.

And he's struck to stillness by the stories of her life. Sometimes when she talks about her family, especially her father Emmett, he is silenced. Words can't find their way out of him when Jessie speaks about Emmett.

At first he was amazed by the stories of Emmett's behaviour and decided the man must have been mentally ill. That time he dragged the little Jessie from her bed, cracking her head on the floor, leaving her concussed with a huge swelling egg on her temple, left his heart thudding and she hadn't even told him about the other kids.

But then other times he hears love in Jessie's voice when she speaks of him, and it puzzles him. How can you love a monster? Why would you?

When she's with her brothers and sister and they're talking about Emmett, then he knows she's lost to him, but he doesn't mind one bit. Seeing her happy and involved and buoyed up by them is a relief. Took him a whole year to work out that whatever is wrong with Jessie is wrong with them all and it's well beyond his simple healing.

But love is a strange beast. He's always thought Emmett Brown was a pompous bore, a chronic alcoholic and probably manic depressive. Sounds simple when you say it fast but give it a lifetime, and make him your father, and it's a whole different thing.

*

That Saturday morning in the hollow of quiet that descends on people without children, Jessie watches the seeds and she sees the shape of the wind moving them, the hills and the valleys. The seeds might seem to have one flight in them but they lift themselves again and again like helicopters into the breeze and then discarded, they mount up near the back door as she imagines snow might in Canada. She always wanted to go to Canada. Neil Young comes from there. When she first heard that thin voice singing 'Harvest', she was gone and Canada was sanctified.

Jessie and Warren's place lies between two train stations and the trains pass rhythmically in a loop of sound that suggests cattle thundering in a canyon. The sound is trapped and early in the mornings when the trains first start up the clattering echos in the basin of the streets.

Next door, up in the flats, the Vietnamese woman lays her washing along the railings and ties it down with plastic-coated wire already in place. Jess raises a hand in a gesture of friendliness and shyly, the woman bows back. Jessie feels moved to say; 'You have a lot of washing today.' The old woman nods and wordlessly retreats into the flat, as silent as air.

There are birds passing in the highways of the air, sluicing their way towards other places. If this were Canada they might be migrating and wouldn't that be something? Great clouds of wings heading somewhere. But we don't have migratory birds, she thinks, and casts the dregs of her coffee into the flourishing weeds that make up her garden. She believes the only thing this place has in common with Canada is air.

Jessie still works in the Rainbow women's refuge and for all that, she's not completely humourless. Sometimes she laughs with the women who come to see her for advice, but she does this just to see them smile and when they do she gets a glimpse of who they might be. Her sense of humour, like her mother's, is held in reserve.

She doesn't allow herself much emotion at work. Keeps a tight rein. It's no accident that she works where she does, she understands the connections, but she's ruthlessly professional and effective.

Feminists who worry about politics are cracked, she reckons. From where she stands, life and death are the things that count and life can be very short when your husband is a brute. Her intensity is legend and intimidating.

*

The sisters' relationship has spun out after Louisa's illness and they never get back to the jokey ease of where they once were. They take turns but usually Jessie taunts and Louisa resents, and each strives to be Anne's Most Beloved Daughter.

Jessie makes up ground with her mother when Louisa is sick with long chats on the phone in the evening. On those nights, over at the desk, Warren sighs beside a cold cup of coffee while he marks an endless, teetering pile of indecipherable school work, half of it on torn paper, one on kitchen paper.

Jess sees him slumped there, giving each child's effort his all, and watches as he writes half a page of encouragement and wonders why she doesn't throw down the phone and go to him, put her arms around him and tell him she loves him. It's a fleeting thought. He knows she loves him, she thinks tartly, of course he does.

After a while on the phone, listening to her mother talk about the other, it dawns on Jess that Anne always loves the one she's not with, and listening to her mother's intimate worries about the others makes her long to ask: what about me?

But the rules say she must continue steadfastly and she reckons she could listen for Australia. She notes the peeling wallpaper in the room, the pile of clean clothes that must be put away and that she needs to cut her toenails. But for Anne the real question is, when is Robbie going to find a nice girl? One who fully understands and supports him.

Anne hasn't been told what's wrong with Louisa but she knows something's up because she hasn't heard from her in a long while and distance makes her special. She will be told, but not until it's almost over. 'Those children are running her into the ground,' she tells Jess. 'Mmm, I know,' Jess says, as the feathery cat settles and curls on her lap. 'I know.'

The solitary light from the porch is still on and it steals through the curtains. Jess can tell that Anne is smoking while she talks, because she hears her mother's long hungry drags. But then Jess is puffing away too. Neither mentions it to each other because each thinks the other is giving up. And suddenly Jess can't talk about Louisa for another second. She could scream. 'I'm sure she's just been busy Mum,' she says calmly, though Anne notes her terseness.

Jess doesn't even consider having children. She's seen them grind her sister down, take all the spark away from her and make her into a sad old bag. That's family life for you, she thinks brightly, and anyway she's got her causes to keep her busy. Battered women, animal rights and now she's become a vegetarian. Pays to maintain your focus, she believes. And anyway, Warren doesn't seem fussed about kids. He teaches so many he reckons he can do without his own, so the pressure to breed is absent. Anne's not pushing it either. 'You've got enough on your plate,' she says and adds ominously, 'and believe me, your life is not your own once you have children.'

*

The old elm tree in Jess's backyard is getting more ragged every day. It's too big for the space. Lost half of itself in Tuesday's recent storm of the century but didn't do much more than fall on the decrepit side fence and split it. So that was good.

Pete and Rob turn up one bright Saturday to trim up the elm, and Rob leaves the place shrouded in swirling sawdust. Pete sweeps a bit and leans on the broom a bit more.

'Lovely day, Woz,' he smiles. He messes around with the dogs, passing the broom in small circles so they jump up and chase it. 'Whaddya reckon Wozza, how're the mighty Dogs gonna go this year?'

'I haven't the faintest clue Pete, it's all beyond me, as you well know.'

'Now Woz, we've had this talk, 'member, and we sorted it. You agreed that you were going to be a staunch and even a defiant Dogs supporter. Don't tell me you're backtracking?' He smiles and waves the broom again at Bert the old kelpie cross and the wind blows sawdust and elm leaves around in eddies.

Warren smiles weakly. 'You really shouldn't tease me Pete, it's hard enough trying to make sense out of Jess. With two of you, I've got no hope.' He brings out the radio and it drones on, a hose of noise in the background, and then out of nowhere, while they are sweeping, Warren turns to Peter and reports shyly, 'The Dogs are doing well this year because of the new coach.'

Pete laughs and says, 'Well, you've floored me there, but I'm bloody proud. It's true mate, he cannot possibly be worse than the old one.'

At lunchtime when he sees the cupboard is bare, Pete nips down to the shops and buys four pies and a bottle of tomato sauce that, amazingly, Warren doesn't use, much to the horror and possibly even to the mild disgust of the Browns.

Pete forgets about Jessie's new vegetarian thing so Rob eats her pie while Pete makes her a toasted cheese. She's a bit snaky about them not remembering she's a vego but even as she tries not to make too big a deal about it, she impales them. 'You're disgusting carnivores, the lot of you,' she says more fiercely than she means. Rob looks up from his second pie and laughs. 'Be surprised if there was much meat at all in these pies,' he says with a wink at Warren. 'Maybe some ears and noses though. And a few tails.'

Jess looks at him and her eyes narrow and some part of her sees the humour. The other part is happier, though, seeing Pete bringing her a hot, melty cheese sandwich.

45

Anne is beginning to think Peter will never marry. He's moved around a bit over the years and now he's back at the shop. One Thursday afternoon, he settles back at his desk in the second small bedroom upstairs and looks through the bamboo blinds into the sideway between the shop and the chemist next door. The sky has taken on the honey colour of early evening and he pulls up the blind to catch more. Some of the gold drifts in but between the two buildings he can catch only a sliver. The computer screen holds itself before him briefly but soon falls into saving itself. He wonders how you save yourself. There's a soapstone owl on his desk, a little gift from his first girlfriend, Gloria, who thought he was wise. He often holds it, looking for a wisdom transfer. He puts it down and decides he needs a walk.

Out in the street, Lily Baxter's barrel of a dog, Ned, charges snorting and snuffling straight at Pete, mouth wide open like some deepwater fish. Lily Baxter takes off after the dog, grabbing at his collar and saying, 'Sorry . . . Ned's a bit of a stickybeak, but look at that, he likes you already.' She smiles. 'It's fine,' he says, patting the squat sepia animal. 'He's a great dog. What is he?'

The dog props magnetically on his shoe, he's not going anywhere. 'He's a Staffie, not pure bred, his mother was a seal by the look of him.' She laughs. Pete grins and keeps patting. He's seen Lily before and knows they went to the same primary school. He recalls it instantly. By grade six, girls were becoming real to him and one lunchtime always stays with him. He was on the bitumen not far from some girls. He spent a good part of the time watching Lily Baxter and her mates play hoppie.

Now here she is right in front of him outside the shop. You'll get nowhere and you know it, he tells himself, sternly turning. They're never interested in you. But Lily has been chatting and he's already stunned himself by inviting her to come fishing with him one day. 'You wanta try surfing,' she says amiably. 'Better than killing fish.' He laughs with reservation, amazed that anyone could think something so dumb.

'Says you.' She looks straight into his eyes. 'Yeah, I say it. Fish are alive just like you are alive. Fish have feeling too.' He's too flummoxed to reply, he's never heard anything like it. He peels Ned off and sends him back, but something makes him turn around. 'You went to West Footscray Primary, didn't you? Year below me. Never forget a pretty face.' He winces at the corny line. 'Wouldn't wanta teach me to surf, would ya?' She laughs as if that was all pretty funny but answers with a 'maybe' that gives him hope.

He's elated as he walks away in the completely wrong direction and must wait till she's gone to come back. Cannot believe how well that went, he says to himself. Upstairs, he settles down in his room and decides, that'll be the end of it, cannot possibly work out. He doesn't expect a thing. So when she drops in a few days later and catches him minding the shop, he's charmed and embarrassed. He makes her a cup of instant out the back and in one of those random, good long gaps between customers that shopkeepers both love and hate, they talk about everything from surfing to school days to the souls of fish.

Lily reckons surfing is what the gods would do if they still hung around here on earth, especially if they had access to Geelong Road. 'Think about it, at one with the sea, with the power of it, the colour of it, with the wind. With every single thing.' There's something in her that lifts him. She's studying nursing and working part-time. 'Bit of the old moolah never goes astray,' she says, rubbing her fingertips together in front of his face, her smile wide.

Apart from fishing, she never seeks to convert him. She gathers information on computer courses and leaves it in the van. She helps him apply. He dithers about kissing her, so she kisses him to get it out of the way. They're standing out the back of the shop on a fresh afternoon when the wind is whipping around and the sky is full of scattered cloud. Peter's being dilatory again, finding it hard to let her go, so Lily leans over, puts two hands on his face and pulls him to her.

Eventually they go surfing. Driving down to the Geelong Road through the flatlands past the You Yangs, the dark mountains on the side of the bay, heading ever onwards to the coast in the van and down there with her, he is healed by the ocean and by talking, and slowly he learns about having another partner against the immensity.

46

When she closed up the shop, Anne put up white nylon lace curtains in the windows out the front. The nylon washes so well, she thinks, and I can see out, but no one can see in. Not during daylight hours anyway. It won't be long now till Emmett's birthday and that means he'll finally be gone, out of the garage and away to the bush. Early retirement and a great fat cheque.

She wonders whether maybe he's got a girlfriend or something. He's rarely there and when he is, he doesn't seem part of the place, he still sits in the garage slaving away at those bloody probabilities. Honestly, if he'd only turned his mind to something useful or even sensible, God, imagine the difference. Still, it's water under the bridge now. Nothing is going to change Emmett. Not one solitary thing.

Anne says none of this worries her at all. He has ceased to be a concern, though she will admit to herself that the sooner he goes, the better and her life will go on with the hum of electricity in the wires out the front. Most mornings she's out there getting the graffiti off the pink-tiled wall between her place and the Indian restaurant next door with the kind of energy the young might envy.

She's absolutely determined that order will prevail. Yet change is everywhere and it springs upon her. The local bank branch closes up and the library branch is gone and so is the swimming pool, the post office is now a shop and the old weatherboard Presbyterian Church is a Chinese Christian Centre.

The fish-and-chip shop is run by a Korean named Mr Kim whom Anne admires for his scrupulous cleanliness; every Friday she gets her tea from him. Once, she gave one of his African customers a dollar when he couldn't buy a piece of flake because he was short. When she handed the coin to him, he looked like he was about to be struck. He held the glowing coin in his palm and was dumbfounded. So was Anne by her unexpected generosity.

The next wave of people pushes through the old suburb. Within a stone's throw, there are two Indian clothes shops, an Indian hardware and a video and grocery store with little speakers out the front, sharing tinny music with the street. The subcontinent has moved to West Footscray. 'Well,' explains Anne to her old friend Maria who lives in Melton, 'the Vietnamese snaffled Footscray long ago.'

*

Emmett eternally believes he's got a chance with Lady Luck. He's in the garage crunching his numbers one sulphurous Sunday afternoon. When the boys arrive for a working bee, he emerges and greets them effusively. 'Mate,' he says to Pete, hugging him and gives Rob a quick pat on the shoulder, which Rob doesn't fail to notice. Then he's off back to his room. 'Be out in a tick and give you a hand,' he shouts through the open door. 'I'm onto a big one now. The numbers are coming out just right.'

It's so hot the sky pulses at them and after two hours Pete sticks his head under the hose and heads off to find Emmett in his old Bonds T-shirt and checked boxers, snoring like a hammer drill.

He stands in the doorway gazing in for quite a while and then he shuts the door softly and goes back to work. 'Dad's taken a sickie,' he says.

Sweat eases things between Rob and Pete. They have long held a deal about helping each other with big jobs. Problem is, Rob does most of the asking. Pete reckons his time will come.

Today the topic is property values. Everyone's doing up the old places and making a fortune. Easy money. 'So there you go. Isn't that just typical,' Rob says sourly to Pete as they shovel under the hot sun. 'The Browns lose out again, but look on the bright side, some things stay the same and we've still got the worst house in the street. Ha!'

It grates that Wolf Street, with its Edwardian trim of three mingey tulips would now be worth far more than the shop. Behind it the petrol station is boarded up and hazard signs sag across the fractured concrete and the cyclone fencing, and down the road there's a bar called Glide or Slide or something evocative. People sit in the sun and smoke and talk on mobile phones and read the broadsheet and drink expensive coffee with far too much milk.

Can this really be Footscray? Louisa wonders, noting with slight concern taut little houses that used to be dumps. She's driving over to help the boys with a bit of backyard blitzing. She's easing herself back in slowly and decides that a bit of physical work might be a good idea.

Tom and Beck are in the back seat bickering over the PlayStation, and she ignores them resolutely with new determination won from her clinic. Her psychiatrist, Dr Emmeline Mackenzie, is a big woman with sad, oyster eyes whose silver crew cut hinges on her cow's lick and gives her the look of an elderly schoolboy. Louisa has never known anyone so composed.

She's trying to become like Dr Mackenzie, so she tells herself she's looking forward to seeing her brothers. Will Jess show up? Regardless of the good doctor, she hopes not, can't face the Princess today. But walking down the narrow sideway between the two shops she feels the vibe between Rob and Pete and realises there's a sulk underway and would you believe it, poor old Jess is nowhere in sight.

'Mum should never have moved to the bloody shop,' Rob hisses at Pete as they shovel up the old tree roots they've dug out of the backyard. They are planning to pave but it's a pure fact that work without pay tends to make him real irritable.

'Stop whingeing Rob. Only makes it worse. This was your idea anyway,' Pete retorts, dragging the shovel back to the beginning of the pile again and wiping the sweat off his face. His dirty hair stands at attention.

'I'm trying to talk to you, you perfect bloody saint, but that's clearly impossible.' Rob waits his turn at the pile and they go on grimly in silence. Louisa walks in and says, 'G'day you lot,' and grabs the shovel. 'I'll have a go, you go get a drink,' she tells Rob who lets go of it and heads for the kitchen. Tom and Beck, ears flapping like flags, follow him inside. A pair of ducklings.

'How is he?' she asks Pete. 'Grumpy as all shit,' Pete says, wiping his face, and they laugh just that bit too loud and she thinks, great, now Robert will think we're laughing at him. 'C'mon Rob, you bludger,' she yells, 'we need you out here.' In the kitchen Rob is engrossed in the classified housing ads. The kids sitting beside him twiddle the PlayStation in turns.

*

Anne ages like a leaf. She goes from being green and strong to lighter, frailer and dry. If you'd told her that, she'd laugh. She likes old autumn leaves, well, she likes most old things. Louisa visits once a week.

They sit at the blackwood table and have a mug of tea. Louisa thinks she comes for tea and grievances. It's always teabags, which really grates on Louisa who hates them but imagines Anne doesn't know this since she never says. All pure foolishness. Anne knows most things. She leaves Lou's teabag in longer to make the tea strong.

Anne's hands are knotted with arthritis and she warms them around her flowery mug. Light shines off the porridge-coloured bricks next door and the glare is cast in. From where she's sitting, you can just see a triangle of sky between the fence and the bricks.

Their conversations ramble around lightly like the spring breeze and they touch on most things – the interpretation of the roses, easy recipes, getting the best out of children, missing bin night and what to do when it happens, worries at work, bills, weight, television – but really they're talking about knowing each other. About the way between them.

Anne often speaks about her parents, George and Rose. 'They look after me, I know they do, and they are always with me,' Anne says in her enduring way. This, as ever, slightly annoys Louisa. Maybe it's just jealousy, maybe she wishes she had these kind of stories too but Louisa has never felt anyone looking out for her.

Anne remembers how her father, apart from the six years he was at the war, would bring Anne and Rose vegemite on toast and a cup of tea in the mornings. He'd put the toast under the griller while the kettle was boiling to keep it warm.

So how then, Louisa wonders privately with a long nurtured sense of outrage, did you allow Emmett to be our father when you had such a father?

Louisa pushes away at the story of her family but the mystery of Emmett is the layer that separates them. Anne wonders why her kids will never let it go but she doesn't ask them, she wouldn't hurt them for all the world. The blessing of these children is in every part of her.

When Louisa presses into the dark landscape Anne will say, 'I don't know why I didn't leave him, but I had little children and he would have come after us and where would I have gone? There were no single mother's pensions then, and I'm glad young women have them now. I couldn't have taken you kids home to Mum and Dad, it would not have been fair, there were so many of you and he was dangerous.'

And Louisa gets heated sometimes when talk turns to Emmett. She grips her mug and the hot tan liquid moves a bit too fast. She looks up at the herbs Anne has placed near the fingers of sunlight just missing the window ledge. They've grown gangly reaching for the light. Listening to her mother sometimes requires an act of will and subjugation of her instinct.

'My way of handling him was to ignore him. His terrible displays. It was the only way, anything could make it worse. I could take what he dished out. I was tough.'

It takes Louisa some effort to speak against her mother but one day she does. Louisa says, 'That's true Mum, you were tough and you are tough now, but we were not tough. We were little kids.'

*

Louisa looks out into Dr Mackenzie's garden and the tall white anemones move in the breeze. She begins with simplicity. 'My father was overbearing. He's still alive but he's sick and old.' She holds her hands in her lap until they start to feel hot and fat. Where do you begin with the story of Emmett? The elastic silence stretches around them. Dr Mackenzie is prepared to wait.

233

And then Louisa blurts, 'It feels like our childhood wasn't acknowledged. That because we survived, well, most of us did, then it's all right.'

'What do you mean "most of us"?' Dr Mackenzie asks. She has a notebook on her lap and her big hand is jotting steadily. Louisa wants to stop her from writing. Writing makes things real.

And so the welling arises in her and her voice goes its own way again. 'There was another one of us.' She coughs to clear the past but it doesn't work. 'He was named Daniel. My brother Peter's twin. He fell over one night running from Dad and he hit his head, fractured his skull actually, and he died.' The doctor writes and then lets her eyes rest on Louisa who weeps for much longer than is sensible, considering this happened so long ago and also that money is being paid and the clock is ticking. And then she smiles at the truth of her being her mother's daughter regarding money, and Dr Mackenzie passes her a box of tissues. Louisa can't stop taking them, she takes at least eight. She wants so much.

When Rob first hears that Louisa will need to take medication all her life to guard against her depression, he's not astonished. He's felt the weight of such anchors within him too. But knowing this hasn't done a thing for Louisa. She's sick to death of the family looking at her as if she's not herself and it irks her that they think they might all get it too, as if it were the flu. All they think about are themselves, she thinks. All anyone thinks about.

Rob was particularly annoying when he slipped into his pet theory that whatever Louisa has, Emmett had too. She wants nothing to do with Emmett. 'Do you think I'm like him?' she asks incredulously. He doesn't answer. She realises she shouldn't have said anything to him, it only fuels discussions later. She can just see Jessie and Anne getting stuck into a bit of character analysis on the side. She decides to say as little as she can to anyone.

Visiting Dr Mackenzie each week and talking about Emmett are the fastest hours of her life. The doctor tells Louisa it would be a mistake to turn her hate for her father back onto herself, and Louisa is clobbered by the realisation that Dr Mackenzie thinks she hates Emmett. 'Oh no. I don't hate him,' she spits out baldly. 'I've only told you part of it, he wasn't all bad.' Then she revises and ends up saying, 'But since I was a child there have been plenty of times when I've just wanted to lie down on the road and let him run me over.' And she groans at her own ineptitude and imprecision.

The doctor writes fast again and, while she does, Louisa tries to correct impressions. Feels like her old interview subjects must have felt. 'It wasn't,' she begins, 'it was just . . .'

So she starts to hold back on detail. The main thing she wants to settle is guilt about leaving Jessie, which still affects her. Talking to Jess is not easy. Emmett isn't curable. 'You need to think about why you felt so responsible,' she hears the doctor say, 'and then you will have your answer.' And then it's the end and Louisa tries to keep Dr Mackenzie talking, but she just rises with her sad smile and opens the door because the fifty minutes are up.

Outside, walking to the train, she recalls in a flash of resistance that she felt responsible because she was. How's that supposed to help? she wonders, watching the city pass and recoiling from the gaudy, suggestive billboards as if they were an assault.

47

Some days it seems too far. Some days Emmett fears he won't get to retirement. He wants it too much. You just can't want things, he thinks, some bastard will always try to stop ya. Days he drives to work wondering whether he'll even live that long. Probably cark it right before the payout, he tells himself, and wouldn't that be just bloody typical? He's got a cold and the headaches just keep coming.

If he makes it to the appointed day he plans to move away from the shop, from Anne, from every single bloody thing he knows. He wants to be clean again, to be new somewhere with people who don't know him. And the bush is where he was born. If he'd stayed there maybe things wouldn't have got so stuffed up. Ah, who knows, he sighs, weaving through the back streets on his way to work, past all the sardine houses jammed together. All this would surely drive anyone mad he reckons.

He's not fussy where he ends up, bush people are much of a muchness to him. Just wants somewhere small, somewhere with a couple of paddocks and a whole lot of sky. He doesn't need his family, believes they're better off without him. When they look at me, he reckons, they see too much.

*

Eventually, Emmett retires to Deakin, a small town of about five hundred people nestled near the granite mountains rising abruptly from the plains near Ballarat. He's been there a while in the crooked little house with three small paddocks. And he so loves all that sky and every inch of it his.

Rob calls Ballarat the 'Prague of the South' and he believes he's onto something with that description because, though he's never been to Prague, he's seen pictures. 'Moving up near Ballarat eh Dad? Not a bad idea, it's a gracious city, not unlike Prague, I hear.'

'What in the name of Christ *are* you talking about?'

Rob's mouth goes dry. 'Prague, you know, in Czechoslovakia, I was just saying they had something in common.'

'Jesus, spare me the crap will ya? It's just Balla-bloody-rat,' Emmett smirks around the room at the others and blows a spray of foam off his beer.

Rob and Louisa stay well away from Deakin. Had enough of the old man to last them forever. Jessie too, though she does write him a letter when he first moves in and in it she lists his faults in exact, concise and lawyerly prose. Everything from violence and drinking to his abuse of Anne and his meanness with money. Jessie feels better for having written it.

Emmett gets out the magnifying glass and reads the letter, all of it, and is proud of the way she put things, bloody well-educated, he thinks. Who would have thought little Jess had it in her? Turned out to be the smartest of the lot. What she actually says is highly exaggerated in his view, but still, you've got to respect anyone who can write a letter like that.

On Sunday nights Peter calls Emmett and they talk, about firewood and cattle and fences and kids, though when mention is made of his grandchildren, Emmett phases out. With grandchildren, he reckons the trick is to compress them all into one bottler, a halfway decent kid. It's the only way.

'Dad, it's coming up to your sixtieth and I think we should do something special for it. What d'ya reckon?'

Emmett's had a good day messing around in his vegie garden. He likes talking to Pete, he reminds him of someone. 'Yeah, ripper mate, what do *you* reckon?' 'Well,' says Peter. 'I could help you with it if you like. I'll come up early that morning.' Emmett puts the phone down wondering what that was all about. And when the day arrives even the birthday is long forgotten.

*

The morning of the big day he's in the kitchen in his tattered old boxers and saggy grey singlet. His legs are thin as sticks and white and nearly hairless but the ghost of the beer belly is still evident. He's standing there in the middle of the kitchen trying to work out where in hell the bloody teapot's gone when he hears a thump at the door.

As ever, his first response to surprise is fury. Unexpected bangs on the door drive him crazy. All visitors risk being sent packing. At the first knock he pretends it's a figment of his imagination but this makes things worse because, encouraged by silence, people just bang louder.

It takes him a while to get to the door because his feet are sore lately and he's hobbling and when at last he opens it, he sees a grinning Louisa balancing a huge box stuffed with food. 'Happy birthday Dad,' she says, stepping neatly over Clancy the dog, ankle-high and just the right height to skittle people. Behind her Peter is yelling, 'Happy birthday you old bastard,' and carrying a couple of bags of ice. 'Louisa,' Emmett says following her, 'what are you doing here?'

Peter called her last night to ask if she could help with Emmett's birthday. 'You're the only one who can really cook,' he points out diplomatically and smiling, and seeing she taught him how to cook in the first place, she reckons this is a hide. 'We can use the van, I've got it all packed up. And I'll come down with you to set up the spit. Okay?'

Though she couldn't explain it to herself, agreeing came easy. Doing it for Pete, she rationalises, make him happy, but there's something else too, something about birthdays. She remembered the time Emmett took her into Myers to buy her a book for her birthday and then to a little Chinese joint for lunch and they got the book out and started it right there in the red glowing restaurant, Emmett whispering different voices for the characters. It was *A Christmas Carol* by Dickens and it was the first time she'd ever been sorry when the food arrived. When they put the book in the bag, it seemed the best of her father went away with it.

*

The morning of Emmett's birthday Peter went to his local deli as soon as it opened and bought six fat loaves of soft Greek bread, all doughy and dense as sponges. 'This bread could be made by the gods themselves, of clouds,' Con the baker told him, pushing the floury loaves into bags. Peter smiled and agreed.

Greeks remind him of Emmett. Dad always loved wogs, he remembered putting the bread on the passenger seat, their food, their language; he thought they made us a better country, yet why did he call them wogs? Right and wrong, how come he was always so right and so wrong? Fair dinkum, you'd have to be a genius to work him out, Pete mused as he drove over to pick up Louisa.

Peter also organised for Nev the butcher in Deakin to get hold of a lamb. It turns out to be a whopper, at least a two-tooth, in fact, the thing's verging on sheep size.

The spit is in the back of the van and a box of supplies with extra-virgin olive oil, garlic, dried Greek oregano, sea salt and twelve lemons.

Pete steps outside into the fresh air with the ice bags, puts them down while he cleans the leaves and sticks out of the old bath in the hay shed. This takes a while because there's some kind of tarry blackness there too, a remnant of some other dubious thing, but he gets it all out and in the end he sits the beer and lemonade in the clean bath and pours the ice around it, loving the crunch and hiss.

Then he gets a nice low coalfire glowing in the half-gallon drum and sets up the spit over it. Tests the thing and after a while yells to Louisa, 'And yes, Houston, we have lift-off!' It's windy now but he realises it's always windy in Deakin. He watches the curtain of air sweep across the open plains, herding gum leaves before it and making washing on lines reach ever outwards like supplicants. At Emmett's old prop clothesline, he takes down a tangled shirt and a pair of trousers that might have been there for months and carries them into the house rolled into a ball.

Emmett means to help but mostly he scratches his head because he doesn't remember where things are but today he's not getting mad about it. He's all right today. Normally not knowing is just the sort of thing that sets him right off. On the tele Louisa finds a calming game of distant cricket and he's drawn in. He mutes the TV and listens to the ABC broadcast on the wireless. There's a little delay between the picture and sound, but he's not watching all that carefully anymore and this way he avoids the hot noise flare of the ads. Before too long, he's dozing in his chair.

Louisa has cake tins and an electric mixer plus all the ingredients for Victoria sponges, including strawberries and cream, and she gets stuck into making a birthday cake. Baking — but in truth, all cooking — settles Louisa. She likes the magic of creation from variable ingredients, likes the mixing and the tasting. Best part of cooking, she believes, is feeding people.

Cakes are special though and deeply satisfying. But no one is harder on herself and her creations than Louisa. She's after perfection and yet when it does come, perfection is not triumphant, it's simply benign and welcome.

The rest of the family are used to her comforting hobby and mostly they oblige her when she hovers holding hot spoons to their lips and asking them to judge. But ultimately her efforts are wasted because most of Emmett's scenes began at the table and they all have a complicated relationship with food. They eat fast and seldom notice how wonderful it is. For the Browns, food is eternally something to be bolted.

They wrap dozens of potatoes in foil and bury the big silver spuds in the coals and while the cakes are cooking, Louisa makes Emmett a tomato and onion sandwich and a cup of tea.

The tomato, a round flat Adelaide she's grown herself, is rich with flavour and still somehow holds the hot smell of summer that emerges from the best tomatoes at the first cut. She scatters salt and white pepper on it and when Emmett bites into the sandwich he taste the richness of love, the love that would last him, and it's so unexpected it makes him shy.

'Not a bad tomato Lou,' he says, glancing up at her away from the TV, 'not bad at all.'

Peter and Louisa clean the table, scrubbing it with sleeves up. They lay the animal out and place rosemary mixed with slivers of garlic (sliced and peeled by Emmett with much comment and complaints about 'fiddly bloody wog tucker') in the small cuts. They rub it down with oil as though they were massaging a sportsman. Both of them sprinkle dried oregano over the lamb. And then outside they hook the animal onto the spit and stand back watching the dull orange coals do their work. Soon the rising smell calls everything to it and Clancy, drooling, sits beside them intently watching the roasting meat.

'Would not call a king me bloody Uncle Bill,' Emmett says and Peter laughs. 'No, me neither Dad. Not today.' Half the people who used to work with Emmett don't make it to Deakin for the big day. Most can't be bothered with him and none of his duck-shooting mates show up either.

Jessie makes a late appearance with Warren who looks lost and puzzled and, as he always does around Jessie's family, left right out. He perches on the arm of a chair and closely examines the label on his beer bottle until Anne takes pity on him and they talk about school.

Rob and Louisa watch from the wings under a ravaged hibiscus, discussing Emmett with the air of experts. Having the old lion in their sights in the open with the protection of others around them is a kind of completion.

There's plenty of beer of course and Emmett's invited his mates around from the pub; there's Reg and big fat Nev brings some special pork sausages he's been working on. The barbie is tamed for the snags. Nev thought a bit of chilli would add that certain zing but as usual he overdoes it. The snags are so spicy that people are gasping like stranded fish and some nick ice from the bath to slide into their burning mouths.

But turning sixty isn't all fun. Emmett and Rob nearly collide on the back step. Emmett happily flourishes the barbeque tongs like a conductor. He snaps them together and tells Rob to lighten up, that it's his birthday. 'Mate, you've got a face as long as a fiddle. It's a man's birthday. You're standing there like a stunned mullet! Cheer bloody up! That's a order.' And he snaps the tongs again.

Rob flinches. 'And what's so great about that? We supposed to be happy that you were born?' As soon as he says it, he's sorry for the remark. He blames the wine. He hadn't meant to reveal anything.

Emmett decides he can't blame the poor bastard but it's about time the boy woke up to the fact that life is shit for everyone, not just for him. Wouldn't mind telling him me own story one day, he thinks, and in the same breath realises it would not make one iota of difference.

So he snaps the tongs again and heads back to the barbie to turn the snags for the hundredth time. Peter carves the lamb and places the fragrant meat upon the bread and the guests fall upon the food like the starving multitudes and for a brief moment Louisa and Pete look at each other and they smile.

Then casually, as if expected, a gleaming red CFA fire truck decked out in blue and white streamers for Emmett's old footy team arrives out the front. Reg leans on the horn. 'Get in you old bastard,' he roars when an astonished Emmett opens the gate. 'You, son, are going for your birthday ride!'

Emmett is both appalled and charmed. 'Well, bugger me,' he gasps, hanging onto the saggy gate. His face crumples and he nearly cries, but he tells himself to be a man and so he roars with laughter and throws his arm around the nearest person and that happens to be Rob.

On being engulfed by Emmett, Rob stiffens but this doesn't worry his father. He just drags him out the gate to sit on the back of the truck, their legs swinging, Rob's reluctantly. Jessie climbs aboard too. Pete handballs a new leather footy at them and Rob marks it, giving it to Emmett who at last has something else to hold. Louisa and Anne, standing beside the fence like pillars of another life, are shocked. This is not the Emmett they know.

And slowly, gingerly, the truck draws away as if it has something special on board. The Browns wave to each other, relieved that Emmett has cooperated. There's a bit of waving and then the fire truck bumps off into the wide empty country street.

48

It's late April, autumn is feeling its power and the pinoaks that line the road to Deakin are becoming as red as the fires of January. Under each of the pinoaks lies a little brass plate inscribed with the name and rank of a man who died in the First and Second World Wars and this is where Emmett goes to talk. He's long given up on God so now he goes to have a yak to the dead soldiers. Reckons his own disappeared old man might even be one of them. Took off when he was a baby. Would you believe, on the night of the baby show too. The night when he'd won most beautiful baby in the whole bloody show; just shows the worth of a pretty bloody face. He laughs and takes a sip from his stubby.

He's sitting in the little striped aluminum chair he brings down here and Clancy's running around chasing myxo bunnies while he talks to the old boys and you know what, he doesn't bignote at all to them, not like he used to with God. No need these days. When he first heard the news about the workings of his brain, it felt like something he'd known, something from way back. Had to be. And it didn't surprise him because life works that way (you pay for every single bloody thing).

It was not long after the ride on the fire truck, a day when he was truly happy, that he got the news that he had a form of dementia that is rapid and irreversible. He'd suspected for a while that something was going on upstairs. He knew he was losing his brains. And he reckoned he deserved it. Served him right. Abso-bloody-lutely.

*

He's stilled by terror as they slide him like a tadpole into the mouth of the imaging machine. He doesn't even hear the technician telling him not to move. He is not connected to his body, he's entered limbo. His left eye twitches. He'd rather be in a pub brawl any bloody day. That Emmett's brain is not normal is not a surprise to any member of the family. But it's a while before anyone explains precisely how bad things are.

Another test in Ballarat reveals more but he must wait to see the specialist in Melbourne. That is the day he knows with perfect certainty that he's departing. He walks away from the hospital hoping a bus will run him over, but he has no luck and he smiles to himself that truly he was never a lucky bastard.

How fast will it be? he wonders, cracking the windows to let the heat out of the car. He drives past the red trees and feels tears pushing at him. On the way home he buys a slab of light beer as a gesture to wellness.

It turns out that Emmett's brain is a sieve of leaking blood vessels. He's had too many small strokes to count. His memory is draining away even as they speak to him. The brain is largely scar tissue. This will be a fast decline. It won't be long before he won't know himself. And yet, for one precious month, he tells no one but the soldiers.

By winter, his chooks have been eaten by foxes and Mrs Thompson the cat has shot through, he hopes to a better place. Clancy was not so lucky, he was run over and a neighbour brought his body back to Emmett and they buried him under the lilac.

He looks at his budgie, Hooley Dooley in the little cage, and decides the time has come so he takes him out to the paddock swinging in his wire cage and releases the little bird. It's one of his last deliberate acts. He watches the small blue speckled wings rising into the blueness with a kind of tearing pain. And though he will never remember it, at the time he believes he's going with Hooley to live in a corner of the sky.

Still, he starts a new diary because he reckons it might save him. 'Diaries give you a new start,' he says aloud to himself. He's always believed in the power of words, and in the diary he asks questions he can read to Anne when she rings to check on him each night. One of them is, 'What is the name of that island where Pete worked? It's shaped like a . . . you know.' He draws a diamond but can't say what shape it is. Anne tells him it's Tasmania. By the time he reads the questions out, he's lost interest in the answers.

49

Anne measures the days of her life by the TV guide. She has her favourites and one of them is the TV judge, a tough old girl who whips hopeless dills right into gear. She's got it all worked out. Possibly Anne sees something of herself in the judge. Tiny, frugal and sensible, but not without a smidgin of compassion.

She still sews for her friends and old customers, the gold light from the desk lamp funnelling upon her. The whirring of the machine is the current between the past and the present. Anne has sewed her way through life, joining one day to the next, her head bent over her labours, her hands smoothing each day through the jaws of the old machine.

She does her best thinking when she sews and some of her thoughts surprise her. To be old is not the way she thought it would be. People listen to you less and even look at you less. But you don't stop being yourself just because you've lived a long time. You get wiser and quieter and less hopeful. Much less.

When Emmett comes home sick, lost and frail, holding the little airline bag he used to take to work, she tells him to put it on the stool.

'Sit down Emmett. Over there on that chair, yes that one.'

'I don't want to get in your way.'

'You won't,' she says, and gets up from the machine. Rob comes in carrying a box of kitchen things from Deakin.

Emmett seems to retreat and Anne watches the decline with a painful honesty about her history with him. She lost interest in him for a long part of the marriage when she believed he was insane. She's not happy about the way things went. But madness is madness and who was going to help the family?

Now she realises that it might have been better to get the kids out of there but at the time she just kept going, plodding through each day not expecting much. Never expecting things to be better. To survive a day was a triumph.

Yet still she remembers the good more than the bad and maybe good comes from the same place as the bad. Who knows? Maybe it's the place where there is no control. And, honestly, Emmett always knew joy more than anyone.

After Daniel died she couldn't bear to be near him, well, he just made her skin crawl. He was more horrified than anyone about Daniel's death. Wallowing around thinking it was all about him, but then Emmett never noticed anyone but himself. So in the way that time moves, slowly and without argument, she gave up on him. Drifted away, didn't question him, hoped he'd move and in a way he did, he moved to the pub.

Now he's sick and back here again and she sees that within the terrible man and even within the pathetic man there's another one, a gentler one. Was he always locked up within Emmett? He wanders from room to room picking things up and putting them down. He smiles at her when she brings him food.

He sits in the yard near the lemon tree, with her little dog beside him. The weather passes through the day. Waiting, just waiting. Seeing this Emmett brings back something of her first love and makes it harder, but then none of it is easy and she thinks maybe I should have told the kids how hard things can be. But they wouldn't like to hear it, she decides. Who on earth would?

50

Food provides the answer to most of Louisa's questions. She often cooks for Anne and for Emmett as if it will just do the trick. She nourishes her herbs and finds a butcher who can prepare the cuts of meat she likes. She goes to the old market once a week and with real discipline buys the best produce she can afford. Often she meets Peter there and they take pleasure in the place.

'Have you ever seen a more beautiful peach?' she asks him on a summer Saturday as they stand before an altar of fruit. 'Let's buy one each for breakfast.' It seems a good idea but the dribbling is excessive and they end up dripping and laughing and flicking each other with peach juice. She tries to dry her hands on him but he gets sick of it and they look for a tap.

After she's towed Anne's ancient jeep to all their favourite stalls, they get coffee, strong and hot, and sit near the small lane that fronts onto the big junction at the top of the market. The lane reminds Louisa of a telescope that looks out to the world beyond. Everything is limpid. People pass in the slowness of their lives and she sees them perfectly.

It isn't far from where Emmett worked as a child and the ghost of him lives here. She imagines him running around, laughing with his mates, a little scavenger let loose to feast on the body of the market. Let loose from the orphanage to his grandma's place opposite the market.

The child who became their father. Wonders again what really happened there. How would you ever know? But the stuff she's heard about orphanages in those days is not good.

She sent away for a Senate report on children who grew up in orphanages and when *Forgotten Australians* arrived she read it in a night. Stories of children with urine-soaked bedclothes tied to them, of beatings and starvation, and she thinks of those children now when she looks at her rapidly disintegrating father.

A coffee machine is revealed though a hole in the wall and the chugging and grinding of beans rips at her ears. In no time, Pete's back with the coffee. Chairs are in short supply and people juggling mugs and rolls bursting with sausage and onion often come chair-hunting. Peter is willing to give the chairs at their table to anyone. Around their feet, drab sparrows as round as hearts stab at the ground with their needle beaks. A couple of bolder ones land on the table in search of crumbs.

Somehow they've started to talk about Emmett, not something they usually do. Pete says that before Daniel died, he once asked Emmett if he loved him, and he laughed. He remembers the mouth opening up like a void. 'And that yellow eyetooth of his, God, I wondered whether he'd swallow me.'

He wished he could have had another father and such wishes took up acres in his heart. Long before he understood Emmett, or at least thought he did, he was held by what he'd seen and what he didn't understand, would never understand. When he decided Emmett was just a poor crazy man, mental for sure, he got over it. But he was lonely; after Daniel was gone, he had no one.

There are things Emmett did that the others don't know about and Peter will never tell them. Some things shouldn't be shared, how does it help? He reckons the others are dealing with enough of their own stuff anyway.

He's also a bit ashamed of the way he gathered his information. For a long time he was the watcher in doorways, listening as a kind of witness to his mother's weeping, waiting until he could hear her no longer, thinking that at least when it was quiet she had some peace. Then he'd go back to bed, his heart so heavy he ached with holding it.

'Most kids have some kind of monster in their past,' he says now, trying to lighten things. He's rolled up the paper tube that held the sugar into the tiniest scrap. He looks up and smiles at her. He won't dwell. The monster is sleeping in Peter's memory, though he's always on the lookout for it, you'd be a fool not to expect it back.

Louisa has not forgotten a single thing her father did either. Indeed, she has indexed them within herself and has a kind of inventory, but somehow she comes to the same decision as Peter. She must let it be. She explains Emmett to herself the best way she can. He must have been sick. Since she worked that out, the world seems less bleak.

But she doesn't tell Peter what she's decided, even though he has arrived at the same place. Neither is wholly comfortable with it, and neither has told Robert what they think.

They halt these talks, slowing down and looking around, and before too long they're discussing the pair of free-range rabbits she just bought. She's considering working some prunes and maybe bacon into the red wine braise she's planning for Anne and Emmett tonight. Pete says, 'How about a bit of mashed parsnip with that? The old man loves a bit of parsnip.' And he grabs the handle of the jeep and is off to a pyramid of parsnips further down the aisle while Louisa gets her coat on.

51

As they age, they all look more like Emmett. The wide face, the big eyes, the cheekbones, they might even be Slavic. But who cares anyway? As Emmett would once have said, 'We're all of us just plain old bastards like every bloody one else in the world. No one is anything special and that includes the Queen her Royal self.'

These days when he walks, Peter keeps his head down a little and there's a subtle stoop to his back. You can only see it from the right angle, but his thinness tells you all about it.

He likes plain clothes, square jackets with deep pockets. Shoes with thick treads that he wears until the uppers collapse. His hair is fading gently rather than going grey. When he lifts his face though, he's mostly smiling. And when he smiles hard, his eyes nearly disappear into the creases.

He lives with Lily in a cream weatherboard house in Flemington not too far from the river. All the trim, after much negotiation, is indigo. There are two windows at the front and a small verandah. Round the back, the park washing up to the back fence is rimmed with peppercorn trees. Peter used to regard them as weeds until Anne said she liked them and then he began to see the stringy beauty of them. He often likes things his mum likes. It seems that she knows the best things.

He works from home servicing Apple Macs. He's a computer technician with his own practice and he fits work around home duties. He cooks dinner every night and sometimes he still rings Louisa to talk about food. 'Tried the new season's asparagus yet? I got some really fat stalks the other day at the market . . .' Or 'Rocket pesto. What do you know about it?'

When anyone's in trouble Pete is on the phone talking a bit of calm into the situation. When Jess briefly wanted to leave Warren once years ago, it was Pete she combed through it with.

'He's such an old man, he just sits and corrects and he lectures me about whether or not I clean up the kitchen properly or not. He can just go jump, I've had him.'

'You're joking Jess,' he said to her, incredulous. 'You're not going to leave him 'cause he wants you to clean up after yourself, you're not really that mad, are you? Warren's got a lot going for him.' And then he listened while Jess talked herself into staying with Warren.

And Anne calls Peter when Emmett goes walkabout. He has the knack of finding the old bloke and that's true enough, though he's not deluding himself. She probably calls the others too but he's the only one who can spare the time. To Pete it doesn't matter much who finds Emmett, he's sick to death of the competitions with siblings, there's always one of them better at something than the others, always bloody will be.

The truth is, he finds Emmett three out of the five times he has bolted and the police get to him the other times. The first couple of times Emmett nicks off Anne is nearly hysterical, not at all like the most serene woman in the world. This day the side gate wasn't shut and Emmett has strolled out.

Peter grabs his coat, hops into the kombi and though he floors it, it still takes a while to move. He's heading from the Maribrynong River over to Footscray. The sky is a darkening dome and in the park the peppercorns are whipped by the cold wind.

Anne has called the police and is waiting in the kitchen in case, by some miracle, Emmett comes home. She's given the description to the young policewoman, a lass named Constable Schultz, who she tells Louisa, is really kind.

The Constable reads the description back to Anne: 'Elderly man, blue eyes, silver hair, wearing bottle-green cardigan, checked blue shirt and navy trousers with black braces, wearing Adidas running shoes. He has a Parker pen inscribed with *Emmett Brown*.' And it takes Anne a few seconds before she is able to speak.

*

Driving through Flemington, it hits Peter that Emmett will go home to the market. He doesn't ask how he knows stuff like this, he's just glad he does. He realises the knowledge is the same as when you're fishing; you just click into the larger consciousness and then you listen and it comes.

He knows he'll find the old man, but it takes longer than he imagined. He trawls those streets around the market for some time. It's not a market day so there are barely any people. A stray sheet of newspaper flaps like a bird past towers of stacked-up crates. And further off, way up in the grey, pigeons are swinging around in the clean wind. The sky is heavy with low-slung cloud.

It feels like there might be a downpour and though the drought is eternal and every single human being in the city is praying for rain, Peter prays it won't. The thought of Emmett getting drenched is not good. Poor old bastard wouldn't know what was going on.

He decides he'll see the old man better in the little lanes where the car can't pass, so he parks at a meter, fishes in the ashtray for a gold coin and then runs off with the coin in his hand, such is his panic.

It's at least another half an hour of scouring the streets around the market before he catches sight of Emmett, barefoot and moving surprisingly fast. Peter jogs up behind him and draws up level before he puts his hand on his shoulder and says, 'G'day Dad, where you heading on a grey old day like today?'

Emmett seems angry when he turns towards Pete. 'No time for that', he says crossly.

He's lost the dental plate that held in the false teeth (most of the teeth on one side went years ago in a fight) so a dark gap looms. He scowls and says urgently, 'I'm bloody late for tea. Nana'll kill me.' Pete agrees that he's late too and this works. 'You too, poor bugger eh?' Emmett says, and they both laugh as if it's the funniest thing they've ever heard.

Peter steers him over to the crates, gets him to sit down on one. Emmett tells Pete he has to see Chook and Eric, his mates. Peter doesn't know what he's talking about, so he asks him where his shoes are. Emmett doesn't hear him but he's jiggling his bloody feet around as if the ground were on fire. Little creeks of blood have sprung up everywhere on them.

Pete finds some jellybeans in his pocket and he pops a red one into his father's mouth. Emmett narrows his eyes and gets ready to eject and then the taste of sugar speaks, and he smiles a little sideways smile.

He chews the lolly vigorously on his good side then Peter puts his arm around him and guides him to the car. He's walking slowly now as if the air is all gone from his tyres. Getting him into the car scares him and he rises moth-like against the window. The glass confuses him. Is it there or what?

He doesn't like to sit, but Peter is patient and finally gets the seatbelt on him and he settles. At a phone box, he calls Anne and tells her he's found him and he hears her tears, though no mention is made. Emmett keeps trying to touch his bleeding feet and gets blood on his face.

They plough through the packed, pushing traffic and Peter thinks of distance and time and how it is so long ago and so far away from the days when Emmett was well. Who'd have thought dementia would improve anyone? Peter reflects. He cleans Emmett up with a bit of spit on the tail of his shirt before they go in.

52

Anne's backyard is as tidy as a ship's deck. Not a speck dares land. She's out there sweeping in the shining morning, when everything is still and quiet, apart from the occasional train down the back and the river of cars out the front. The crab-apple Louisa gave her years ago is about ready to release its rosy blooms. Anne touches one of the plump pink pouches and hopes the mean old wind stays away this year. Last year it stripped the branches bare. Still we live in hope, she thinks grimly, sweeping away a few last grains of something before storing the broom on its hook and going inside to sew in the alcove between the shop and the kitchen. Emmett is sitting in the kitchen at the blackwood table with his hands in his lap. At the end of the week he's going into the Woolamai Hostel.

The little tele is turned into Kerri-Anne on the morning show. She's so bright, Anne thinks, she gives you a lift just by being there but Emmett's not watching, he's looking at the light out the window. His head is still and it is impossible to know what he sees.

Anne's working on something for Noreen Nugent, one of her oldest customers. Noreen just keeps getting fatter and she rounds up her wardrobe every few months and gets Anne to let out all her clothes. How long the seams will keep offering something to her is anyone's guess. Still, while it lasts, it's a breeze for Anne and will bring in a good twenty bucks. Money is an eternal comfort to her.

She's never more herself than when she sews. Something about the busyness of it and the noise of the machine; she becomes part of it. She thinks she will leave the old machine to Louisa when she dies, but she's not sure why.

She glances over to check Emmett and hopes a sparrow or something passes occasionally to interest him. He doesn't ever look at the tele, just watches the light. Anne wonders whether there must be someone who would care to know about Emmett. But there's no one. Drinking friends don't count, never did.

The only person she can think of is Chook Sash, his old mate from North Melbourne. She knows he moved to Werribee not long before Daniel died, she remembers he came to Danny's funeral and that meant something – and still does.

Emmett had once told her he used to call Chook 'Dugong' at school because he looked like one, whatever that was. Emmett had laughed and she had offered a tiny smile, though she never considered calling people names to be funny. He didn't notice her lack of commitment. 'But most of the kids didn't know what a dugong was so I changed his nickname to Chook 'cause he sold eggs.'

He'd told her Chook had been with him in most of his fights at school. 'Always loyal, always available,' and he laughed again, 'but he was a plain boy, old Chook, a very plain boy. Used to wear his hair long. Gave him something to hide behind.'

Anne had liked Chook instantly, had seen in him that inconceivable thing, a man she could talk to. At Daniel's funeral he was a consolation. Though she wasn't noticing much, she always remembered the home-grown roses Chook had thrust at her with their kindly smell.

He was a gentle presence in the family until Emmett had banished him after a fight over politics. Chook was never a confirmed Labor voter, unlike Emmett who was violently passionate about Whitlam and, surprisingly, even about Hawke. Chook never could see much difference between the sides.

Being an adult had improved his looks. Still pale and large, he kept his faded hair short and he was no longer troubled so much. His face was studded with scars gouged by acne. His eyes had become amber and were flecked with leaves of light. He made a reasonable living as a plasterer. The pay was okay and he got to be inside most of the time which suited him because in the sun he was toast.

When she rings, Anne gets hold of his wife, Wendy, and there's a bit of enquiring about kids (they have three girls, one's a worry, the others are fine). It isn't easy for Anne to reveal herself to Wendy. There's an ache there and she wishes she could just talk to Chook and not parry with details. Wendy says she'll pass on the message to Mervyn (she doesn't like people calling him Chook) that Emmett isn't doing too well. Anne thanks her, hangs up the phone, and sits looking at it.

53

The next day Chook is at the door of the shop banging away with no intention of not being heard. She opens the screen door and it takes a while to recognise him. But when she does, she sees that he's a roomy man and still shambolic. And now, standing there engulfed in plaster dust, there's a ghostly quality to him. His hair is streaked with plaster.

He edges into the kitchen shyly, as wary as a horse moving uncertainly into a stall way too small for him. They get a cup of tea going and then go out to the backyard to look at Anne's lemon tree in a pot. Chook seems more comfortable outside. It's easier to talk out here under the shade of the peppercorn. A wind picks up and touches the lemon buds lightly. Emmett is upstairs in his room sleeping in the cradle of the afternoon.

'I don't know, Chook,' Anne says, and then she surprises herself and starts crying. God, it's a rotten nuisance all these blasted tears. She tells Chook about the brain scans and the dementia and how fast it will go. 'I just wanted to talk about Emmett with someone who really knew him.' Chook puts his hand on her shoulder and tears slip down their faces.

And even Chook is suddenly and fiercely amazed that Emmett means this much to him. He has been gone from him for so long. Then they sit at the green plastic table splattered with chalky bird-shit circles and after a bit Chook starts talking and thinking together. 'I knew that I had grown to love Emmett as a mate, but I knew he didn't ever love me. It didn't matter in the end, he was something else. I've never met anyone like him.'

He tells Anne stuff about Emmett that she has never heard. About the orphanage. 'He got sent there time and again, poor little bastard, when his Nana couldn't afford to keep him or when he went wild or when his mother decided he should go back in the orphanage to be with his little brother, Jimmy, but it wasn't just one he went to, he went to them all over, even went to that awful one at Royal Park. It was bad in there and worse in the foster homes. He wouldn't tell me what the foster father did to him, but as I got older I could imagine. He hated that bloke.

'He wasn't an orphan as you know, he just had a useless mother who couldn't be bothered looking after him and then she kept having more kids by different fathers, all over the place, there were at least four halves, you know, half-brothers or sisters. Springing up everywhere.'

Sitting there in the yard, their eyes are towed to the lemon tree as if by mutual consent. Over the fence, the top of the Uncle Toby's Oats silo just shows and goods trains hustle by along the fence-line making long clacking in the afternoon. A couple of Screen-master James Stirlings spread upwards near the fence, a mesh of olive green leaves as big as raindrops. A daisy bush takes the sun and a mauve hydrangea, its singed leaves as wide as wings, clings to the mercy of shade.

But the lemon tree in the cobalt blue pot is the undisputed star of the yard. It even has its own shade cloth cape constructed by Anne to fend off the sun on killer days. Today it has four lemons hanging from it like yellow balls.

Their eyes shuffle from one lemon to the other. Anne knows some of this stuff, but she doesn't let on what she knows or doesn't know. She's mining a rich lead here. She asks Chook how Emmett ended up in North Melbourne with his grandmother and he speaks as if this was something he's been waiting to say. He's an authority on Emmett.

'Eventually it was his uncles who saved him from the orphanage. I think it was his Uncle Spud who said he should just stay put with them at Nana's. Left the other poor little bugger Jimmy in the home though. Don't know what happened to the other halves. Unbelievable, the way they treated kids in those days.

'You know, he loved my mum so much. She'd ruffle his hair and make him eat and tell him he was a handsome boy. I came home one day and Emmett was sitting in the kitchen having a cup of tea with her. Now I know she was a kind woman and everyone loved her and she was not a bad mother unless she was pissed, which was most of the time if I'm honest, but I got a bit shitty seeing Emmett Brown sitting there helping himself to a slice of bread and dripping and a second cup of tea. After a while, I made Emmett uncomfortable with my bad manners and he got up and left. He gave Mum a peck on the cheek and it seemed to me they had some kind of understanding.'

Chook pauses for a while and then says, the fact was, he was only a kid himself. Left unspoken is that he was always touchy about his mother, probably still is. In the quiet that follows his words, Anne knows she's just gathered more about Emmett than she ever has. She puts her head down on the table and leaves it there resting on her arms.

Chook reaches over a white hand, still flecked with plaster, and puts it on her head. He pats her hair softly as if she were a child. This is so affecting, a wave of feeling for him washes up in her heart.

He offers to help Anne in any way he can and she's grateful, but she never calls him again. She thinks of Wendy and their girls and she doesn't want to be taking up their time. She's just glad he knows.

*

When Emmett goes into the hostel, there's often a note in the visitor's book saying that M. Sash had called in. When he comes, Chook always brings a piece of fruit, a pear or a peach or if it's winter, a thick-skinned navel orange. Peeling it, the spiky citrus smell springs into the stale air like a song.

Though Emmett stares ahead resolutely as if he's concentrating, Chook firmly believes that Emmett remembers the smell of oranges from when they were boys at the market, tossing them around against the grey gully of winter. Chook divides the fruit into segments and sets the pieces out on a flowery plastic plate he brings along. And then, with the patience of the humble, Chook places a fragment of orange into Emmett's papery hand and guides it up to his mouth.

He waits the long minutes until it's time for the next piece. Sometimes it doesn't get to the mouth. Emmett throws it away. When this happens, Chook places the next piece into Emmett's mouth. Sometimes he spits it out. Sometimes he chews it. He looks solidly ahead. Whatever happens, Chook wipes his old mate's mouth with the bit of paper towel he brought along and then he wets it at the tap and cleans him up before he sets Emmett free to roam the corridors once more.

54

Woolamai Hostel is built on the principle of a circle, never Louisa's favourite shape, and now, in a fog of confusion, she's lost again and doing laps of the beige place. Imagine how the patients must feel, she thinks furiously, aiming her rage at the anonymous designers of the joint. Instead of giving these poor people a signpost, a big red lamp or a pot plant, no — they make it all beige. Of course they bloody do.

Most of the inmates are in for dementia. She passes knots of them standing near the main desk. One old man is groping an old woman's sagging breasts and her face is as empty as a clean plate. Nothing. The old man rubs himself against the old woman's behind and as he bumps at her, she holds on to the wall to steady herself.

Louisa wants to go over and slap the old man away but no one else seems to notice or mind and so she thinks she might be imagining things. Anyway, there's not one single staff member around and Louisa is once again a reluctant witness.

Women and men, she sighs, seething at her quailing heart, at the cold fear the sight raises in her. At the sadness it stirs, knowing she should do something. You are still a gutless wonder, she scolds, forcing herself to look away. Another patient, a tubby little woman named Nancy, startles her, appearing into the void of memory. She gently touches

Louisa's hair. 'Do you know Mrs Golightly?' she asks, 'I do. I know her ...' Louisa feels stinging tears spring up. Wintry tears for Nancy and for the old lady she didn't help, for every single thing.

She tries to get a grip on herself and her memories but they well up like flood waters. Everyone tells her she lives in the past and she thinks well, so bloody what? You live where you want to and I'll live where I want to. It's mainly her brothers and sister who chide her about it. They can all get stuffed anyway. She finds she's muttering 'get stuffed' and thereby proves that she is truly losing it.

She presses on through the pale sealed circle, through the sour piss-seasoned air, searching for Emmett as if he has the answer, and the very idea of this is so insane she utters a harrumph without even meaning to.

Some days she finds her dad standing by a wall pulling at his cardigan. Memory is sharper than reality because whenever she first sees Emmett at the hostel, she irrevocably believes this can't be him. A mistake. Cannot be him, someone has taken him and replaced him. Emmett is huge and terrifying and smart and cruel. He can't be this poor old bloke fiddling with his buttonhole.

And then her eyes adjust to the truth that the first one is gone and in his place is this poor scrap who walks miles round and round all day every day, walks until he can walk no more. Getting him to sit down seems to cause him pain.

She is always astonished by what she feels. Understanding love is hard for her, she's never really grasped the concept. And Emmett should be hated by all of them. How could he not be? And yet, seeing her mother with him, she is again humbled by love.

On each visit to Woolamai, Anne takes a picnic of things Emmett used to like: fruitcake and his own mug and good strong coffee. Little square ham and mustard sandwiches cut up as small as stamps and placed into his mouth.

'Love doesn't come into it,' Anne says dismissively, 'he was my mate and I spent most of my life with him and here he is now and he's suffering and if I can make him one little bit happy, then I will. He is a human being and he gave me my kids and now he is a poor old thing.'

Once Emmett seems to wake from the place that holds him and with the old blue look, he says, 'My baby girl. Little Louie.' Then he is drawn away by the light on the wall and she thinks she must have heard wrong and wants him to say it again; but she's too surprised to speak and her voice stalls. She'd thought he was gone, now here he is again. In that little sentence, all the sorrow and all the sweetness of him come flooding back. Her father knew her. Despite everything, he knew.

She leaves Emmett and Anne and walks to the window, leans on it looking out at the red dahlias reaching for the sky. She turns towards her parents and it seems that they explain everything about her. She wants to laugh and to cry out in their defence, 'It's not your fault.' But that would be mental so she just wipes her eyes and heads back over to them.

Louisa watches while her mother feeds her father and is astonished by the quality of tenderness in the face of memory. The monster has become the lamb and through it all her mother has maintained her humanity.

55

Louisa has taken the morning off because Anne needs someone with her today. 'Lou,' she'd said low and even when Louisa told her that today she didn't care about the old man or how sick he was, 'he's still your father.'

So she asks Mr Conti and he waves his heavy hand at her in answer and says, 'Make it up another time dear girl.' She heads over to the shop, picks up Anne in the dented green Mazda 121 she calls Olive and drives to the hostel. She's decided her new policy is that if she's going to do something she will not begrudge it. This is Policy number 5431. She is trying to be more positive. Maybe it will help. Dr Mackenzie thinks it will.

They enter the hostel and loop the building looking for him. He's nowhere. They ask at the staff desk and are told to their astonishment that he's locked in his room. The key is passed to them.

Flinging the door open they see Emmett lying in pain on the pencil bed, in that stinking room. And this is far more than they bargained for. It's an outrage. Louisa feels the bile rising and thinks she might heave and fights it down.

In that small cave of a room, the tight hot smell of urine fastens Louisa to the foot of the bed. To see her father, to see anyone, like this is shocking. Poor old bastard lying there in his own piss, I can't believe it, and this is supposed to be a civilised bloody country. Anne takes the chair over and sits next to Emmett.

Louisa flings the window open as if there's a fire. Then she strides to the front desk and bails up the matron. 'Emmett Brown is really sick,' she says raising her voice, 'and blind Freddie could see that.'

But casual cruelty is a way of life for Matron Knight, a wide woman with a long pointy nose and the startled look of a rabbit. With an affronted expression, she peers up from her ledger at Louisa.

'I face immense funding problems and since Mr Brown became doubly incontinent, his care category has increased. We have staff shortages every day, it's not a job people are reliable about. Besides,' and she turns back to her ledger, pen scanning figures, 'I thought he'd benefit from a day in his room.'

Louisa hears something about funding and wishes she were Emmett in the old days because chucking a mighty tantrum would feel real good right now. She looks at the matron as though she's never seen anything like her but decides restraint is required. 'I'll be in Dad's room. I'll speak to you there.' Tearing along down the beige corridors, she feels time slowing, even while her heart is thudding like an engine.

In a while, Matron Knight cracks open the door to Emmett's room and peeps in timidly. She thinks it'll be safe to step in and when she does, Louisa goes for her. 'What do you think you're doing here, leaving a sick old man locked up, all alone like this? It's not human. What are you, some kind of a sadist?'

This is a pretty long speech for Louisa and now she's lost for words, except for one more thing. But, her voice has gone on her again. 'We want to see a doctor,' she croaks, assuming this will be a simple matter, but nothing, it seems, is simple when it comes to hostel etiquette and procedure.

Matron Knight is ready for this one and smiles patiently. 'The doctor was here yesterday and he saw your father and decided it was nothing serious.'

Louisa stands up and in her new boots is about a foot taller than Matron Knight. They look like a sideshow act. Trump the old witch, go on she urges herself, and says, 'Okay, I'll pay for it myself, I don't care, just get the doctor here.' Matron exits with as much grace as she can muster.

The tentative air slips in through the window and Drysdale's image of *The Drover's Wife*, the one Emmett cut from a calendar and Anne framed, hangs sideways. Louisa straightens it. Emmett periodically clutches his stomach.

The walls of Louisa's life are high, and this day she holds her emotions tightly to herself because Anne won't appreciate her tears. This is the first time Louisa's seen Emmett in a while. She hasn't been able to stand it. She hasn't brought Tom and Beck because she can't explain this to them. Seeing Emmett being subtracted from the world before your eyes is harder than she would ever have believed.

The last time she brought the kids had not worked. She had told them that Grandad was not the way he used to be, that he'd changed, that his brain was sick. Even so the kids were excited to see him because Emmett always made them feel special.

Tom, at fifteen, stood tall, with blue eyes and long dark curls and Beck, though she was olive skinned, looked very like him. She was almost thirteen. Louisa had been keeping them away from Emmett since he'd gone into the hostel, because she found it as much as she could handle on her own. But now it was holidays and, because they had no extra money for going away, here was a Saturday they were all free and the kids wanted to see him.

As soon as she walked in with them, she knew her strategy had been wrong. She should have introduced them to the deterioration more gently. Emmett was staring by a wall and Tom walked over and put his hand out to shake hands as they always did. Emmett didn't see him. So Tom dropped his arm and came back over to his mother looking hurt and puzzled, and Louisa thought, this is too much for them. The stranger with the staring eyes frightened Beck. She could see nothing of the funny old Grandad and the tough adolescent veneer she was pursuing dropped from her like a curtain. She began to cry.

Dealing with the kids' sadness over their grandfather made sense of Anne's need to quickly get back to normal after her Nan died. But Louisa reflected that perspective is always hard won. And driving away from Woolemai with the silent children, she decided they'd seen enough reality to last them a very long time.

Now Emmett is old and skeletal and he knows no one and is all but dead and time just keeps marching on. The pity of it all wells and she turns away to look at *The Drover's Wife* and recognises the lost eyes of her father.

Finally Dr Edward Roote appears in the small room. He positions himself at the foot of Emmett's bed as if he's a contagious proposition. Anne holds Emmett's hand. It lays there like a dead fish until the cramping pains come and then he clutches at his stomach.

Louisa feels herself reddening in the face of authority, something that hasn't happened since high school, but quite firmly she says to Dr Roote, 'My father needs to go to hospital now and if you don't arrange it, then I'll put him in the car and take him there myself.'

The doctor is a thin young fellow with ears like small fine wings. His eyebrows and his hair are so light as to be no colour at all though palest green is hinted at. 'I examined, err' – and here he consults his clipboard and scans until he finds the name – 'Mr Brown, is it? Err yes, yesterday, and he had a mild cold. There is no need for further treatment.'

For a man clearly so unsure of himself, Dr Roote is pretty arrogant, Louisa decides. She controls her anger. 'I don't care about yesterday,' she says quietly. 'I care about now.'

The doctor glances at her with his clam-like eyes and fiddles with his pen and scans yesterday's notes again. He reminds Louisa of one of the gilded youths in Banjo's 'The Man from Ironbark', the ones whose 'eyes were dull, whose heads were flat' and who 'had had no brains at all . . .' Just recalling the lines makes her want to flatten this little creep and fight for her father. The class system, she thinks, alive and bloody thriving.

Once again she says, 'I don't care about yesterday,' an undertow in her voice. 'Today is what matters. Look at him. He needs medical attention now and you are clearly not giving it to him.' She considers calling him an appalling dolt but thinks better of it; that would just be indulgent.

Dr Roote fudges some more and blinks and steps back, then in a few hollow seconds completely caves and scurries off to ring the ambulance. It's a victory that doesn't feel like one.

Louisa puts her hand on Emmett's head and his hair is baby hair now and suddenly the grief is pouring out of her. She has to go outside to compose herself. It's been a while since she stopped having shock treatment but she's still reasonably fragile, she's coming to terms with the new medication and she's still on anti-depressants and she still sees Dr Mackenzie. She stands near the door with the sad old lost people wandering around and lets out a breath.

An old woman touches her face and Louisa sees that she only has one shoe and her cardigan is hanging off her. Just under her mouth a clump of whiskers sticks out like a paintbrush. Sometimes everywhere you look makes you sad and she reminds herself that sometimes sad is normal, sad happens to us all. Sad isn't the end.

And in a while the paramedics plough their shining trolley up the hall and into Emmett's room. The ambulance men are bald blokes with flushed faces and big polished cheeks, one a head shorter than the other, and they pick Emmett up gently as if he were a baby and tuck him in on the trolley.

They call him mate and shake his flapping hand as though they mean it. They pat his shoulder and let Anne hold his hand and pretty soon Emmett looks better already and then they put a brave red rug over his legs.

As they leave, Louisa shuts the door on the stinking little cave. The tender paramedics have made her teary again but then she's a great sook. She strides ahead to lead the way to the ambulance, up front where she can get some privacy. Her father groans again and Anne walks besides Emmett still holding his hand.

Ambulances are common at Woolamai and they provide a break in the day but today nobody's that fussed and most miss the exit of Emmett. One old woman waves as they pass and then there's Nancy who waves at everybody. At the ambulance Emmett looks straight at Louisa and salutes and she salutes back. And then the old man's laughing with the paramedics. She puts her arm around Anne's shoulders. They laugh. Emmett always did love a fuss.

56

In the wrap of greyness pushing through the long windows of the Geriatric Ward, Jessie holds Emmett's hand and digs out faeces, hardened and trapped like fossils, from beneath his nails. God, she thinks, who would ever have thought it?

Emmett doesn't move. He's not aware of anything but pain. He's resting between bouts of the clamping cramps that seize him. His liver is dying and his brain is almost gone. He will be aware when spasms take him and hold him. And then he will be helpless, will fix faces with the look of a child in agony. Help does not come.

The doctors avoid him, to them it's just waiting. The nurses tolerate him; some are sensitive and some are not. One, a tall woman with zany purple glasses named Sue, remarks on the beauty of his eyes while changing his adult nappy. 'When you were a young man, it's Emmett isn't it? With eyes so blue you could have had all the girls,' she says, chatting to Anne as much as to herself to ease the time it takes to tend to an incontinent, rigid old man.

Jessie and Anne remain standing like sentinels beside the unravelling bed watching the performance. Anne, in a jumper the colour of stones, smiles her weary smile and says, 'He did all right,' and in that insect second Jessie wonders again about the life between her parents.

'Strange isn't it,' the nurse continues as if anyone cares, 'how things turn out. Once a handsome young man and now poor old fellow, eh Emmett?' Long pause before she blathers on. 'I like that name. Is it American?' And she turns to the shell of the wasted man none too gently and pats his translucent stick of a thigh. And Jessie wants to kill her for one rough gesture.

Anne tells her it was his father's name and it comes from the Bible, Old Testament. And Jessie adds, wildly over-the-top, 'Then it must be American!' Her fizzing anger is lost on everyone and disintegrates into the stale stillness of the hospital. She turns to the window and feels even more wretched and realises she doesn't get it. She'd always thought the death of Emmett would be something to celebrate, so why does she feel bad? Emmett clenches again with the pain and Anne touches his hair.

The clenching lasts and he begins to sweat. He moans and mutters, 'Get away get away get away,' and 'piss off'. He clutches the sheet up under his chin and it's not possible to ignore his suffering.

The nurse moves across to Edith in the bed across the aisle. Edith is a whale of a woman with a voice that penetrates skulls like a flat violin. She's watching *The Bold and the Beautiful* with genuine enthusiasm. A forgotten plastic jug of urine that looks oddly like orange cordial stands on her bedside table. Jessie considers tipping it all over the floor or maybe even over Edith, just for some kind of release.

In the milky light of the hospital at dusk, the big window by Emmett's bed frames the west of the city. Clouds are pushed together like smoke and the idea of rain is raised again.

Seeing Emmett in this state stirs something in Jessie. The illness makes him look dismantled and watching him in such devastation makes her want to cry. The bile the thought of him brings up is at odds with this particular poor old bloke. And why, she asks herself, does she now think of the good things?

She wills herself to remember the bad bits. The pushing of her mother, the beltings, the slaps, the lewd language. The fights. It isn't hard. She looks into those moody clouds and thinks of one of the nights at tea, of the terrifying presence of Emmett Brown throwing his plate or the teapot at the wall or at them, or mocking them for their pathetic pronunciations of hate. How he laughed when they said they hated him and he mocked them with: *You ate me do you? Well now, that would be something to see*, and roared laughing as a child fled, sobbing with a mouthful of cold mashed spud dropping, dropping. The taste of tears and cold potato were complimentary but it wasn't one he would ever know. He'd down the beer in one gulp and against the stripe of light on the ceiling and through the glass, the amber liquid illuminated the giant man.

And so Jessie has him back. Has him all locked away again, all square. Emmett the bastard, not Emmett the poor old bugger.

57

Apparently when hospitals call people to tell them their loved one is gravely ill, it means they have already died, but at the time of Emmett's death, the Browns don't know that. Anne hears this titbit much later on talkback radio, where she gets most of her information.

Jessie is at work the day he dies and Anne rings to say the hospital has called. It's a bit over a week after Christmas and she's volunteered to go in because the women she works with have family and there are plenty of other people to look after her own mob. Anne says, 'Dad's very sick, darling. Dad's dying. Do you want to go to the hospital?'

'Will I pick you up?' Jessie asks her. The boys will go straight there. When Jessie gets to the shop Anne is sitting with her hands clenched in front of her on the old wooden table. She seems to have fallen into a rift in time.

*

Rob and Pete can't find the damned entrance to the hospital carpark. They're driving like maniacs in Rob's ute, hurtling around corners and coming to jerky stops at traffic lights that change just as their breath starts to slow. The bright smell of sawdust surrounds them.

Peter looks over at Rob and sees his hands on the steering

wheel and recognises Emmett's hands. His own are the same, though maybe not as brown. These are the exact hands that thrashed them when they were kids. That hurt their mother. That showed them how to knot ties. That made beer that exploded in the shed. That sheared their dog Frank in summer. That showed them how to bat. The legacy that lives within the genes lives within the mind. Nothing is withdrawn.

Then he remembers how the Footscray gardens run down the hill like something green spilled into the brown river. On hot nights sometimes Emmett took them there and everything felt alive. Funny to remember the good things, Peter considers, just while they're getting lost.

Earlier he had been glad they were lost because it meant it wouldn't happen. He had the street directory on his knee in an effort to help but still it took so long threading through the sluggish traffic that Rob snapped and chucked a U-ey and nicked through the back streets. Finally, they find the carpark entrance, leave the car illegally parked and sprint to the lift. Peter remembers hesitating there for a second and then Rob sees the curving concrete stairs and he's gone, taking them two at a time. He follows, moving fast, but soon he's beginning to breathe hard.

They fly down the corridor, find a nurse and Rob says urgently, 'Where is Emmett Brown?' She says a room number and waves them towards a ward and they burst in, rush to the side of the bed and stand there panting and sweating.

The sun is slanting in. In the next bed, Edith, the whale-woman is snoring. The pink cotton curtain between the two beds is half-drawn and the day is rapidly moving past.

*

The last thing Emmett sees is a rural scene in France. A haystack and a farmhouse and green trees and some chooks pottering around in a print at the end of his bed. His eyes are still settled on it when his sons get there. By the time they arrive Emmett is yellow, hands clutching his chest.

It's just before twelve o'clock and it seems he's been dead quite a while. Peter reaches over and closes Emmett's eyes and takes his cold hands in his own. He would like to make them warm so he pulls the sheet up over the old man but keeps hold of Emmett's hand.

He looks around for Rob who by now is surging toward the nurses like a force unleashed to blast them for leaving Emmett to die alone. 'NOBODY should have to die alone,' he yells. And the nurses are sorry. Nothing is their fault, they are so few and so busy. And then it hits him that Emmett's life is over. There's no turning back. He stops fighting as if someone has turned him off. Next door Edith snores on, ploughing the deep fields of sleep.

Peter puts his hand on Emmett's head and waits for Anne and Jessie. He feels such a weight holding his heart down. He can barely raise his head but he sees the window and through it the west is spread out like a map. He knows his face is wet by the freshness of the air touching it.

Rob comes back and sits in the chair in the corner and a skin of anger, like something alive, revives and settles on him and he imagines the anger is to do with the hospital leaving his father to die alone.

He knows he's crying but he doesn't wipe his face. Caring doesn't edge into his thinking at all. He stares ahead, tries normality but it doesn't fit. He even wants to laugh but the feeling passes. Though he's still, his heart is racing. They stay beside their father for long minutes guarding him, tending him.

58

Since she broke her hip, Anne has slowed right down. It has been replaced and the new part works well, it's just that she's well down on speed. She and Jessie get to Emmett within half an hour of the call from the hospital. Footscray, as Emmett always said, is not far from anywhere.

They wait for the lift because Anne is not able to take the stairs. When they reach Emmett, Rob is in the chair and Peter is close to Emmett with his hand resting on his head.

Rob says quietly, gently, 'He's dead Mum, there's no rush.'

Jessie feels the world shooting by and she reaches out to hold the bed. Anne puts her hands to her mouth and Rob steers her to the chair but she's not ready for that. She walks to Peter and takes the sheet away and she leans over and kisses Emmett on his cheek. Then she raises the sheet, and still looking down into that mysterious face she says, 'Louisa. We will have to tell Louisa.'

59

When Emmett dies, Louisa is in Venice. It's reliably beautiful, glinting with echoing lights across black water. At the moment of his death the light is yellow in this hollow of Europe because she's in an ancient church lighting a candle for him of all people. Faded paintings of saints look down on her. Outside the church, it rains the languid rain of Europe.

Much later she works out that the moment of the candle is about when he died. At the time though, she thought, isn't it pleasant wandering around Venice all on your own? Dodging pigeons as you walk through the salty breath of the city and gazing for much too long into the windows of handmade paper shops.

And she thanks Mr Conti for sending her here. He'd decided that now she was settling back into her life, a little trip to the most beautiful place in the world would do her good and it seemed that Emmett was stable. She and Anne had even picked out a nursing home for him.

*

That night, after she's been asleep for a while, there's a strange ringing and the phone call is from Rob, who in the swimming void of the phone line says, 'It's happened Lou. Yes, it's happened. Dad died today.'

And she breathes steadily as she holds the heavy Italian phone and remembers the times hiding in the shed or under the hedge when the two of them had prayed for this death, when they thought he'd kill them unless God intervened. But nothing had happened because God was never where you wanted Him and that was the only, the always truth. Even when you prayed for a death, it didn't come and now here it is in Venice on the Dosodura at the shadow of dawn on a rainy morning.

Emmett's voice is the past, she's in this watery place full of old beauty and luminous shops and she has to get home and face it. The death of the tyrant. The chain of memory is thick and strong but reality doesn't seem to belong.

A gulf of distance defines Australians. Breathe deep because getting there will take a long time. She takes the water taxi (hang the expense) to the airport at five am and sees the sky become faintly glassy as the boat skips over the choppy sea. At the airport, lights like torches line runways and every other column is red.

Rain falls in circles on the polished tarmac and Louisa stands in the bus taking her to the departure gate, the travel agent going home. As the bus moves, she leans into the curves holding the freezing metal pole.

She knows her father has died but it's not real. To herself she chants, my father has died, and moves aside politely for more Italians wedging themselves onto the bus at every stop. Most of her life she hated him and now she weighs hate in her heart and finds it light on. So was this really hate? Some questions lie in the air unclaimed.

She has the knowledge of the oceans between here and home, and the knowledge that the hate has her in a holding pattern stills her. The balances are out and she's heading the long way home. Into the distance she sees her water taxi moving away and feels towed with it. Go back, a voice inside tells her, run away, hide in Venice and never come out, but she shakes her head.

And besides, she doesn't get it. How can you hate so much and then, when you hear about the death, feel swept up by the sea of sorrow? Because it wasn't real, comes to her, and because hate is a waste of time. Big thoughts when you feel small.

She sees a water taxi's hull reflecting the lagoon and she holds it because it stops the image of Emmett as an old man in the hospital, demented, liver rotted, a lost man who wanted to be a poet but who gave up on everything because, apart from Anne, not one person ever helped him or believed in him. He hated the way the world treated him but never found of a way of changing it. The idea of loss does laps in her head. Love and hate are plaited together.

On the bus, she feels elated to be free of him and then heartbroken in quick succession as if she were riding a merry-go-round. Light lies in gold stripes across the ground and other buses heading to planes going to other places pass with Louisa's reflection in their eyes. A man on the bus says: 'Ciao Aussie' and she wonders if it's that obvious, and then she remembers the little Australian flag the kids got her to sew on her backpack.

She smiles at the man and wants to tell him she's lost her father but then decides that she doesn't, she says farewell to rude Europeans in fur coats, preening themselves and smoking wherever they want to and slamming change down on counters when you have your hand out ready to receive it.

She thinks, goodbye Italy, I won't be back, and smiles to know that they won't miss her. She sees the moss green islands in the lagoon between the tarmacs and remembers Emmett's vegie garden, the one thing he truly seemed to love apart from beer and occasionally her mother.

Take it out and look at each piece of it. Weep for the tyrant, the poor old tyrant bastard, hear him again in her secret corner. Hear him in the good times reading *The Man From Snowy River* on long hot nights in the warm heart of the southern city when the cicadas call greenly and the light stretches out thinly all the way down to Tassie.

She hears her mum's voice on the phone after Rob saying, 'Darlin' the truth is, Dad's face wasn't good at the end. He went yellow. Must have been the liver disease that got him.'

She wonders what will get her. What will get Mum? What will get her children? What gets us all? She wants to be home, to lay her hand on Australia and unwrap her sorrow for her father.

60

The funeral has been hard. They've all cried too much and now there are many people they don't know, people who know Anne mostly. Anne, it seems, is popular in Footscray, known and loved by all. So after the funeral a swarm descends on the shop looking for sandwiches and cups of tea.

One man stops Louisa near the kitchen and begins to tell her about rigging a yacht. She has a tray of antipasto in her hand. The man is shorter than Louisa and is clean shaven but for a snow-white neck beard. His face is the colour of corned beef. He tells her about rigging a sail. He didn't know Emmett. He eats a few olives and holds onto the pips.

One of the Deakin farmers talking to Rob says he always remembers Emmett describing Ballarat as the Prague of the South. 'Amazing man,' he says 'knew so many things. Learned, he was. I was much taken with his brilliance.' Rob nods and sips his tea. A smile moves across his mouth and he says, 'It was truly individual wasn't it?'

Louisa looks over at Rob standing near the front of the shop holding a mug of tea and watching the street. She turns away but when she looks for him again he's shot through and left his tea making a ring on Emmett's desk.

Then Jessie arrives and the yacht man pops his pips into his pocket and places a sundried tomato on a piece of bread with infinite care and he turns his attention to her with the force of something magnetised and she listens to how sails are rigged with grudging gratitude because it saves her from thinking.

Louisa slips outside and finds Rob sitting in his car with the airconditioning on, the sun glinting off the dirty window. She gets in. 'You all right?' she asks, not expecting anything.

Rob says, 'I don't know. I thought it would be over when he died. Thought I'd feel released. Still feel stuck in the shit of it all.' In the stale churning air of the car, the heat is still barely tamed and Louisa looks washed out. He reckons they should go back into the wake, such as it is. 'C'mon,' he says.

'Yeah, but I just want to say one thing. I want to say that we are free now. The day has come. Finally.'

He still has his hand on the keys in the ignition and thinks, Not for me, I won't be free of this bastard for a very long time and neither will you. But if it makes you feel better to imagine it, then go right ahead. Yet all he says is, 'Yeah Louie, finally eh?'

61

When they were kids, Emmett had a Panasonic projector. Best projector money could buy and, according to Emmett, a bloody humdinger. Now, looking back, Louisa realises that Emmett was always looking for protection from things that might go wrong and buying the best was just a dear form of protection.

After the funeral, Peter sets up the Panasonic in the old shop. The rickety screen stands there on its skinny tripod legs with that great rip in the reflective fabric that Emmett taped up all those years ago. Louisa thinks of Emmett fussing in the spirit of his sons as they ready the gear. And the photos seem like a kind of love.

They laugh and they're respectful with the pictures of each other, the youngest kids are in them all and the older kids aren't in many because they never liked the camera much, certainly not after Rob tried to boil it when he was ten by dropping it in the billy. Another picnic that didn't end well.

They're perched on the ends of the couch, some stand behind it, so many of them now that others have joined the family. Peter holds the globe in with a tea towel because the old projector is on its last legs but the globe overheats and cuts out intermittently.

Everyone laughs at the shot of the four of them, Louisa in

those pink bathers with the little skirt and her plaits carefully folded into a shower cap and Rob, Peter and Daniel all in blue Speedos. In the picture the light is yellow and the sun not past burning them. Anne is sitting on the crate having a smoke, watching. She's wearing khaki shorts and a striped top and on her feet her thongs are worn to the thinnest shaving of rubber. Her hair is brown curls and as she looks at the kids her smile is love itself.

The children grab onto each other with some concentration because the floor of the pool is slippery on the concrete and Emmett has them all leaping in at once. The hose fills the pool with shining water. They hold each other with reliable comfort as if the other's arms were there just for them.

Frank's tail is caught in the picture as he moves about in the cycle of here and there that is dogs. They gaze at this photo as if it's a cure and ignore the warning of the low buzzing that begins just above silence and is coming from the projector.

The life-sized picture of the four of them is still up on the screen. Seeing Daniel again connects them with the loss that breached them. Looking at the picture lasts many heartbeats and then someone notices the smell of burning and yells, 'Something's bloody ON FIRE!' And Peter jerks his hand away and the tea towel falls into a small burning knot on the floor. He stands on it to put it out. When that picture fades, childhood is finally over.

62

Within weeks of his death, dreams of Emmett move into their nights. Louisa dreams Emmett picks up her hand and turns it over as if it were an oyster prised off a rock. In the room, square windows hold the sky at bay.

He begins to tell her the dream and she says, 'I know, I know.' Behind her, someone walks though the windows and blood springs up like red umbrellas. Louisa will always wish she had not interrupted her father in that dream.

That same night, Peter dreamed about him too. 'There was a boat and the sky and there were others and I was trying to get people to sit down so they wouldn't fall. The sky was green and Dad said he was going.'

It's another hot day, a month after the funeral. Peter and Louisa are driving up to the bush for the scattering of the ashes. Rob, Jessie and Anne are following them. Louisa hears Peter's dream and stares through the smeared window. So much does she want to hear more, she can't speak.

Peter doesn't say anything for a long stretch of road. He looks into the rear-vision mirror at Rob in his ute and wonders if he's had a dream. How he will be today? Will he be able to handle it?

When they have a break and a cup of coffee at a roadside stop, Rob and Anne, it seems, have also dreamed about Emmett. In

Anne's dream, he came into the room and sat down and put a bunch of flowers and her little dog on the bed. 'Goodbye my darling, Annie,' he said. She woke up gasping at the vision of Emmett.

In Rob's dream he spoke to him on the phone, told him he was a bastard, a hard man, but that he wouldn't have had it any other way and Emmett said goodbye. Jessie missed out on a visit that night but the dreaming has its own rhythm and goes on for months.

The windscreen is coated with the fine mesh of the day the car collects and the sun blurs through it. The kombi trails over the shimmery road and the black wing of a dead crow flaps up as they pass.

Back in the car, Louisa and Peter peer through the windscreen at the long road that takes them to Emmett's uncles' place up in the river country. Talk of the dreams preoccupies them for a hundred kilometres. No one believes in ghosts or in God but they believe in him. 'It's him, he's come back to tell us he's goin', to tell us he's all right,' Peter says. 'Definitely.'

Louisa wonders. Doesn't seem in character for the old man to be so caring. 'Maybe it's not intentional, just the leftover spirit of him like the tail of a comet fizzing out, finishing. What d'ya reckon?' Pete holds the wheel and the car hums. 'Dunno, but the coincidence gets me, it seems intentional. Honestly, I can't even think about it yet.'

Louisa grabs the bottle of water between them and knocks back half of it, hands it to Peter. She says, 'I mean, shit, what if there is a bloody God after all this certainty that there isn't? What d'you think? Angels, you reckon there'll be angels Pete?'

He grunts and laughs at that idea. She keeps at it. 'What if there's heaven and hell? Where d'you reckon he'll go? Poor old bastard. What if he's in heaven? And that's why he's being nice.' Peter drinks the bottle dry and crushes the plastic with a crack and tosses it into the back and starts talking about anything else.

Then after a while it goes quiet and they drive on, spearing through the day towards the river, a place Emmett held sacred. This was one of the many places he'd wanted to wind up in. The others were the backyard under the beer bottles, Newport Power Station because it was beautiful, or in the Mallee because he was born there.

They have his ashes in the urn. Peter has made a lid for the urn out of something hard and Emmett is duly contained. When they get close to the river there's a floodplain spreading out before it and the earth is brown, a cracking dry place with scraggly leaves barely hanging onto the trees. Everything is taupe and it doesn't look like much at all.

Peter steers the van up the embankment and fears with a sinking heart that they might not make it. He doesn't say anything out loud but he's thinking, oh shit. But as the kombi has never failed him before, he hopes it's not going to start now, and finally after a long, high-pitched straining in the engine, it gets them there.

It feels like Emmett is offering advice from the back seat and they both recall times when their father had bogged the car and then thrown mighty tantrums and stalked away, leaving them all waiting in the baking sun for him. Once in a country town when the car broke down they played cricket in the middle of the road and the local kids joined in. By the time Emmett emerged from the pub, it was night and the other kids had gone home.

*

Around the soft edges of the inlet in the river, bulrushes stand straight and weed cast on the water like a blanket is moved by the breeze. A nearly submerged beer bottle lingers close by and they all get the joke, at least Emmett will have something to drink.

Further out fish push their mouths up to slice through the surface and when they move on, they trail furrows through the dark water. Dragonflies busy themselves and their silver wings shiver an inch above the water.

On the big island in the river, shots blast. Duck-shooters, says Rob. This news causes a comradely argument about duck-shooting because Jessie takes it personally when bad things happen to animals. The others don't like it much either but don't claim to be missionaries on the subject, but because it's ashes day they let the disagreement fall away.

No one knows in what order they should do things, never having scattered ashes before, and they long for a bit of leadership on the subject but there's none. Everything will be done by consensus. Finally, they settle on a strategy.

They get the six deckchairs out of the car, one for each of them (Daniel included), and set them around a circle in the sand and then they collect firewood. They're after dry stuff which isn't a problem because most of the wood is practically explosive due to the drought.

It's late afternoon. There's a bit of summer moon out thinking about the night and the bush is readying itself for that too. Alone in the bush, Louisa starts talking quietly to Emmett.

She stands on a dead sapling and pushes it down, waiting, concentrating on the moment of the snap. It comes and she's ready to go back to the campfire when she comes upon another tree with a red trickle of sap: tree blood. 'Dad,' she says, 'look what I found,' and imagines he'd have patted her head and treated her like a scientist if he was in the mood.

Again, like a ship coming to grief on a reef, she is holed by the loss of her father. By the absence of her father he could be.

So she hangs onto the tree as if it's someone's arm and, in time, recalls the many realities of Emmett.

Then she hears the others dragging wood and getting the billy on then looking over cups and saying, 'Where's the milk?' and 'Did you bring sugar?' and 'Why don't we use the mugs from before, save us washing them?' Little questions hanging there in the evening like clean washing on the line.

She listens to her brothers and sister for a while then joins them sitting with their legs stretched out and their feet pointing towards the fire like spokes in a wheel.

It's decided that the tree should be planted first. Emmett liked the idea of having a ficifolia planted for him, he liked to think of their scarlet coats in the summer, and so Anne had ventured into the vast acre of the local Bunnings and picked one out.

Concerns are mounted: that this is a State Forest, that the tree will die because there is no water, that it will be rabbit food. They decide to look upon it as a gesture to Emmett. Possibly to his fathering, Jessie jokes.

Rob does an impersonation of a full flight Emmett: 'It will live or die like the rest of us and will probably have a hard go of it. But THAT is LIFE.' He gets out the shovel and digs a big hole for the small tree. Jessie fills a bucket of water from the river and waters it. They stand back. The tree is small beside the bush, just a little bloke.

It's decided that the child believed to be the most loved by Emmett will be the one to disperse him. So Peter kneels at the foot of an ancient river red gum with the urn. The tree must be two hundred years old and with the lower limb removed it makes a rough altar.

Rob wants to smash the urn but really he just wants to break something, anything. Make a big show of it. Smash the bloody thing to smithereens. 'Go on,' he says, 'act like Greeks, they smash urns. They do,' he says, looking around for agreement. The family looks doubtful.

Then Peter and Louisa say, 'No, it's not happening.' The word 'dignity' is used and Rob gets mad. Says, 'He wasn't being very dignified when we were kids, was he? Don't get all sentimental about him just because he's dead. Anyone can be dead. We'll all be dead, nothing mystical in that. He was poison. Pure and simple.'

Rob steps back, vanquished in his attempt to smash the urn and so finally to smash Emmett all at once and gloriously in front of everyone. His anger is understood but no one else feels like being destructive today. It's just time to let the old man go. Scores, they reckon, don't get settled at ashes-scattering ceremonies.

Rob seems to shoulder his hurt as he always has by taking it into himself and looking out at them, daring them to disagree with him. The others look back, there are times when Louisa and Peter see that Rob has borne more than anyone, other times they wish he'd just give it up, even for his own sake.

Jessie watches them in their endless banter. The three-parter they play again and again, as if she's part of the audience. God, she thinks, let this be over. Anne says nothing.

Peter walks over to the ficifolia and touches the top of it lightly. Louisa is looking at the sky as usual, a bit of rose is smeared on the clouds stretched out up there in the acres of blue. Louisa hears her Nan saying, 'Pink clouds in the evenin', sailor's warnin' ', and regardless of what's going on, as always, misses her savagely.

And then, in a moment's flash, she sees how isolated the Browns are. Always alone when it comes down to it because no one else shares the legacy of Emmett. Alone there and missing no one really but Daniel.

And had he lived, how would he have turned out with

a father like Emmett and a mother who worked so hard you feared she didn't have time to breathe? How had they all turned out? How was it possible that they were not all basket cases? Ah, maybe they were. No point getting all high and mighty when you're talking about the original latchkey children.

Peter pushes the urn under the water because the bugs and yabbies might make a home there and that would be a good thing. Tears make lines down his face as he kneels.

Leaving Emmett behind is harder than Louisa thought it would be. She takes a stick and stirs him into the water; one of the others tells her to leave things alone and yells, 'Come on Louie,' so she chucks the stick down.

Then they stand in a circle and put their arms around each other's shoulders like footballers after a big victory and weep for the old man. For what he was, for what he wasn't, for what he might have been. Rob and Peter shake with the sorrow of it.

And then to break the solemnity, Jessie laughs and says, pulling her hands across her face to wipe the tears, 'It's time Emmett got a move on, hanging around here, wasting all our bloody time.'

They laugh remembering his performances on the subject of time-wasting when they were kids. 'NEVER be late; it is a discourtesy to those waiting. Politeness is free and everyone can give it and receive it; you don't have to be rich to have manners.'

They move from tears to laughter so fast, their faces are still wet.

Anne declares she has nothing to say, except that the kids are better at such things. She's quiet in the bush because it reminds her of Emmett. He said this place was as holy as any cathedral and it feels like he's come back to somewhere beloved.

Louisa reads a bit of a poem by a German poet who thinks that we're all nobody really, except maybe fragments of stars. Or some such typically dilatory stuff, thinks Rob. In the bush standing on leaf litter smelling eucalyptus like a memory, the poem is read in her usual halting, stumbling, croaky way and makes little sense. She should have read from 'Clancy', she knows this as soon as she opens her mouth. But there you are, stuffed it up again.

After a silence, Rob tells them that when Emmett was up here as a young man his uncles would leave a tin of jam hidden within these giant old trees for him in case he didn't catch a fish. Then he says, 'Now here we are, the kids, those endlessly bloody annoying kids, not the beloved long dead uncles, just us wretched kids, we are the ones releasing him, the ones letting go.'

Peter shuffles about on the spot, clearly ready to disagree but not wanting to. He reads out something he's written about Emmett taking him to this river when he was a small boy. How he taught him to look hard at everything he picked up on the riverbank. How, because of Emmett, Peter would always be 'investi-gate-ing'. He smiles as he remembers Emmett telling him that there's a gate in the word and gates take you to many places.

Is this what love looks like? A campsite with six seats, the sky full of rose clouds. Insects touching them lightly. All of it connected to Emmett, who in his leaving becomes human again, becomes himself?

And then Rob stands up and sings, 'I Know Where I'm Going', the song Emmett taught them on those couple of nights when he decided they might make a reasonable choir. His mother's song.

*

They take the cars out an easier way and in time the road hauls them home.

Louisa drives with Peter again and they listen to the Cat Stevens' songs she played when he was a boy. It's his idea this time. Then they sing Joni Mitchell and Dylan songs, the words engraved on them. Eventually, they put some Floyd on to ease themselves.

Then the hypnotic road consumes them. The headlights fan out and touch the sides of the road lightly. There's a rhythm in the driving and then, out of nowhere, a bat hits the windscreen at speed and they leap forward absolutely together, shocked by the randomness of life and by the death of the bat.

Outside, they see a stripe of red fire burning in the long grass in a faraway paddock and soon they pass the luminescent orange of a haystack on fire, the heat drawing in all within its orbit. Behind them the lights of Rob's ute are steady eyes in the hungry night. And then they press on and the dark folds itself around them and the light retreats like a fallen army.

Acknowledgements

In the writing of this work of fiction I'm grateful for all the help I've had. Despite his busy schedule, my husband, Alan, read early drafts and with his encouragement helped me more than he can ever know. And later, my friend and editor Nadine Davidoff was both bracing and liberating. Being accepted by publisher Meredith Curnow was special enough, but hearing her speak of the characters as if they were real was completely unforgettable and will always stay with me. And Brandon VanOver has been a kind and thoughtful editor with that rarest quality, a sense of humour. My RMIT teacher, Antoni Jach, was also helpful and my dear friend Margaret Geddes listened to more than her share of potential plots along the journey that this book has become. My sister, Sarah, and my brothers, Anthony and Russell, were generous and patient during the writing of the novel, and I thank them for it. Finally, thank you to my children Phoebe, Alice and Christopher; you are always inspiring.